Necessary EVIL

LINDSAY WELSH

Necessary Evil
Copyright © 1995 by Lindsay Welsh
All Rights Reserved

No part of this book may be reproduced, stored in a retrieval system, or transmitted in any form, by any means, including mechanical, electronic, photocopying, recording or otherwise, without prior written permission of the publishers.

First Rosebud Edition 1995

First Printing April 1995

ISBN 1-56333-277-9

Cover Photograph © 1995 by Trevor Watson

Cover Design by Julie Miller

Manufactured in the United States of America
Published by Masquerade Books, Inc.
801 Second Avenue
New York, N.Y. 10017

The house had been cool and refreshing when I rushed from the air-conditioned car to the front door; it was so hot outside that even that short exposure made the change in temperature welcome inside. I kicked off my shoes and stretched out on the sofa.

Then the call had come, the insistent ringing, the voice on the other end. Colder than any refrigerated air. Quiet, forceful, one word only in greeting. "Jennifer."

My insides went icy. Even though she was just a voice far away, I immediately dropped to my knees instinctively. Hardly daring to breath, I whispered, "Mistress?"

"I want you here at midnight," she said, and then there was a click, followed by the steady drone when she hung up. I looked at the receiver for a long time and then slowly put it back in its cradle.

I hadn't had the opportunity to serve my Mistress for more than two weeks and I went weak with the knowledge that I had been summoned. It was an honor and just as importantly, a turn-on, even if I knew that my own personal satisfaction would have to be forsaken for my Mistress's.

Also by LINDSAY WELSH:

A Circle of Friends
A Victorian Romance
Private Lessons
Bad Habits
Provincetown Summer

Chapter *One*

In the South, the summers are almost obscenely oppressive. Even as the sun goes down, the temperature does not. As I take off my clothes, the thick sweet air, heavy with moisture, seems to wrap around my body like a lover's arms.

The high ceilings built into this old house are supposed to make the rooms light and cool, but tonight they aren't much help. My long blond hair is plastered to the back of my neck.

I look over longingly at the grille of the air conditioner, and I sigh. With one quick, light flip of a switch I could flood this whole room with refrigerated air, but

I don't. It would destroy the mood. I want to be uncomfortable. I want to be miserable.

It all began several hours ago, shortly after I got home from work. I had been in a particularly good mood, having just landed an important contract at the office, and I felt in complete control. I had won over the customer, I had made a great deal of money both for the company and myself, I was victorious. I had enjoyed the accolades from my supervisors when I had been taken out for a victory drink afterward. I was on top.

The house had been cool and refreshing when I rushed from the air-conditioned car to the front door; it was so hot outside that even that short exposure made the change in temperature welcome inside. I kicked off my shoes and stretched out on the sofa.

Then the call had come, the insistent ringing, the voice on the other end. Colder than any refrigerated air. Quiet, forceful, one word only in greeting. "Jennifer."

My insides went icy. Even though she was just a voice far away, I immediately dropped to my knees instinctively. Hardly daring to breath, I whispered, "Mistress?"

"I want you here at midnight," she said, and then there was a click, followed by the steady drone when she hung up. I looked at the receiver for a long time and then slowly put it back in its cradle.

The heat outside was nothing compared to the heat that started up in my pussy. I hadn't had the opportunity to serve my Mistress for more than two weeks and I went weak with the knowledge that I had been summoned. It was an honor and just as importantly, a turn-on, even if I knew that my own personal satisfaction would have to be forsaken for my Mistress's.

I knew I had to get myself ready for this session. The first thing I did was turn off the air conditioner, albeit reluctantly, and open all the windows. The hot air came in like a blast furnace and before long the whole house was stifling. It was necessary. A submissive cannot be permitted the luxury of comfort.

I took off my clothes, preparing for a shower, for I could not appear before my Mistress unless I was perfectly clean. I wanted cool water but I turned on the hot water tap and stood beneath it, scrubbing myself hard, until I was dizzy. I used the rough soap and the coarse cloth reserved for this to get my skin clean. I felt raw when I was finished. When I stepped out of the shower, the thick towels were damp in the sticky air. Even when I had dried myself I still felt wet and clammy.

I stood before the mirror and looked at myself. I hoped that my Mistress would like what she saw. My legs were firm from countless miles walked, my belly hard from exercise. My hair was long and thick, reaching almost to my waist. My breasts were large but firm, the nipples huge and hard. I wanted to touch them but did not. I let them ache.

Standing there looking, I realized suddenly that I was admiring myself, and quickly I closed the door so that the mirror was no longer visible. Admiration meant that I was worth looking at, but I was only a submissive, a slave! Vanity and pride were pleasures I was not permitted under any circumstances. I was only fodder for my Mistress's desires and apart from that I had no use at all.

I put on a light, Hawaiian-style caftan that allowed me some respite from the heat until the time I would have to dress to go to my Mistress. I did not want to sweat too much for that would require another shower. I could not appear before my Mistress unless I was perfectly clean. Of course, if she so desired to leave me wrapped in heavy clothing in the heat until I passed out, that was up to her. I would go to her washed, fresh, almost virginally innocent. How I would leave her was not my decision.

Now I sit on the edge of the sofa, in the dark, listening to the heavy ticking of the clock. It sounds far away and the noise comes to me through the humid air thickly.

It amazes me that I can sit like this. At any other time I cannot be still for more than a minute unless I have something to read. Even a quick run to the bathroom cannot be carried out unless I first look through the piles of books on the coffee table or the nightstand and select one to look at while I am sitting there. It is impossible for me to just do nothing.

But then my Mistress will call and my mind goes into what I call "submissive mode." It is as if someone has tapped into my brain and flipped the switch that turns me from an ordinary businesswoman, indistinguishable from any other you might meet in a regular day, to a whimpering, boot-licking, frightened slave.

The changeover is complete and all-encompassing. In my "regular" mode, a paper cut or a bruise from banging the corner of a desk is a painful, brutal injury. When I become a submissive, I not only tolerate but often even enjoy a chrome-studded paddle across my ass, a whip across my shoulders, a huge dildo that cruelly spreads my rectum and forces its way inside. One night I almost came when a Mistress beat me with a thin wet cane that drew blood in exquisite scarlet slashes across my back.

My attitude changes. At work, or even in social settings, I take crap from no one, and I've been known to tell the odd co-worker or barfly to fuck off if I'm not in the mood to put up with them. I don't go through life with a chip on my shoulder, but I don't let people take advantage of me either. After all, I didn't get to be my company's top producer by letting people walk all over me.

If only they could see me in a scene! No matter what my Mistress tells me, no matter what she commands, I accept it. I offer her respectful silence, or I thank her for what she has given me, or I simply say, "Yes, Mistress," depending on the response she is waiting for. If the response is not correct then I accept my punishment without complaining. I have cleaned muddy boots with my tongue, so that hours later I still tasted the filth and felt the gravel grinding between my teeth. I have polished a single silver tray for more than an hour, until my fingers were so cramped they would not bend. I have listened to a Mistress call me scum and dogshit, and I have agreed with her and then thanked her for telling me.

And I have learned to wait. When my mind moves into my "submissive mode," I will wait for hours with nothing to do save kneel on a hard floor. I have turned into a submissive now, and I think that I would reject a book or other diversion if it were offered to me right now. Slaves wait for their Mistresses without complaint and without entertainment, and right now I am a slave.

While I sit and wait, however, something does go through my mind, and it is something that bothers me. It almost frightens me, for it is not the sort of thing that a submissive should even consider. It nags at me, when I am sitting like this and when I am with my Mistress. I am not completely satisfied with her.

I am frightened because that is not what I should be concerned about—after all, I am there to satisfy my Mistress's desires. If I allow myself just a little bit of pride, I believe that I do that very well, judging by the number of times this particular Mistress has demanded that I return to her and submit myself.

Still it seems to me that often she is not the Mistress that I dream about, the Mistress that leaves me hot and wet when I merely think about serving her. She is not the Mistress that makes me wake up in the middle of the night, sweat-soaked and gasping, dreaming of her whip raised to strike me.

She is quick to punish, and her icy voice snaps out commands that I am eager to obey. I have no dissatisfaction there. What I miss are the mind games, which this Mistress does not use. There are commands, there are punishments, but there is little intrigue.

My last Mistress had turned these mind games into a fine art, so that I never knew where I stood with her. Sometimes I would be allowed to become her perfect slave, until I really believed that everything I did was pleasing to her. Then, once she had allowed me to fall into this comfortable niche, it would become a trap, and I would be severely punished for transgressions I did not know I was even guilty of. I would be commanded to do something, and she would find a way to twist it so that I was disobedient when I carried out her wishes.

I was constantly in fear, always torn apart, not knowing if what I was doing would be acceptable or if my back would be lashed repeatedly all night. I had never been in such a state in my life. Under this treatment, my pussy was always soaking wet and every nerve was ready to break apart. I had never known such satisfaction, such joy. When I knelt on the floor to kiss that Mistress's boots, I thought my heart would burst with love for her.

It did indeed break, the day she told me that she had been accepted for a major promotion at her job and would be moving across the country. I tried, but could not control the sobs that racked my body when I realized I would not see her again. She beat me ruthlessly, for selfishly thinking about my own feelings. Then, as a reward for holding her in such high regard, I was permitted to suck her beautiful wet cunt until she came. Before she left, I was given to the Mistress I now had, bartered in return for a suitcase and some books.

How I remember that night! I can feel my pussy-juice on my thighs as I think about it; it always gets me wet. My Mistress took me to my new Mistress's house. I wore a collar under my shirt and as soon as the door closed behind us, I was ordered to strip and a leash was snapped to the ring of that collar. I was commanded to fall to the floor and then, like a dog, I had to move on my hands and knees across a hard stretch of polished wood through the hallway.

My new Mistress was waiting, dressed in a very tight dress that accentuated every curve of her delicious body. She got up and kissed my Mistress deeply. At least, that is how it sounded, for I was ordered to keep my eyes on the floor once I had my first quick glimpse of my new owner. I would have to wait before I could look at her fully.

"I'll miss you, Laura," my Mistress said to her friend. "I brought this by, like we agreed. Of course, I'll also leave you something else more valuable to remember me by."

"This," of course, was me. I was pulled up to my feet by the collar, gasping as my breath was cut off. My Mistress was very strong and she often dragged me around in this way, so that I was completely helpless. I loved it.

"You might want to examine it," my Mistress said. "I never purchase anything unless I've looked it over very well. Of course, if you decide you don't think you like it, you won't hurt my feelings. I can sell it elsewhere."

"Oh, it doesn't look too bad," Mistress Laura said. She lifted my chin with her fingers and I was able to look into her large green eyes. They were icy.

I knew then how a horse must feel when it is sold. Mistress Laura felt me all over just as a horse trader would, running her hands over my arms and legs and feeling my breasts to be sure she approved. My hair was lifted, my eyes were checked. I was even ordered to open my mouth, so that my teeth might be looked at. Then I had to run around the room until I was breathing hard with the exertion.

"She seems to be adequate," Mistress Laura said. My own Mistress smiled. "Perhaps," she said, "you might want to make sure that everything is in order."

Mistress Laura looked at my Mistress and then smiled. "You are right," she said, and without warning she reached across and smacked me hard on the side of the head, so that I was thrown to the floor. I was so shocked I could not move, but stayed there on the cold floor, waiting, wondering what would be next.

It did not take long for me to find out. Mistress Laura stood before me, smiling, and very slowly lifted the hem of her short skirt. She wore nothing under it. My eyes were treated to the sight of a luscious pussy, the lips shaved clean, the hair on her mound artfully sculpted into a tempting oval. I glanced at the woman who still technically owned me, and I saw that she was also looking at this hottest of sights. By the expression on her face, it was obvious that it was not the first time she had seen it.

She came over and stood beside me, and immediately it became clear what was expected of me. I got up to my knees, the heavy collar around my throat, and I put my face close to that sweet pussy.

I was almost embarrassed to be doing it, for my own Mistress, the Mistress who I loved and served, was standing there watching me pleasure another woman. I got over that quickly, though, for my momentary hesitation earned me a decent cuff on the ear from my Mistress. I did not want to risk the consequences of disobeying and so I applied my tongue to the cunt that was waiting for me.

No matter how many times I was awarded the honor of pleasuring a Mistress, each occasion was like the first. There was nothing in my submissive life to compare to it. I liked to think that I was quite good at it (my Mistress, to my chagrin, often used this lack of modesty to her own advantage and to my misery) and I always tried to be better than the time before.

I used the very tip of my tongue to burrow deep into the cleft of Mistress Laura's hot, wet folds. It was an unusual feeling, for her neatly trimmed pubic hair scratched at my nose and lip, while my tongue glided effortlessly over the smooth hairless lips. Her nectar, which had seeped throughout her cunt, was hot and sweet and I relished the taste of it. What could be more delicious than another woman?

My Mistress had always been very particular when

it came to being pleasured. Often, for her own amusement, she would command me to finger my own pussy, although I would be ordered to cease just before I reached orgasm and would be left panting, frustrated, my belly and pussy aching with unrelieved pressure. Because my hands had touched my own cunt and were thus "soiled," I was never permitted to put them between her legs but could only use my tongue.

This limitation had made me much more proficient with my mouth, and now I was able to push apart Mistress Laura's cunt lips with my tongue and press the tip of it into the opening to her tunnel. It was silky smooth and unbelievably wet, and my lips came away soaked with her. I licked it off and then flicked over her clitoris, at first gently and then much more firmly. I could feel her thighs tightening and I knew that I was having an effect.

I had never known a Mistress who would lead me to believe that I had made her come. They were experts at controlling their trembling and never did they gasp or moan, for it would show that their lowly slaves were able to create such feelings. Instead, I had learned to identify climaxes by the subtle ways that Mistresses used as a disguise. I knew well the spasms that went through a Mistress's pussy and the way the rings of muscle at the opening to her vagina would pulse on my tongue. I recognized the quick breath and the tiny shudder that would go through her. These gave me as much satisfaction, if not more, than if my Mistress had cried out in the throes of climax. When I made a Mistress come, it was better than coming myself.

I was determined to show this Mistress that I was a capable slave. I licked her from front to back, leaning in between her legs and craning my neck so that I might pleasure every inch of the pussy that was above me. I nibbled gently at her clit with my teeth and was rewarded with a quick breath from her, so that I knew I was succeeding. I lapped at the warm place where her thighs curved up to meet her pussy, and I pressed my tongue against the tight opening of her ass. I did not miss anywhere, and gradually I worked my way back to the front of her cleft so that I could concentrate on the sensitive little button of flesh there. I knew the signs and I knew she was close to coming.

I was so involved that I never heard my own Mistress's footsteps behind me. Suddenly my head was on fire. It was my Mistress, who had wrapped her hand in my long hair and was using it to drag me away. Gasping, crying, I could only fall helplessly on my back. When my Mistress let go of my hair, a handful of it fell away. I sobbed, both with pain and with the shock, but fortunately I was able to hold my tongue. I knew that if I had questioned her, I might have ended up thrown across a table with a whip applied to my buttocks.

My Mistress was naked, having undressed while I was pleasuring Mistress Laura. The two of them walked across the room to the sofa, Mistress Laura pulling her dress off as she walked. Mistress Laura reclined on the cushions, while my Mistress got on top of her, and within moments they were licking each other's pussies.

I could not control my tears, which ran unchecked down my cheeks. I had been so close to making her come, and now that had been taken away from me. Since they were both dominatrixes, there was not the stigma of being licked by a slave, and they vented their emotions by gasping and sighing even as their tongues were firmly in each other's cunts. I sobbed. Never would I have the opportunity to make a Mistress cry out like that! And my Mistress's cunt, which I knew so well and had pleasured so many times, was now being served by another.

They made each other come, and I could only stay on the floor and watch. My own pussy was throbbing at the sight of them, for a sixty-nine was one of my favorite positions to watch. For a moment, I considered putting my fingers there to relieve myself. They were so caught up in what they were doing, I was sure they wouldn't notice. But then the whole picture came to me, almost like a flash of blinding light. These were dominatrixes and I was but a lowly submissive! It was my lot in life to lie on the floor, a leather collar about my neck, and wait for commands. Even the threat of punishment wasn't as much a deterrent as the fact that this was something a slave simply wasn't supposed to do.

When they were finished, they lay for a moment caressing each other. Then they sat up, their arms about each other, kissing gently and running their hands over each other's bodies. Chances were that they would not see each other again, and this was good-bye. I could not believe my good fortune at being permitted to watch them. Such rare displays of compassion and love were almost unknown to such lowly creatures as myself.

After a long time they got up and dressed again, and I was hauled to my knees, left there on the hard floor while my legs ached. The suitcase and the books, the barter for me, were brought out, and my Mistress looked them over carefully, checking for the tiniest details. It was not lost on me that these goods were examined much more scrupulously than I had been. These items were of a greater value than I was, a fact that was driven home when my Mistress refused to take more than two books. Four books, she said, meant that she was getting the better deal and the exchange would not be entirely fair. Finally, she accepted a third volume when Mistress Laura pointed out that she would also like to keep the leather collar I was wearing.

I was taken, on my hands and knees, to a closet, where I was ordered to kneel inside. The closet floor was protected by a nubbed rubber mat and I moaned quietly as it made contact with my legs. The hard, tiny nubs were like needles pressing into my skin. Then the door was closed and I was plunged into darkness.

I could hear their voices but they were muffled, and I was unable to understand what they were saying. They talked for a long time and then they walked away. I never saw my Mistress again.

All of this came back to me as I waited in the stifling room, watching the clock. The hands seemed cemented in place, and the sound of people outside on the sidewalk and cars going by only reinforced the fact that I had to sit and wait. But wait I did. I was a lowly slave who had been given her orders.

Finally, at eleven, I got up and stretched my stiff legs, then quickly dressed. I thought it would be cool outside, but the summer night was almost as hot as the day had been. I walked up the sidewalk, slowly, hoping that I had given myself enough time. Walking quickly would make me sweaty, which would be difficult to explain. Being late, however, would be deadly. When one was only a possession, there simply was no excuse.

Chapter *Two*

The porch light is on at my Mistress's house when I arrive, and it affords me enough light, standing at the sidewalk, to see my watch. It is three minutes to midnight. I stand close to the magnolia tree in the corner of her yard, hidden in the shadows from cars driving by, hoping that no one sees me there. I have to wait for those three minutes to pass, for my Mistress ordered me to be at her house at midnight. For a submissive, that is not three minutes to twelve or thirty seconds after. It is midnight, on the dot.

At exactly the moment that the hands on my watch meet, I go to the door and ring the bell. I always thought it strange that her door held a decorative brass pineapple, the Southern symbol of hospitality. Hospitality was something I would definitely not be receiving here.

My Mistress opens the door without a word, and silently I step inside. The door clicks shut behind me, and I close my eyes and wait. I do not know what to expect or what to do. That is what being a submissive is all about: My life is completely in another's hands.

"I see that you replaced that watch of yours," she says. "Yes, Mistress," I say. I had overspent and would have to play serious catch up with my credit card, but the pricey watch I wore was a necessity, not a luxury. My old one often lost time, and using it to make my Mistress's appointments had resulted in more than one cruel beating.

"It's about time," she says, smiling quickly at her pun. I lift the corners of my mouth slightly—my Mistress has made a joke—but only enough to show that I had heard it. Laughter is only to be permitted under certain circumstances and I instinctively know that this is not one of them.

I stand rooted to the spot, for I have not been told to do anything. My Mistress stands in front of me, no doubt so that I might admire her. This I do. She has prepared herself for me just as I have prepared myself for her. She wears a soft suede vest with no shirt below it, and I can see the swell of her lovely breasts beneath it. She wears a garter and stockings and the tiniest panties, formed of soft leather that molds to her hot pussy. I hope that tonight I will be deemed worthy enough to pleasure her, and my mouth waters in anticipation. For me there is no higher prize.

She walks behind me, and her stiletto heels ring

out on the hard floor. I cannot see her, and I do not know what she is going to do. It is difficult for me to control my breathing. Is she standing with her arm raised, about to strike me down? Is she sizing me up, deciding what type of punishment will be best? This is what I really love about a scene, the fact that she is in control, and I know nothing until it is actually done to me.

I am somewhat disappointed when all she says is, "Take off your clothes." I had hoped for a little more than that, but then, it is not my place to complain. Silently, as quickly as possible, I shed the light dress that I am wearing. The house, in stark contrast to my own, is cool. There is no suffering for a Mistress, ever.

"On the floor," she orders, and I drop like a stone to obey her. She walks away and snaps her fingers. I am to follow her, heeling, like a well-trained dog. My knees slap hard and painfully on the floor as I struggle to follow her quick steps.

I see that we are heading down the hall to the room at the very end of it, and I can feel my pussy start to ooze its hot, thick juice even as I look at the closed door. I know this room so well, and when my Mistress opens the lock and the door swings open, I close my eyes and breathe deeply. I love the smell of this room. The hardwood floor smells of rich lemon oil, polished to a high shine by submissives on their hands and knees. There is a faint wisp of the vanilla-scented candle that my Mistress sometimes burns inside. And as I take the cool air into my lungs, it seems that I can smell the women who have been in here. I can smell the sweet heat of my Mistress's pussy. I can smell the thin film of sweat that glistens on a submissive's skin as she hurries to obey a command. I take in the smell of their fear, their desire, their womanhood. My own is mixed in with it all.

My Mistress stands at the door and waits for me to crawl inside. Although I am hurrying, I am not fast enough for her, and I am given a kick as I pass by her. When her boot connects with my flesh, I gasp and speed up. The room is dark, the only illumination coming from the thin slice of light admitted through the open door, and I hope I do not run into anything. Of course she does not tell me where I am to stop, and when I have gone far enough for her, she grabs me by my hair and pulls so hard that I am drawn back onto my haunches. I wait there, my scalp burning, my chin down, my eyes on the floor.

She turns on a single shaded light hanging on the wall. The room is filled with various lights in different positions, and she likes to set the mood by using them in combinations, depending on her preference at any particular time. The small bulb casts deep, gloomy shadows, and the devices along one wall appear even more gruesome and hideous than usual.

I had been a little sleepy before I came out this evening, but now I am wide awake, my entire body on edge as I wait. I love the way that being under a Mistress's command keeps me in a state of sexual excitement that will not abate, no matter how horrific the punishments that are meted out to me. The lack of relief, the emphasis on my Mistress's satisfaction only, heightens all of it.

Walking behind me, my Mistress circles my body with her hands, and then I feel the rough fibers of the rope on my bare skin. It is thin rope, made of nylon. If I squirm when I am within it, it will leave long, cruel burns on me.

She wraps it around my chest, just under my breasts. Then, with quick, practiced motions, she loops the ends around my tits. My breath is squeezed out of me as she tightens the circles. When they are as tight as they can be, she wraps them around me again and knots all of it firmly behind my back.

I can hardly breathe. My tits swell up almost immediately and the pain floods through me. My nipples are engorged with the blood trapped in them and my skin is as tight and shiny as a balloon. I take tiny, gasping breaths and my lungs feel as if they are empty. I desperately want to suck air into them and I feel dizzy and oxygen-starved. But I know that if I expand my chest, those ropes will bite hungrily into my flesh. I try to calm down and breathe slowly through my nose.

"Close your eyes," my Mistress orders, and I do so. I hear her heels on the carpetless floor as she moves about the room. I concentrate on that sound to take my mind off my hideously bound breasts.

She comes back and stands before me. I wish I could look at her and know what is coming, but that is forbidden. She waits there so long that I begin to tremble with anticipation and fear. I don't know how much longer I can hold out.

When she reaches for my nipple, her touch is so soft that at first I think I have imagined it. Only when she touches me again do I realize that her fingers are brushing up against me. I cannot stop the soft moan that escapes my lips, for it feels so good on my bloated, firmly bound breast. It slips through the pain and sends a heated chill throughout my entire body. I love this, when pain and pleasure cross their thresholds and mingle throughout me. At times like this, I don't really know which sensation it is that excites me more.

Then she hisses, "Stupid slave!" At the same time, I all but scream. My eyes fly open and I look down in horror.

She has deftly snapped clothespins on my nipples. They hang grotesquely from my flesh, and when one threatens to fall off, my Mistress rudely opens it and closes it back in place.

The pain sears through to my ribs and my skin is on fire. I try to breathe slowly through my nose and I swallow several times, trying to control the nausea that rises up in me. My eyes are once again closed—it doesn't seem to hurt as much when I can't see those wooden tormentors!—but it is too late. My Mistress saw them open when the pins were first applied, in direct violation of her orders.

"I notice," she says, "that a Mistress's command is not enough for you. Did you think I did not see you, when I ordered you to keep your eyes closed? Did you think I would miss it?"

"No, Mistress," I whisper, barely audible. "I do not hear you," she says. "No, Mistress," I repeat, a bit louder. She makes me say it four times, each time with more emphasis. It is not lost on me. Each time I must take a deeper breath to project the words, and when I do, the pins tremble on my nipples and send shock waves throughout me.

"Do you believe this is a forgivable offense?" she asks, walking behind me. I answer immediately, in the negative. She is not listening, for she knows that no other answer could possibly be forthcoming.

She continues walking in back of me. I long to turn around and look at her, to see what she is doing, but I know that such action is, of course, impossible. By her footsteps I know that she is at the cupboard on the wall, the one secured by a lock which contains her favorite torture devices. I look straight ahead at the shuttered windows. I try to avoid looking down at my breasts, so monstrously bound with rope, the nipples distended by these ordinary household devices which have become horrible instruments of torture in my Mistress's hands. I try to avoid looking at the far wall, with its frames, its rings, its harnesses, all even more imposing in the half light of the room.

She walks around in front of me, but I keep my eyes closed, following her instead by the sound of her footsteps. Then I feel her boot on my chest, and when she pushes me onto my back I have to bite my tongue hard to keep from screaming. The ropes cut into me deeply and the clothespins bob on my distended nipples. For a moment I almost pass into blackness, but just before the blessed unconsciousness overcomes my pain, my head clears and I am thrust back within the circles of torment.

She uses her boots to kick my legs apart. The agony of her roughness is offset by the delicious coolness of the leather as it touches my naked skin. She is standing between my legs now, and I know she is looking at my distorted breasts and my cunt, now spread open to her view. I can feel the heat in it and I wonder if she notices the glimmer of wetness on the pink flesh. For just a moment, I engage in a most forbidden fantasy, of her bending down to apply her tongue to it and relieve the almost overwhelming passion that has built up in it. That lasts for only a few seconds. I have a better chance of living on Mars than I do of any Mistress carrying out such a dream.

Nevertheless, my body longs for a touch on that swollen nub, where all of my raw sexual nerves begin and end. Eventually I receive it, but it is not what I have been waiting for.

"You may open your eyes," she says to me, and I let them open. The pain is so strong that I see stars at first. Then I look down and to my horror I see the clothespin. This mate to the ones stuck on my nipples has been clamped onto the wet, swollen flesh of my clit.

My Mistress laughs coldly at me. My eyes are wide and my mouth is open in a silent moan of pain. When she reaches down and flicks at it with one red fingernail, I do black out for a few seconds, and it is only when my head hits the floor that I come out of it.

"Hung out to dry," my Mistress chuckles, and she walks away. I cannot remember when I have had to work so hard to regain my composure. I swallow to control my nausea and concentrate on my breathing to keep from gasping and thus pulling the ropes tighter. My hands clench and unclench and it seems like hours before I can finally lie on the floor and work myself through the agony.

When I eventually do, I can smell vanilla. It is the candle that my Mistress enjoys burning, and soon she appears before me, with the candle in one hand. In the other she holds a thin metal rod.

"I find," she says, "that it is much too cold in here. Poor little thing, you'll be shivering soon. I guess it's my duty to keep you warm."

With that, she holds the end of the rod in the sweet-smelling flame. When she brings it out, it is glowing red. She holds it for just a moment, until the cherry color fades slightly. Then she presses it against my belly.

I have worked around so much pain that the bitter touch is only a dull ache on my skin. I find, instead, that I am fascinated by the flame as it burns with its deceptively sweet, candylike smell. My eyes cannot leave the rod as it slowly changes color within the fire. When it is withdrawn, brimming scarlet, a shiver goes through me. My arms are not bound, and it would be simple for me to lift my hands and push it away as my Mistress brings it down to brand my skin. I do not. I almost welcome its thrust onto my pale belly, for it pleases her to do this to me.

She is an expert at this. She knows exactly the right temperature for the rod, so that it burns with exquisite pain and yet will only leave its marks temporarily. I do not know how she has come by this knowledge, what trial and error has brought her to this point. I long to see the woman who still carries the scars that she must have left before she learned.

I am able to control myself when the rod is applied again and again to my skin, but I shudder and moan uncontrollably when she tips the candle and lets the drops of hot, sweet wax fall onto my swollen breasts. The wax runs in molten streams, scalding as it moves, and when I jerk away involuntarily from it, the clothespins tighten. Through my ruby haze of pain, I can see my Mistress's glistening red lips as she smiles coldly. She is thoroughly enjoying my condition.

Abruptly she blows the candle flame out, and I breathe a shallow sigh of relief. Her eyes do not smile. In them I can see a convoluted sexual satisfaction, even though I have not been allowed to touch the hot cunt that I long for.

Inexplicably, it is over. She rips the clothespins from my clit and nipples without opening them, and I can control myself no longer; a muted scream rises from my throat. She kicks me onto my stomach and unties the ropes, then pulls them away. They burn as they are whipped across my skin. My breasts throb as the circulation is returned to them. My whole body feels like the skin has been peeled away from it, layer by precious layer.

"You can find your own way out," she says, and her heels click on the floor as she leaves the room. She turns out the light, leaving me lying dazed in the dark.

I lie there for some time, waiting for the feeling to return to my body. Bruised and burned, I get up slowly and stiffly and make my way back to the front hall. I do not know where she is; the lights are all out, and I have to rely on the faint glimmer that comes through the windows from the streetlights. Fortunately I know the house well, and I am able to find the door and my dress discarded beside it. The door clicks closed behind me and I am once again wrapped in the thick, humid heat outside.

As I walk home along the deserted streets, I am confused, and at the same time, upset by my confusion. I served my Mistress well tonight, I am sure of that; I saw her smile, saw the look in her eyes as she enjoyed my discomfort. But at the same time, I know that all I received tonight was torture, plain and simple. There were no mind games, no intrigue. There was none of the sweet entrapment that so many Mistresses used to disorient a submissive and then use as justification for punishment. Instead, I had simply been summoned, tormented, and then released.

I crave pain; that was part of the reason I had chosen the role of submissive so many years ago. But I crave pain when it is intermingled with cunning, and that was something I had not received this early morning.

Arriving at my own front door, I turn on the air conditioner as soon as I walk inside, and once again discard my dress on the way to the bathroom. I turn on the light and assess my body in the mirror. I like what I see. The lines left by the ropes are still there, and some of them are raw burns in my flesh that will scab over and be visible for weeks. My nipples are still red and so sore that I cannot touch them. My belly is criss-crossed with thin red marks, and slowly and patiently I use a fingernail to scrape the hard wax off my tits as gently as I can.

I take a cool shower, but the water on these punishments is an agony, and the soft towel irritates them as well. My clit is too sore for touching, but that does not prevent me from taking a vibrator and placing its gently rounded tip at the opening to my cunt. It slips effortlessly into my soaked tunnel. I think about a Mistress who will hold my mind captive as she punishes my body while the plastic device buzzes delightfully against the soft walls of my hole. My tongue slips out to lick a pussy I have been ordered to pleasure, and I fuck myself with the vibrator at the same time. When the forbidden waves of orgasm course through me, leaving me sweat-soaked and gasping, I know that this cannot remain a fantasy any longer. I have a need, and I will fulfill it.

Chapter *Three*

"This is the only part of the job I really and truly hate," Cleo says, as I get out of the cab and wait for her to slide over on the seat and follow me.

I certainly have to agree with her, standing on the hot sidewalk, looking up at the huge hotel. This will be my home for the next four days as I work through the bane of my existence, the trade show.

Both of us have come to detest the trade shows even though we do so many of them each year. Long ago, when I was new in the business, I found them incredibly thrilling. Taxicabs would pick me up and whisk me to the airport, where a plane would be waiting to take me to a new city, perhaps a few hundred miles away, perhaps all the way across the country. Another taxicab would take me to a hotel, where I would have a room to myself and meals in the dining room (or even room service—what a rush!). And all I had to do in return was stand for twelve or fourteen hours a day at a booth, showing the benefits of our company's fasteners over all the other companies represented there, and keep on smiling no matter what.

It didn't take long for the novelty to wear off. The early-morning or late-night flights the company booked to keep costs down were no longer exciting, but aggravating when they meant waking up at 4 A.M. My destinations were still exciting cities that I had always wanted to visit, but all I got to see of them was the airport and the three or four blocks around my hotel. Living out of a suitcase was bad enough when my attire was sweats and blue jeans, but even worse when I had to wear a business suit or dress everyday. The hotel food was overcooked and bland, and standing on my feet all day took its toll.

Worst of all were the businessmen who thought all I wanted was to spend the night with them. Little did they know that I would undoubtedly have preferred their wives!

It wasn't long before, instead of looking forward to the trips like a child at Christmas, I was begging my superiors to find someone else to send. My ability was my downfall. It was beyond me to turn in an unprofessional performance—no doubt a result of my training as a submissive!—and I remained the top trade-show producer, signing on new clients in numbers no one else in the company could exceed. My talent meant that, at least for now, I would be the first choice whenever a trade show opened anywhere in the country.

Cleo was my only saving grace. Three years ago she had started with the company, and as part of her training, she was assigned to accompany me to a show in Chicago.

She had intrigued me from the very beginning. She was small, lithe, firm-breasted and cheerful, even if she did drop her eyes whenever I looked at her. She had worn her hair cut rather short, in a mannish style that somehow seemed to bring out her femininity, and for a moment I had wondered if this might be a clue. But then we got caught up in the show, and for the rest of that day I worked alongside her, without a moment to myself to think about the possibilities.

When the show wrapped up for the evening, I suggested a relaxing drink in the lounge, which she quickly agreed to. We no sooner sat down than two loudly dressed, obnoxious, and decidedly soused businessmen tried to put the make on us.

"Perhaps a drink in the room might be a better idea," I said, and we left quickly. Her room was closer and we went there, to enjoy a bourbon and ice from the minibar.

She excused herself to go to the washroom and I absently played with the television remote control while she was gone. This particular hotel featured video machines in their rooms, and out of boredom I hit the "play" button, even though I wasn't expecting to find a tape in the machine.

My boredom vanished immediately when I saw what was in there. The television screen came to life and to my surprise, I was watching a movie that definitely hadn't been scheduled on HBO that night.

A woman, obviously a dominatrix, was standing in the middle of the room. Her costume gave her away: a skin-tight, soft black leather corset, black fishnet stockings, impossibly high stiletto boots that went almost to her knees, black leather gloves to her elbows. She wore a small black mask over her eyes and in one hand she held a black riding crop.

There were some sounds offscreen, and then a young woman crawled into view and over to the dominatrix's feet. I sucked in my breath and my pussy almost exploded with heat. The woman was naked, and I could clearly see red welts across her back, no doubt from the riding crop. She had pierced nipples with gold rings in them. Attached to each ring was a short, thin gold chain, and each chain ended in a small weight. These swung as she crawled, and they must have been painful, for they dragged her tits down and distorted them. She stopped and put her head down, and I gasped when I saw her pink tongue snake out to lovingly caress the high polish of the leather boots.

I was so caught up in the film, I didn't notice Cleo had come back into the room until I heard her gasp. I turned. She was staring at the screen, her eyes wide. Her face was completely white, then, rapidly, it changed to a brilliant scarlet. She was so embarrassed that the flush went right down her chest, as far as I could see over the top of her blouse.

"I didn't mean for you to see—," she gasped, reaching for the video control, but I held it away. I was surprised as well, but for a completely different reason.

"You brought a movie with you?" I asked.

"Yes," she said, close to tears. "It excites—no, please, don't take this the wrong way. Please, just give me the control."

"Are you a—I mean, are you into this?" I asked. Out of the corner of my eye, I could see the dominatrix gently caress her slave's ass with the tip of her riding crop. My pussy tightened, for I knew that such a caress almost inevitably ends with a welt-raising blow.

Her secret out, Cleo sat down on the edge of the bed. "I'm a submissive," she blurted, looking at the floor. "That means I like to obey orders from a superior."

"I know," I said, hardly daring to breathe. "I'm a submissive too."

For a moment I could see that she didn't believe me. But I nodded to her and held out my arms. In the next moment, she was holding me, and I was breathing in her perfume and smoothing her hair with my hand. We held each other for a long time, rocking back and forth, both of us complete in our discovery. There are thousands of us out there, but when we find each other, it is like we are the only two on earth.

Wordlessly, our arms still around each other, we turned back to the television screen. The woman on the ground was still busy polishing those delicious boots with her tongue. The dominatrix raised one foot, and her slave fellated the thin spike heel. I trembled at the sight of her cheeks sucking in to clean the heel thoroughly.

I didn't even realize that my hand was making its way slowly between my legs until I let out a tiny sigh. It was the result of my fingers reaching the soaked panties under my skirt. I heard a similar sigh beside me and turned to see that Cleo was also fingering herself. It was just so natural for both of us that we could not resist a quick kiss before we returned to the screen.

Without taking her eyes off the television, Cleo slipped off her skirt and her panties. I could see the wetness glisten on her pubic hairs. I did the same and now we were both sitting on the bed, naked from the waist down, with our hands firmly on our throbbing clits. We had to have relief; this was just too much for us.

I kept averting my gaze from the screen to watch Cleo and discovering that she was sneaking glances at me as well. The atmosphere in the room was electric. The air was heavy with the rich perfume of our cunts. The slave on the television screen was now groveling at her Mistress's feet, her face contorted with pain, while the tall dominatrix used the pointed tip of one boot to set the small nipple weights swinging. We were on the bed, feeling ourselves up, two virtual strangers who were now bound together by an inescapable need to submit.

Our orgasms were positively explosive. Cleo, who later confided that she was usually very quiet, threw her head back and moaned as her hand twisted and shook across her swollen clit. My own orgasm almost sent stars to my head, and I was left gasping. We collapsed into a satisfied heap on the bed. Since we are so very rarely permitted actual sex, when we do receive it, it is amazing.

Ever since that day we were the best of friends, and business trips actually became tolerable again when Cleo was assigned along with me, which she usually was.

Tolerable, but still not completely enjoyable, I tell myself, as we walk into the lobby of the hotel. We sign in at the desk and receive the keys to our rooms. The company always gives us separate ones, but it is not unusual for us to rumple the bed in one and then sleep together in the other. As we ride the elevator, I pray that this hotel has video machines in the rooms; I know that a tape from Cleo's extensive collection is packed into her suitcase.

Alas, it is not to be, and I mutter, "Shit," as I look around the video-deprived room. It is a lovely room, well appointed and expensive, but it is nevertheless just another hotel room, and I quickly shower and dress. The show is being set up this afternoon for an early start in the morning, and I might as well go downstairs.

The show is being held in the hotel's cavernous basement, and at least I will be spared the aggravation of trying to get a cab in rush hour to get to a convention center. I knock on Cleo's door, and she answers it in a bathrobe with a towel wrapped around her head. "Soaps," she says, and I smile. Cleo has a passion for soap operas, and I know there is no point expecting her to get ready before the last melodramatic moment has spun itself out on her favorite series.

"I'll see you down there later, then," I say, making my way to the elevator.

The huge room is a bustle of activity and half-erected displays. My own booth is being set up by the "roadies," as I call them, and I watch as the components gradually take shape. I take a few minutes to assess everything: my proximity to the door, the layout of the show, the booths that are going up on either side of mine. I have known all of this for weeks from the floor plans I have studied, but I still like to get an up-close view of it all as it is coming together.

"Excuse me," a voice says behind me, and I turn. My mouth almost drops open.

The woman standing there is a goddess. Tall, slim, well-built, perfectly dressed, she is stunningly beautiful. Her long dark hair is carefully drawn back and her eyes are large and friendly.

"Are you Jennifer Dobson?" she asks.

"I am," I say, trying hard to keep from staring at her in awe.

"I'm Lyla Kirk," she says, and puts forth her hand. I shake it. Her grip is warm, dry, assertive. I must have a puzzled look on my face, for she continues, "Weren't you told about me?"

I shake my head. "I'm surprised about that," she says. "Head office sent me. I'm in charge of trade-show accounting there."

"Now I know; I thought your name sounded familiar," I say. It does. When I submit my expense accounts for the trade shows to head office, they are returned a few days later with a stamp signifying that they have been accepted. The name signed above the stamp is Lyla Kirk's.

"I'm going to be here for the show," she continues. "All of my previous experience has just been through paperwork at the office. Under the new training program, they wanted me to come out and get an actual feel for the whole thing, and they told me you would be the best person to work with."

For a moment I stiffen. Cleo and I have worked together for so long that the idea of a third party, especially an unannounced one, is an unwelcome intrusion.

Lyla mistakes my reaction. "Don't worry," she says. "I'm not here to audit you or make sure your expenses are legitimate. I'm here to learn something, and hopefully you can help me."

In spite of myself, I find myself relaxing. For one

thing, she seems sincere in that she will not be taking over from us—Cleo and I take great pride in our company performance. For another, she is so gorgeous that I can hardly stop myself from drooling over her. Perhaps I can make the best of this situation.

"I'm also supposed to be meeting someone else," she says.

"Cleo," I tell her. "She's still upstairs getting ready. We don't really start until tomorrow morning, so we just take our time and unwind from the rushing at the airport and the flight."

"But they send you in the day before?" Lyla asks. I smile. "Obviously they didn't brief you completely," I say. "Everyone else is going to be on this floor at seven-thirty tomorrow morning." I realize she isn't an early riser when her eyes open wide in disbelief, and I can't resist adding, "Cleo and I will be down here at six-thirty."

"Why so early?"

"Because it's little tricks like that, that make us the best in our field," I say. "We'll have a head start on the competition and they'll never be able to catch up. When the doors open, we'll be ready. They'll still be drinking their coffee and trying to wake up."

"So what do we do now?" Lyla asks.

"There really isn't much," I tell her. "I know Cleo will be a while. Why don't we have a drink in the lounge?"

The lounge in this hotel is extremely inviting, all dark paneling and comfortable, richly upholstered chairs. We order our drinks. Now, sitting across the low table from each other, without the trade-show background, we are almost shy. Finally she asks where I live. To my surprise, she lives only a few miles away from me.

"So what does your husband think about you taking off to all these trade shows?" Lyla asks, as she sips at her drink.

"I'm not married," I tell her. "I live by myself. What about you? Do you have a family?"

"No," she says, and for a moment I can tell that she is wrestling inwardly with herself. She looks around and then says, quietly, "I want to tell you this, right from the start, because some co-workers aren't really comfortable with it. I'm a lesbian."

I suck in my breath, and for the second time that day she misreads my intentions, thinking that I disapprove. Quickly, I tell her the reason for my reaction. Once I have, we sit back and I feel almost satisfied. Through the admission of a shared secret, we are now immediate friends.

Exactly what happens next is something I know I will never be able to remember, not in its progression; the precise series of events will evade me forever, but I will not forget the result. I finish my drink and we order two more and sip them while we talk. Lyla asks me about loneliness when I am zipping back and forth across the country, staying in strange hotels in strange cities. She tells me about her own loneliness and her needs. Before I know it, I am in the elevator with her. I am walking down a hallway that seems longer than any I have ever walked before. I watch her push her key into the lock, see the room, a mirror image of my own. And I watch her as she unbuttons her shirt, and the delicious breasts topple away from her clothing and beckon to me. This, I know, I will always remember.

Chapter *Four*

When we are both undressed, Lyla takes me into her arms. Her skin is delectably cool and smooth against mine, and her lips are warm and sweet as she pushes her mouth against mine. Her tongue snakes into my mouth. A thrill goes through my entire body.

I am captivated by this woman, but at the same time I am confused about what I am feeling. It has been many years since I have held a woman in this way and have been treated as her equal. It is difficult for me at first, even though I want Lyla as badly as I have ever wanted anyone. When she kisses me, I feel as if I am doing something terribly forbidden, which I will be punished for later on. At the same time, her forward manner excites me. I am being taken here, there is no doubt about it. This is a woman who does not wait to be asked what she wants.

She is luscious. She obviously works out and her body is firm, although it gives just where I want it to. My fingers appreciate the softness of her breasts and the smooth curve of her throat as it meets her chest. She moves me over to the bed, her arms still around me, her tongue deep in my mouth. She explores me with the tips of her fingers and my skin reacts with a warm quiver wherever she touches.

When we get to the bed, she lies down on it, spread out fully. I cannot help but admire her. She is so strong, so sensual, and for a long moment I want nothing else but to throw myself at her feet and put myself at her mercy. Of course I know that she wouldn't understand, and so I kneel on the bed beside her. Her hands are on my breasts, playing with my hard nipples, making me groan. My pussy feels soaked and it throbs with desire. She puts a hand between my legs. I close my eyes; her touch makes me almost come.

Then she turns over, lying on her stomach. Her spine is a delicious curve down to the smoothly rounded, firm globes of her buttocks and her long legs. Her hair, now untethered, spreads black against her milky pale skin.

I run my hands up and down that creamy back. She almost purrs as I caress her. My hands play with the thick hair and trace the design of her backbone. I slip a finger into the space between those asscheeks. She is hot there.

"I love having my back scratched," she sighs, and like a cat she seems to undulate under my touch, trying to get every last bit of pleasure from my fingernails.

"Yes, Mistress," I whisper, and then, horrified, I put a hand to my mouth. It slipped out so automatically!

"What did you say?" she smiles. Lying with her face on the pillow, her arm wrapped around her head, my words came through muffled. Fortunately, she did not fully hear my submissive reply.

"I—um, you're lovely, Miss Kirk," I say quickly. "I said you were lovely."

"Why, thank you," she says, "but at this stage of the game, I think Miss Kirk is just a bit too formal. My name is Lyla, Jennifer."

"Of course," I say, and cool my burning cheeks against the sweet skin of her shoulders as I continue to move my hands along her back. How I long to call her "Mistress Lyla"! But that will have to remain a dream, and right now, it is reality I am interested in. She is here in front of me, all mine for me to enjoy.

I have never seen anyone enjoy the touch of a hand on her skin as much as Lyla does. She squirms and writhes under my fingers, sighing, moaning as much as if I were touching the hot wetness between her legs. Her thighs are parted and I can see that this area is indeed waiting for a touch as well. Her clit is huge, and my mouth waters at the sight of it. I want this hot candy between my lips. It protrudes beyond her cuntlips, looking almost impossibly pink against the black hair curled against it.

I run my hands over her asscheeks. I can feel the delectable flesh under the skin, and I can't resist grabbing them until they give gently under my fingertips. Lyla moans again and I can't wait. I let my hand slip into the hot crack between them, and down, until I can feel the juice on my finger. She twists and groans loudly and whispers, "Oh, touch me there!"

At this point I don't need a command, even one spoken in passion rather than domination. Gently I manipulate her legs and turn her body, so that she is lying on her back. Her nipples are swollen and hard, and I have to touch them first. They are hot and sweet in my mouth, but right now they are not the prize I want.

I find it between her thighs. Her taste is sweet and salty on my tongue at the same time, and I lap the liquid from the folds of her cunt before I tickle her clit.

A Mistress always holds her emotions in check, and one of the things that I often find frustrating about being a submissive is that I don't always know when I am pleasing my superior. There is no question of that here. Lyla is the most animated woman I have ever met. It is difficult for me to keep my tongue on her steamy clit, for she moves around so much. When she bucks her hips, I move my tongue sideways, and she moves her clit up and down on my mouth.

Her hole is positively gushing nectar, and I can't get enough of it. I rim all around the opening and then push my tongue right up inside of her. Meanwhile my fingers are caressing the tight opening of her ass, hoping that I might gain access. When I do, with the tip held firmly by the ring of muscle there, Lyla almost goes wild.

"Too long, too long!" she gasps, and for a moment I think that I have entered this forbidden zone too deeply. I pull my finger back, but to my surprise, she reaches down and takes my wrist, motioning for me to remain inside of her. I do, pushing slowly and firmly, until I am in right up to my knuckle. "It's been too long," she smiles, and suddenly I realize that she has been without this pleasure for a while. I am all the more determined, then, to make this very special.

I am now very busy between my lover's legs. One hand is busy at her tunnel, two fingers deep inside of this wet heaven. My other hand is inside as well, and I can feel my fingertips through the wall of flesh that separates them. My mouth is firmly on the pink clit that she moves for me. I lap at it, I push it back and forth, and I feel it swell between my lips as I caress it with my tongue.

She builds up so slowly, I know she must be controlling herself to make this last. This is where my expertise comes in. I take forever with her, building her up and then moving back at the right moment to let her catch her breath before the next tongue-lashing on her slit. It is easy to tell when she is close. She moans, writhes, spreads that beautiful body for me.

I am surprised that she makes no effort to reach for me, but instead of feeling put upon, I am joyous. In this position, even though we are not dominatrix and submissive, I feel like I am here only to provide her with pleasure at her command. In the unusual way that my preference works, I am more excited by being left alone than if Lyla were to caress me or insist that I crouch over her mouth for a licking of my own.

My tongue moves on her clit like a trip-hammer, and I could keep this up for days. I love eating pussy! I back off and build her up twice more until she is almost out of her head. Then I concentrate on that sweet nub of flesh, not to give up until I have achieved my goal.

With this attention it doesn't take long. If I thought

she was vocal before, this time she is right over the edge. She positively howls and reaches for her tits, rolling the nipples between her fingers as I try to keep my tongue on her clit. She writhes, bucks, pulls every last bit of pleasure out of my mouth through her cunt. When she has finally finished, I lap her soaked pussy dry and then crawl up the bed until I am at her hip, lying there. I am as satisfied as she.

I want to stay here, in a submissive position beside the woman I have just helped to a climax, but she takes my arm and motions me to lie up beside her. I move into her arms, and she kisses me deeply.

"That was magnificent," she gasps, as if I cannot tell. "I haven't come like that in a long time."

"I'm so glad I could do that for you," I tell her.

"You are wonderful," she says. "I wish I'd met you long ago." She kisses me again, slowly and tenderly.

Still she does nothing more than this, only lies there basking in the afterglow of this explosive orgasm. Finally, she reaches for my tits and massages them with one hand, but I can tell that she really isn't into it. She seems much happier just relaxing beside me.

I am thrilled by this, and gently, I take her hand and put it down at her side. "It isn't necessary," I tell her. "You just lie there and enjoy."

"But you haven't come yet," she argues, although I realize it's only a halfhearted response.

"I don't need to," I tell her. "It's enough for me just to do that for you."

She hesitates for a moment. "Are you sure?"

"Absolutely," I smile. She kisses me again, and runs her hand along my arm lovingly. "Thank you so much," she says. "When I come like that, I haven't got the energy even to lift my little finger. All I want to do is lie back and enjoy how relaxed and satisfied I feel. It isn't often I get to do that."

I hold her close. My fingertips draw lazy circles on her throat, around her breasts, down to her navel, and she obviously enjoys it immensely. "You know," I tell her quietly, "if you enjoy being pleasured without giving it back, you can have that. There are women who just want to please, without any thought for themselves."

"I only wish," she smiles; she does not believe me.

"No, it's true," I tell her. "Just imagine it, Lyla. Pleasure without reciprocation. In fact, pleasure any time you want it. All you do is demand—er, ask for sex, and it's given to you immediately without question."

"Sounds like something in a fairy tale," she says.

"I know it does," I say, "but there really are women like that out there. Trust me, I know."

She is quiet then, and it is obvious that she is relishing the idea. For me, it is enough to be close to her. The fact that I may have planted a seed is too much to even imagine, but I hold her tightly, tickle one nipple, and try my best.

Chapter *Five*

The evening breeze is so slight that the Spanish moss hanging gracefully from the trees barely even sways. The city is firmly in the grip of another heat wave, complete with humidity. Even now, at eleven o'clock at night, it is brutal.

I sit on a bench outside the restaurant. Through the huge window, I can see people sitting at the bar, laughing and drinking, obviously enjoying the air conditioning. Those on the upstairs patio have fans moving the air around them and long cool drinks in front of them. I have my moist skin, my clinging dress, my lank hair, as I watch them with longing.

How simple it would be to just get up and walk inside, stand in front of the icy blast of the air conditioner, and order a drink. But my Mistress has ordered me to be here, sitting on the bench outside in the heat, waiting for her. I know she will leave me sitting here for forty minutes, for that is what she does every time she gives me this command. I would have enough time to walk in there, cool off, finish my drink and come back outside. She would not know that I had done this. But I am a submissive, I have been given my orders, and I will sit on this bench until dawn if necessary.

My mind wanders back to the four glorious days at the trade show. I was invited back to Lyla's room three more times. The shows usually wore me out, but during this one I became even more invigorated as the days went on. Cleo smiled knowingly and suggested that the head office consider sending gorgeous lesbian newcomers along with every team to promote productivity.

Each encounter seemed better than the last as I learned Lyla's likes and dislikes, the most sensitive parts of her body, and her reactions. Each time, the lack of reciprocation seemed to be what Lyla enjoyed most. She was a taker, not a giver. I preferred to think of her as a top to my bottom, but of course, it was a little too early to introduce such an idea.

All good things have to end, and in this case, it was the first trade show I'd been sorry to leave. Lyla kissed me in the hallway as I got ready to go and assured me that it would not be the last time we would be together.

That lifted my spirits, but as I got closer to home, I also came to the realization that I had been unfaithful to my Mistress. I struggled for quite a while with that, and even now as I sit on the warm bench, it bothers me. My Mistress has many other submissives, but that is not an issue here; she is superior and does whatever she wants. I am inferior and I do not.

My confusion is compounded by the fact that I am becoming more and more frustrated with my Mistress. I will receive little satisfaction this night. Not the sexual kind—there is no satisfaction ever for me, just the aching need that I have accepted and even longed for as a substitute for orgasm. No, what I will not have is the satisfaction of being properly dominated.

I know exactly what will happen tonight; I knew it from the moment my Mistress called me and commanded me to come here.

I was ordered to leave my car at home, and I took the four buses necessary to get here. Two of them took me through the city's seamiest area, and none of them made their connections at the right time, so that I had to spend most of the trip standing at bus stops in the sweltering heat.

The trying journey is the whole point behind this. My Mistress will pull up in her Cadillac, the air conditioning cooling her all the way, and I will crawl into the back seat and stay on the floor as she drives me straight back to her house, within walking distance of my own. I will be beaten and tortured almost perfunctorily and then sent out the door to return to my house.

The trip is only done to inconvenience me. The fact that this is a restaurant is academic; she only uses it for a landmark. We will not go inside. We never have, and I expect that even if I make this trip a hundred times, we never will.

My previous Mistress, the one who sold me to Mistress Laura, used restaurants as cunningly as she used handcuffs and chrome-studded paddles. They were instruments of torture, wielded with imagination into plots that took my breath away.

Ordered to wait at them during their busiest times, I would have to bully headwaiters into allowing me to occupy a huge table by myself while angry patrons lined up and looked on, glaring furiously, until my Mistress arrived. Commanded to stay at them at closing time while waiting for my Mistress to show up, I would have to convince the staff that I had to be allowed to hold them up and keep them from going home. At expensive restaurants, I would have to try to second-guess my Mistress—never successfully, of course—and order her meal, hopefully to her approval, before she came in. In cheap barbecue joints, I would have to sit like a fool in my finest clothes, stared at by the other patrons in their blue jeans and sneakers, trying to keep from staining myself with the sauce from my ribs.

I sometimes wondered if Mistress Laura just didn't want to pay for a restaurant meal. But I knew she had a very high-paying job and it would just be a minor expenditure for her, so that couldn't be the reason.

Besides, an imaginative but miserly Mistress would find a way around that. My previous Mistress one day called me and ordered me to an expensive restaurant, explaining that dinner would be her treat and that I was to leave my purse at home. When the dessert and coffee were finished, she excused herself to go to the washroom and did not come back. Only my good luck at finding Cleo at home, with a desperate phone call and some pleading, avoided the horrendous embarrassment of not being able to pay.

Two weeks later, my Mistress gave me the same instructions. Suspecting another trick, I slipped a credit card into my pocket. Sure enough, she left before the bill came, but I was ready and paid with my smuggled card.

Unfortunately, I found out that she called the restaurant and asked. Bringing the card along had been a breach of my command and the beating she gave me, with a cruel length of cane, left me bruised and sore—but unbelievably happy and excited—for weeks.

A couple passes by me on their way into the restaurant, giving me a very strange look. I remember the night my former Mistress ordered me to wait for her outside a popular nightclub, dressed in high heels, skin-tight miniskirt and low-cut top, and only rescued me at the last minute from two cops who were determined I was a hooker on the prowl. There was no doubt about it, she had been an expert at the fine art of humiliation.

Mistress Laura does not deviate from her regular plan at all. The Cadillac pulls up right at the time I have expected, and she sits at the far end of the parking lot with the engine idling almost silently. I walk the length of the large lot, and as I approach the door, I can hear the distinctive click of the electric door locks as they pop up. I open the passenger side rear door and get inside, without saying a word. The sedan has a huge space between the front and rear seats and I crouch on the floor there. The carpet is spotless, the result of many hours of attention by submissives ordered to clean it.

I know the way home very well, having been in this position so many times before. There is a right turn here, a stop for a light—everything is so predictable that the light is almost never green—and a long straight stretch before another series of turns. Then the final turn into the driveway, and the big car's engine is silent.

We are in the garage; I can hear the electric opener bringing the door down. Hidden from prying eyes on the street, my Mistress gets out of the car, walks around it, and opens the door where I am. I have to crawl out of the car, on my hands and knees, and on to the garage floor. It is much more difficult than one would think, since I am not permitted to stand up even halfway at any time. My Mistress's love of fine clothes always results in the command to wear a short dress, for it would bother her to see an expensive long skirt or pants ruined from their contact with the concrete floor. My knees bang painfully on the hard, cool surface, unprotected by any fabric.

I crawl across the garage floor to the door. The floor is spotless; I have often scrubbed it myself, on my hands and knees, with detergent and a brush. She opens the door, and I struggle over the raised threshold into the house. The door is closed before I am completely through, and it bangs painfully into my legs.

Once the door is closed, I am ordered to undress, which I do. Again, it is difficult, for I cannot sit back on my legs and stretch my arms over my head. I have to wiggle out of the arms of my dress, one at a time, while my other hand stays on the floor to steady me. My Mistress watches me the whole time, obviously fascinated. This guileless torture may not overly excite me, but it has an amazing effect on her.

When I am naked, she snaps a collar around my throat. It buckles tight, and I am immediately aware of it. If I am calm, breathing regularly, it is only mildly constricting, but I know that if I start gasping for air it will cut me short. My pussy stirs at this knowledge. I am completely under her command now. More than that, the fact that my actions will determine the degree of discomfort excites me. I only hope that she will use this to her advantage.

She leaves me there in the hallway, on the hardwood floor, with the tight collar around my neck. I can hear her shoes moving toward her bedroom, and I hear the door close behind her.

When she returns, she has changed from her severe business suit into a delicious outfit I have not seen before. It consists of a very short, very tight skirt, black stockings with stiletto-heeled shoes, and a gold chain that glistens enticingly about one ankle. Her top consists of a halter bra with no cups, just sweet red straps that outline each breast and make them stand out invitingly. How I long to touch the tip of my tongue to the tip of that nipple! Perhaps, if I am very good, I may be allowed this most singular pleasure.

"Come with me," she says, and I follow her into the kitchen. On her command, I stand in the middle of the floor, under the harsh fluorescent lights, my head down and my eyes trained on the pattern in the tile.

She opens a drawer, takes something out, comes over with it. I recognize it immediately as she holds it out for me to put on. It is a maid's uniform, an apron with a bib that goes up between my breasts. I wrap it around me, tying it securely in behind. My tits are exposed, and while the apron covers my pussy from the front I am completely naked under it.

My Mistress takes up a writing pad and a pencil and stands before me. When I look back at the floor, she puts the pencil under my chin and uses it to raise my head up so that she can see my eyes.

"This house is filthy," she begins, even though it is spotless. She begins to write on the pad. "The floor needs scrubbing. The carpet in the living room must be vacuumed. I want the bathroom sink cleaned and the wastebaskets emptied. That will do for now."

"Yes, Mistress," I say, and take the list that she has ripped off the pad and held out to me. I begin to walk toward the cupboard, where I know the cleaning supplies are kept.

"Not so fast," she says, and I stop immediately. "On the kitchen table."

"Mistress?" I ask, unsure of what she wants. I see her arm move, but as a well-trained submissive I do not flinch, and she cuffs me hard alongside my head.

"Get up on the table," she hisses, and I hurry to obey, sitting on the edge of the heavy pine table. At another command, I move my ass back from the table edge and put my feet up, so that my knees are spread wide and my pussy is completely exposed and open to her view.

She reaches for me, and I can hardly control myself as she runs one manicured, blood-red fingernail up and down my slit. Her touch is warm and smooth, but her eyes are cold, and when she smiles at me, my blood almost freezes. I know that look well. She has a particularly cruel punishment in store for me. I dread and anticipate it at the same time.

She makes sure I am watching as she walks over to the refrigerator and removes a large stainless steel bowl. By the sound, I know that it contains ice cubes. That is bad enough. What else it contains almost makes me faint.

The collar tightens cruelly about my throat as the panic starts to rise in me. The object in her hands is a speculum.

It is so cold she holds it by just her fingertips. The icy water drips from the surgical steel onto the floor. I tremble and involuntarily I shake my head "no." That earns me a hard slap across the face.

"I am going to insert this now," my Mistress says, incredibly calmly. "I am sure you would like to move away. I would advise you not to. You will not move again until I grant you permission."

"Yes, Mistress," I whisper, and I try to calm myself. The collar is tight around my throat and I am afraid of hyperventilating. If I do, I will definitely pass out.

I bite my tongue hard and breathe through my nose at the first touch against my pussy. It is so cold, it burns my flesh. I try to think about how hot it is outside, how the people sat in the restaurant, even the carpet on the floor of the Cadillac—anything to keep my mind away from the instrument about to violate my body.

It is useless, for she orders me to look. The flattened metal arms of the horrible device enter my pussy very slowly, and my Mistress pushes them steadily inside. I feel as if the very core of my body is frozen. Then it is completely inside of me.

Now she turns the screw to open the arms, and I gasp and try to control myself. I have always hated these things at the best of times, when they were warmed and wielded by a kindly gynecologist trying to put me at ease. When it is inserted ice-cold by a Mistress intent on causing me agony, it is a punishment beyond words.

When the device is completely open, I feel as if I

will split in half along the line of my cunt. I am giddy from lack of air, and I long to take a deep breath and fill my depleted lungs completely. Of course I cannot; I can only sit on this hard kitchen table, collared, spread wide, at the mercy of a woman I am bound to obey.

"Are you going to sit there all day?" my Mistress snaps. At the same time, she flicks her hand against the speculum. The shock waves go right through my pussy and once again I struggle to gain my composure. "You have work to do."

"Yes, Mistress," I whisper, and as quickly as possible I get off the table. This certainly isn't as easy as it sounds. The horrible device forces me to keep my legs far apart and it pinches me inside when I move. The only advantage I have is that I am so excited by my punishment that my cunt is sopping wet. My nectar lubricates the steel jaws and I can feel it seep out of my wide-open hole and down my inner thigh. It is burning hot against the icy metal and I think that if I were any more excited it would sizzle.

I go to the cupboard and get out the cleaning supplies. Every movement is torture. When I am not quick enough to get to my knees, I am kicked soundly.

"I will give you half an hour," my Mistress says, and she turns on one heel and leaves the room.

Half an hour! I don't know if I can stand this thing in my cunt another half-minute! Of course, I could always reach down, loosen the screw that holds the jaws apart, and slip the despicable tool out of me. At least, physically I could. Mentally I am as helpless as if it were chained in place. I am a slave, tortured by my Mistress, and that is reason for excitement so strong that I can barely contain it.

Scrubbing the floor is difficult. I must keep my knees so far apart, because of the appliance inside of me, and at the same time I must maintain my balance as I push the scrub brush. It is hard work and my breathing increases, but this only puts pressure on my throat as the tight collar draws closer. Although the room is air conditioned, my skin shines with a thin film of sweat. My hair hangs in my face and I am constantly pushing it back. I wish I could tie it up, but my Mistress has not given me permission to do so. I work with it in the way.

When my Mistress comes back in half an hour I am almost finished. I have tried to hurry but it just isn't possible, with my throat constricted and my pussy dilated.

She comes up behind me and I dare not turn around to look at her. I can hear her footsteps on the floor and my whole body is tuned in to that. I don't know if she is watching, scowling, smiling, preparing. My whole body is on the edge, waiting. My nipples are so hard they ache.

Crack! The paddle she holds comes down on my ass and I can't help but scream out. The blow not only cuts into my flesh but jolts the speculum. It has warmed up, but its steel jaws still invade painfully.

Three more times she brings the paddle down. Tears run in hot rivulets down my face, as I try not to sob. Sobbing pulls the collar tight in spasms that make me giddy.

"Half an hour!" my Mistress hisses. "I gave you half an hour! You should have been finished long ago."

"Please, Mistress, mercy!" I beg, but this simply earns me another smack. Then I am pulled up by the hair, gasping for breath, my cunt on fire, until I am up on my knees. In one smooth movement she is before me and her naked cunt is at my mouth.

"Thank you, Mistress!" I whisper before I plunge into it. I cannot believe my good fortune. The agony of the speculum and the collar melt away as I dart my tongue into this hot, sweet recess.

"I hope you pleasure me better than you wash my floor," my Mistress says coldly, and I am determined to show her that this is true. She holds the paddle threateningly over me, but I do not need the warning. This I do out of love, not fear.

It does not take long, with my tongue dancing over her soaked clit, for me to bring her to her orgasm. After Lyla's writhing and screaming, my Mistress seems even more detached than ever. Still, I recognize when she is building up to her climax, and I ride out her cunt on my tongue, until I have squeezed every bit of pleasure I can for both of us.

When she has come, she steps back quickly. I see her movement and in that split second I close my eyes. The paddle crashes into my cheek and knocks me to the floor. The speculum jabs painfully and the collar cuts off my breathing. Gasping, moving stiffly, I stretch out on the floor as she orders me.

She bends down and unscrews the speculum. I sigh with relief as the horrible jaws close. Then it slides out of me, and it seems as if the pain flows out of me and follows it.

She holds it up; it is thick and shiny with my juice. It is thrust into my face and I am ordered to clean it. I do, tasting my own hot juice on the now-warm metal. When it is spotless I am commanded to kiss it and thank it for what is has done to me.

Finally, the collar is removed, and my deep breaths

are shaky at first. The flood of air into my lungs is intoxicating.

Then, methodically, I am ordered to dress and told to leave. Almost before I know what is happening, I am outside on the porch. I realize when I am outside that I was not even permitted to finish all of the cleaning jobs I was given on the list.

The walk home is torture. The speculum has been inside me for so long, my belly is racked with cramps. My pussy feels raw and horribly violated, and I relish every painful step. It was done to me against my will, by someone who has complete domination over me.

Still, as I walk along the deserted streets in the heat, the doubts come back to me. The predictable trip to and from the restaurant had the potential for so many variations, none of which were exploited or even explored. The speculum was an exciting deviation, one I had never before experienced, and I am impressed with my Mistress's choice of the iced contraption.

But, I tell myself at the same time, it had just been presented and inserted and then I had been left on my own. Knowing my Mistress, it will be used again, but in exactly the same way. Just off the top of my head, I can imagine gynecological examinations, being fucked with it, or having it combined with some of the even more insidious orifice spreaders I had seen in catalogues. I know such alternatives will never be mine to enjoy.

I walk along, enjoying the quiet of the night and the heavy perfume of the flowers. A face comes to my mind, one that excites and intrigues me more than I can possibly explain. I struggle to uphold my Mistress, but no matter what I do, I cannot get Lyla Kirk out of my head.

Lyla, Lyla! Do you know that I dream about you, that I would give anything to throw myself at your feet and beg mercy from you? Do you even realize the potential within yourself to control me?

My step quickens and I search in my pocket for my keys as I approach my house. It is too late to call now, and I long for daylight more than I can imagine. I have to talk to her and see her, and it upsets me that I still have several hours before I can do so. I try to be patient. Only a few hours, I tell myself. I can wait that long, but that is all.

Chapter *Six*

"Do you want me to take off my clothes?" I ask.

"I do, I do," Lyla whispers, and despite all my training as a submissive, I tremble visibly at the sound of her delicious husky voice.

We are in her bedroom. She lives in a magnificent house, one of the huge old Southern estates that has been passed down in her family from long before the War Between the States. I have spent more than an hour looking through it, admiring the heirloom furniture, the thickly woven carpets, the hand-carved wooden accents.

Its historical significance makes me so excited that

I feel almost giddy. I have seen these houses many times before, for they are situated all throughout the city; but I have never been inside one before, just dreamed about them. Now that I am within, I am completely captivated. It is so perfect that it seems to have been created out of thin air by a Mistress with only one thing in mind: the total domination of her submissives within its walls.

This house was the home of a wealthy landowner, Lyla's great-great grandfather. The acres and acres of surrounding farmland have been sold through the years, and most of the outbuildings have been torn down, but the renovated garage remains as the last clue of the house's legacy—it had been one of the slaves' quarters.

As I walked through the house, my whole body came in tune with the history. It is thick, almost tangible, built right into the massive walls along with the lathe and plaster. I can see myself owned by the Mistress of this house, bound to obey her through fear and love, ordered to do anything she commands. Servitude and domination were always part of this house and I want to continue the tradition. At that moment, I knew that there was only one path for me—and it led here. Now I don't care what it will take; I will have to become Lyla's slave. Without thought, without debate, right now, I know that becoming her property is my life's ambition and nothing can stop me, and it will have to begin here and now.

I want to be owned in this house again, in keeping with the tradition of this old-world Southern mansion. I want to obey my owner and be controlled by her within these old rooms.

We have found our way to her bedroom slowly, and I know that this was her idea. During the tour of the huge house, she deliberately walked by the closed door twice. When I asked what was behind the door, she brushed off my question with a quick, "Oh, just my room." My pussy was on fire right from that moment, and I could tell that hers was too. Did she know how badly I wanted to be in there, running my hands over her gorgeous body? Was this part of her plan? I could only hope.

Then, finally, she asked, "Would you like to see my room?" My answer was swift and in the affirmative, and so we climbed the huge staircase—that looked so much like a set out of *Gone With the Wind* that it was almost unreal as I went up the carpeted steps, past the bronze statues at the base of the banisters and under the huge chandelier above, fully expecting to see soldiers in proud gray uniforms on the lawn through the window on the landing—and walked down the long hall together to the white door. The sound of the brass knob turning sent a thrill through me.

Like the rest of the house, the room is enormous and richly furnished. Most of the items are period pieces that have not left the house in more than a century. The door is closed behind us, and I take in all of the pastel-shaded room. Like the rest of the house, it conjures up visions of domination that take my breath away. One wall is taken up by a large fireplace, flanked on both sides by mirrored walls that reflect the bed and open up all sorts of interesting possibilities for me. The dressers and vanities are large and heavy, with thick legs, and I can imagine having one wrist tied to them, or an ankle chained there, and sleeping on the hard, unforgiving floor while my Mistress sleeps comfortably under her covers a few feet away. The bed is a king-sized canopy style and again, I can see myself tied to the posts. When one is a submissive, there is a sinister use for even the most mundane items!

Now I ask her if she wants me to remove my clothes for her. She does, and I know instinctively that this must be the signal for our first lesson. It seems strange, almost confusing, for this lowly submissive to think that she will be able to "train" a Mistress. But I know that I want Lyla, and I know that when she is exposed to the world I live in, she will come to understand that domination is as much a part of her as her hair, or her skin, or the cunt that I so badly want to lick. Perhaps I will not be training so much as I will be pointing out the obvious.

I sit her down on the bed and stand before her. I think about what I am going to say very carefully; I know that this is the session that will make or break me, that will either make her think seriously about what I am going to say or dismiss me forever as a pervert. I have never done anything like this before, but the aching between my legs, the antebellum mansion around me, and the gorgeous woman sitting before me give me the courage I need.

"Lyla," I say to her, "this may seem strange, but in the short time I have known you, I believe I have learned a lot about you."

"How so?" she asks, curious, leaning forward. I can see down her low-cut shirt to the beautiful swells of her firm breasts. How I want them! How I want to hold them—no, be ordered to hold them and pleasure those stiff and inviting nipples!

"Well, you're very independent," I say, and with

relief I see her nod slightly. "You're not used to being told what to do. You tell others, and you are gratified when they do what you tell them. Am I correct?"

She thinks about this for a moment. "Yes, I think you can say that," she says. "I've always found myself a bit too bossy for my own good."

"Oh, not bossy," I counter quickly. "I think 'assertive' is a much better term. You know what you want, and you insist that you get it. There's nothing wrong with that."

"No, I guess not," she says slowly.

"Now, up until recently, I've noticed that you've just been assertive about your job and things like that," I continue. "When you want something at work, you insist on it, and you get it."

Lyla looks puzzled. "Jennifer, what are you getting at?" she asks. "What does this have to do with you taking off your clothes and making love to me?"

Bingo! It is as if a lightning bolt has crashed into the room between us, and I can almost shout with joy. "That's what I'm getting at right there!" I cry. "You've figured it out!"

"I have?" She's still in the dark, watching me, wondering what I'm going on about.

"You said, 'making love to me,'" I say. "Not 'us making love,' but me making love to you."

Suddenly she's embarrassed. "I didn't mean it that way," she begins.

"No, no, that's what it's all about," I tell her, and almost instinctively, I kneel on the carpet in front of her. Right now it's the only thing I can do, and in this familiar position, I am as gratified as if she had reached down and touched my throbbing pussy with her fingers.

"I have made love to you," I continue. "For all of

that weekend at the trade show I made love to you. You didn't reciprocate at all. You offered to, but I refused. What was your reaction?"

"I suppose I was selfish," she says.

"No—don't think about how you *should* have felt," I say to her. "Tell me how you *did* feel. How did you like not having to give back what you got?"

"I liked it," she admits. "I liked it very much. I love lying back and having someone make me come, but I really don't care much for doing it to them."

"It's a powerful feeling, isn't it?"

"Very powerful," she says. "It makes me feel powerful, and I like that."

I get up on my knees, hold her hand, look into her eyes. "Power," I say to her, "is what this is all about."

The glimmer in her eyes lets me know that I have found the right words after all. "That weekend, I told you that I like to give," I say. "Now you admit that you like to take. That sounds like a perfect relationship to me."

"You don't want anything in return?" I struggle with myself for a moment, and then I decide that this is both the time and the place. "I do get something in return," I say, "but it's completely different from what you receive. It may be difficult for you to understand, but my satisfaction doesn't necessarily come from physical pleasure.

"I'm not really into conventional sex. I like to be dominated by the woman I am with. I like to be ordered around. I like to be commanded. That is the satisfaction I receive in a relationship."

Lyla thinks about this for a moment. "I've read about this," she says. "They call that a 'submissive,' don't they?"

My heart leaps. "Exactly," I tell her. "I submit to the will of the woman who commands me."

"Your 'dominatrix,'" she says, as the article comes back to her.

"My dominatrix, my superior, my Mistress," I say. "A lot of people think it's very weird or perverted, but I can't help it. That's what turns me on."

"I don't think it's perverted at all," Lyla says quickly, and again my spirits rise. "So you enjoy pain and being beaten?"

I actually have to stop and think about this for a moment before I give her my answer. "Well, I don't really enjoy pain," I admit. "Some people do, but being hurt isn't the turn-on for me. It's a little more complicated than that. I like the fact that my Mistress likes to beat me, and by accepting the punishment, I'm pleasing her. She has complete control over me, even the fact that she can whip me or spank me if she chooses. I like it when I'm sore for a while afterwards, too. If I try to sit down and my ass hurts because I've been caned, it brings back the scene to me. That's what I like about the pain. Does this seem strange to you?"

"No, no it doesn't. I've thought about it myself, after reading about it. I don't like to give sex in return. It's too much trouble for me; I just want to come and then lie back and enjoy it. But you can't just go up to someone and take without giving. That's why I rather liked the idea of just getting sex from this 'submissive' that I read about, whenever I want it, without worrying about anything else."

I am so overcome that I have to close my eyes and lean back. "Then, Mistress Lyla," I say to her, "command me to remove my clothes."

"Will you take them off?" she asks, almost shy within this new role.

"That's a question," I say, my eyes still closed. "A Mistress doesn't ask, she commands."

Lyla takes a deep breath, and I wonder if her eyes are closed as well. We are at the crossroads about to embark on a journey and it is momentous for both of us. Her voice is quiet and even. "I command you to remove your clothes," she says, and a searing chill goes through me from my head to my toes.

"Yes, right away," I whisper, and my fingers find the buttons of my shirt.

It is not long before I am completely naked, still kneeling on the floor. She does not ask me to get up, and it is at this moment that I instinctively know that I will never feel Lyla's hands on my body in a display of love as an equal partner again. It is a heady, emotional revelation for me.

"Now I would like to be undressed," she says to me, and pauses for a moment. Almost as an afterthought, she adds, "I think I would like to have you stay on the floor."

I am almost overwhelmed. As I struggle to obey, it is obvious that she is trying her new role on for size, and seems genuinely astonished that I am obeying her command. Her expression is that of someone who has tried a sip of a new wine and is pleasantly surprised to find that she likes it.

Her command is not easy to carry out, but I do it gratefully and happily. As she sits forward on the bed, I unfasten the buttons that hold her shirt together. Her delicious breasts tumble from it, unfettered. I touch them first with my fingers and then with my mouth, and both of us enjoy this immensely.

Of course, if I were with an experienced Mistress I would never dare do such a thing, for I have not been given permission to do so. But Lyla is a novice and I know that she does not yet understand that when a Mistress is in command, a submissive must obey only her orders and go no further on her own. All of that will come in time. For now, my mind still reels with the progress I have made this afternoon.

Her skirt is a bit more difficult, for it closes with a side zipper and I must gently ease it off of her. To my delight, she wears nothing under it, and when the skirt is removed, I am treated to the sight of her hot cunt. When she spreads her thighs a bit, I see the juice glistening on her dark pubic hair. I was right all along.

"I think that needs pleasuring," I suggest. She sits on the bed and thinks for a moment. I am sure that she still believes that I am going to come out of character and tell her that I won't be pushed around, or something of the sort. Oh, Lyla, how much you have yet to see!

Finally she comes to terms with herself. "My pussy needs to be licked," she says. "I want you to do this to me."

It is the most wonderful command I have ever been ordered to perform. Gently I spread her legs open, kneeling on the floor between them, for I have not been given permission to rise. My tongue touches on that most sensitive place. Lyla shudders, and sighs loudly.

This is what I have been waiting for. I feel as if I have just been newly born. I have eaten Lyla's pussy many times before, but always as an equal. Now I am eating it the way I always wanted to: as her submissive, commanded by her to do her bidding.

Her pink slit is soaking wet and I lap up the juice greedily. I take each of her swollen cuntlips between my own lips in turn and suck them dry, letting them slip slowly and smoothly out of my mouth. My fingers find the opening to her hole and I slip some of the hot nectar out of it and spread it around so that I can lick it off again.

"I like that," Lyla prompts, and I keep my fingers there, inching them into the vortex and then slipping them back and forth inside. My tongue, meanwhile, rides along the grooves on either side of her clit. I can feel the hard pink nub of flesh throb under my tongue and I can only imagine how good it must feel.

It is obvious, for Lyla is as vocal as ever, sighing and moaning with each movement of my tongue on her burning vulva.

"Right there," she says, and I concentrate on the spot she has selected. It is the very top of her clit, where it is both hardest and hottest. My tongue stays glued to this spot, flicking over it and pushing it back and forth. This movement seems to drive her wild.

My face is soaked with her juice and her wonderful heady perfume fills my nostrils. I can hardly breathe, I am drowning in her. She holds the back of my head, pushing my face into her. I am her plaything now and she exploits it fully. I am only there to give her pleasure.

It seems that I can't lick her fast or hard enough. This is the Lyla I have come to know, but it seems to me that she is even more animated than usual. Surely she needed to command me just as I needed to be given the order by her!

I lap at her, push my tongue into her hole. My fingers play with her ass and my nose brushes against her clit even as I try to get all of my mouth inside her cunt. All the while, she is gasping out orders. "Lick my clit! Your tongue there, harder! Right there, eat me there!" I struggle to obey. It is difficult because she is bucking her hips against me. I want to ride her out to the very end.

She explodes. I am ground into her pussy; her thighs close hard on my head and hold me there. Her cunt throbs on my mouth. Her exuberant moans fill the room and we hover, trembling, as she takes her climax hard from me.

When she falls back she is spent. I lick my lips, wipe my face with my fingers, and then savor the juice from them in my mouth. I watch the rise and fall of her exquisite tits as she gasps for breath. I am filled with a glow that must be almost as strong as her own at the knowledge that I have done this to her.

I remain kneeling on the floor, for she has not indicated to me that I should join her on the bed. She looks down at me and gasps, "That was wonderful," but still I am not invited up to her level. That excites me, for it seems to cement our relationship of dominatrix and submissive even more. No Mistress would ask to be cuddled after she came, and I believe that this is not an oversight, but that Lyla understands that I am her plaything, not her lover.

"My robe," she says. "Bring me my robe." There is no "please," no gentle respectful request, as I would have received during our weekend at the trade show. My spirits lift even higher.

I rush to bring the robe she wants, a beautiful thick terrycloth one that hangs from an ornate hook on the wall. When I come back to the bed with it, she very slowly gets up. I stand there, holding it ready for her, but she takes her time. Finally she is in position, her back to me, and I slip the luxurious robe over her lovely shoulders.

"I would like a bath," she says, and then for just a moment, she is once again shy, unsure of herself. She looks at me and asks, "Is it proper for me to ask you?"

"If you want me to run a bath," I explain, "you don't ask. You tell me to run one for you, and I will do exactly that."

"Then run me one," she says, and I can see that glimmer in her eyes again, the one that tells me that this is something she is getting used to.

"How hot?"

"Very hot," she says, and then in a husky voice, "I like it really steamy. There's a jar of oil on the shelf; put some of that in it."

"Yes," I say, and then slowly add, "Mistress." I stand for just a moment, watching her reaction. She is letting it sink in. Her expression slowly changes. I can tell that she wasn't expecting this, but now that it has been broached, it fits her just fine. Then she looks over at me and her eyes narrow a little.

"Are you going to keep me waiting all day?" My heart pounding, I race out of the room down the hallway to open the taps on the tub. As the steaming water fills the spotless tub and the musky scent of the bath oil wafts up, I look around at the old walls. The tradition continues. I think that they approve.

Chapter *Seven*

"So," Cleo says, as she lifts her wineglass daintily to her lips, "do you really think you're making any progress with Lyla?"

"I certainly do," I reply, as I take a sip of my own wine. Have I ever been more sure of anything in my life? "Cleo, I would have to be blind not to see it. She only wants pleasure, lots of it, and she doesn't want to give anything back."

"That doesn't necessarily make her a dominatrix," Cleo says. "She might just be lazy or greedy. I'd want more than that before I made a decision."

"No, there was more to it than just that," I tell her.

"I got her to order me to pleasure her. It wasn't difficult to convince her, and I could tell that she enjoyed doing that. It was obvious."

Cleo thinks about this for a moment, sipping her wine, stretching out on her sofa. I can't help but admire her long, beautifully muscled legs, made even better by the very short, loose nightshirt she is wearing. At one point I can catch a glimpse of her tantalizing dark pussy between her thighs. She is not a dominatrix, but I am turned on by the sight of any woman's cunt, no matter what her persuasion. We often get together on nights like this, enjoying the air conditioning, good wine, and fine company, both of us very relaxed and informal, as often as not with popcorn and a good video. Sometimes it is a blockbuster from the video store; just as frequently, it is a treasure from Cleo's extensive private collection.

"It could be rather dangerous, what you're doing," she says.

"I suppose so," I reply. "But surely I'm not the first submissive who ever thought she might make a dominatrix out of someone."

"Maybe not," Cleo smiles over her wineglass. "The trick is being the first successful one." She sips again, and then looks at me, serious now. "Have you thought about what your Mistress is going to do when she finds out?"

A momentary chill makes its way swiftly down my spine. No matter how much I want Lyla, no matter what my disappointment with my own Mistress, the facts are there. I belong to her, I am pledged to her—I was sold to her, for that matter! She is still my Mistress, and even though she may have as many submissives as she chooses, it is not my place to pick and choose Mistresses and go from one to the other.

"I honestly don't know what she would do," I say. "Perhaps she would punish me severely." This excites us both; when Cleo moves again and I peek at her cunt hairs, they are shiny with juice.

"Perhaps so," she says. "She has a rack, doesn't she?"

"The kind that she can tie my wrists and my ankles to," I say. "It's the standup kind, so that she can leave me there until my legs give out and I'm just hanging by my arms." I'm warming up to this very quickly. "After a few hours, when she lets the restraints go, I can't lift my arms at all and my legs won't work. I just fall on the floor, and then she always beats me with a whip or a riding crop because I can't stand up."

"She might take a harness, and bind you so that you can't move, and then just leave you there for a while," Cleo says. Her hand is slowly making its way down to that place between her thighs. This is being done for both our benefit. "Then when she finally unfastens it, she might demand that you run around the room, and beat you when you can't make your cramped muscles obey."

"No, she always unfastens the harness and then kicks me over," I say. "Then she kicks me a few more times, so that I can feel the point of her boot, and then I must kiss it and thank it for what it did to me. I always have to clean the heel with my mouth, too. She fucks my mouth with her stiletto heel."

Cleo's hand is now inching up to her pussy. "She might throw you across a chair and spank you," Cleo says. She is brushing the dark hair, and giving me a good look at her fingers as they work their way between the delicious lips of her cunt.

"She always puts me over her knee when she does that," I say. I can almost feel the harsh slap of her naked hand on my uncovered buttocks. She hits hard enough to leave cruel red marks on my flesh and I can't sit down for hours afterward. "She puts me over her lap and spanks me hard, and then she gets up so that I fall on the floor."

"Then what?"

"Then the session's always over," I say. Suddenly my passion has dissolved completely, and Cleo feels it also.

"What's wrong with that?"

"Well," I confess, "nothing really, I suppose. There are women out there who would give their eyeteeth to have a Mistress who does that sort of thing to them. I should be grateful."

Cleo sits up straight. "So why is this a problem?"

"Oh, Cleo," I say, and my voice feels like it is breaking. I have a lump in my throat and I can feel hot tears behind my eyes. "It's what I've just told you. I can tell you exactly what my Mistress will do in each of those situations, because that's the only thing she *ever* does at times like that. She has a routine with each of those things, with spankings, with harnesses, with the rack, and it never varies. She goes through the rituals and I'm thrilled to be her submissive, happy that I am giving her pleasure. But there's never any intrigue, never any wondering what will happen to me. I can't kneel on the floor with my eyes closed in mortal fear of whatever punishment is coming, because I know exactly what it will be. I feel like I'm in the same play every night, reciting the same lines."

Cleo looks at me and I am almost overwhelmed by the love and friendship I see in her dark eyes. "Then there's only one thing to do," she says. "It's time to see if Lyla will be the Mistress Lyla of your dreams."

"You make it sound so easy," I say, sniffling just a little, but in a much better frame of mind.

"One day soon," she says, "you'll sit back and wonder why you ever thought it would be difficult."

I come over to the sofa and take her into my arms. We kiss, not a kiss of raw passion, but an exchange of love, between two women who are sisters under the skin. I have never felt so close to her as I do right now.

She pats my shoulder comfortingly. "Come on," she says. "Sit down here beside me. We can both use a treat."

I love the sound of that. She picks up the remote control and I know that tonight's offering definitely won't be *Casablanca*. I snuggle up to her, comfortable in the loose lounging pajamas I am wearing. I don't expect to be keeping the bottoms on for much longer.

As always, the film is one I haven't seen before. I'm always amazed at the movies that Cleo gets, and she won't reveal her source, but they're always the hottest, kinkiest, and most interesting I have ever seen. I've never seen her whole collection but it must be in the hundreds, possibly thousands. I have never seen one twice; each time it is always a new one.

Some of them are just collections of sessions, but this one actually has a plot, thin as it is, and Cleo has made a bowl of popcorn in its honor. The hot, salty corn reminds me of the treat of Lyla's hot, salty cunt. No matter what I do, everything comes back to her.

"I think you'll like this one," Cleo says, as the credits start to roll. She's wound it right back to the beginning, teasing me, making me wait through the duplication warning, through the credits. It seems to take forever. I toss a piece of popcorn at her and she grins.

The acting in the video is terrible, but that isn't the reason we're watching it. A gorgeous woman, haughty, well built, with delectable chocolate skin, has asked her secretary to come to her house to finish up a report late in the evening. The secretary, a small, thin, blonde woman, doesn't really want to do the work, but she doesn't dare refuse. She shows up at her boss's house with her briefcase in hand, ready to take dictation.

Of course it's obvious that a financial report wasn't anywhere near the boss's intentions. She answers the door in an outfit that has me gasping, a pair of skintight leather pants and a close-fitting corset that looks like it's made of thin red leather, decorated with chrome studs and laced up between her ample breasts. I take a peek over at Cleo; she is glued to the screen and her hand is once again making its way between her legs. I smile and then realize that, unconsciously, I have begun to reach under the lounging pajamas for my own clit too.

There are a few more stilted lines, as the secretary is shocked to see her boss in such an outfit, and she is ordered to come inside and remove her clothes at once. She is deliciously built and the soft hair on her cunt indicates that her blond hair is real. I love women with really blond cunt hair; they look like their slits are shaven smooth.

Once the dialogue is out of the way, the women are into an environment they both understand and desire. The terrible recital of the lines is over and they are comfortable as they fall into their roles of dominatrix and slave. I fall right in alongside them. I want desperately to kneel before this red-corseted woman and do whatever she demands.

The plot doesn't explain how the young secretary, who was surprised to see her boss so dressed, immediately knows how to kneel and address the black woman as "Mistress," but that doesn't matter to either of us. The sound of the word inflames us, and my cunt begins to throb. Sure enough, I wiggle out of the pajama bottoms and toss them on the floor; I know that I won't be able to stay away from my cunt for long. The dominatrix orders the young woman to crawl behind her, and the camera follows them as they make their way down a hallway into another room.

The room has a ceramic tile floor, and both of us wince as we watch the submissive crawl across it. My knees hurt just watching her, and she is obviously very uncomfortable doing it. Of course we know this is the true mark of a submissive! Any of us, under the circumstances, could just as easily get up and walk out if we truly wanted to. But we don't. We exist to serve, and if serving means crawling naked across a mile of marble floor then we will do it. My heart swells and feels like it will burst when I think about it. I love to please a Mistress so much!

The Mistress now has a riding crop in her hand, which she has picked up from a table that obviously contains many other goodies that we can't clearly see just yet. She drives her submissive around the room with it, much like a mule-driver might, using flicks of the crop to turn the blonde woman this way and that, make her stop, make her speed up.

"You seem like a well-trained horse," the Mistress says, and I am so excited that my finger finds the tip of my swollen clit and pushes it back and forth. The shivers go up my spine, and I pray that it will turn into the kind of scene that excites me so much.

It is, it is! "I told you this would be a treat," Cleo says, for she knows my preferences well. I hug her close and kiss her, and then return my attention to the screen.

One of the "goodies" on the table is a small saddle, specifically made for this purpose. My fingers are now tweaking my clit hard, and my other hand is playing absently with my nipples through the thin fabric of my pajamas.

Using the riding crop, the black woman positions her blonde horse to kneel in front of her. The saddle fits her back perfectly. It is an Eastern-style saddle, and the pommel fits just behind the young woman's shoulder blades. The girth fastens around her just below her breasts. Her Mistress pulls the girth hard and she gasps. It is buckled into place and I sigh. I wore a saddle once, many years ago. I would love to have this one buckled into place around me again.

Now it is time for the bridle. This is a beautifully crafted piece of work, and like the saddle, it is not intended for a real horse. Rather, it has been specially made to fit the contours of a submissive's face, and for this reason it excites me even more. Someone has actually designed and made this, and someone has purchased it for this purpose! I am thrilled when a Mistress uses an everyday item to keep me in line, but I go off the deep end when she presents something that was specifically made for the type of sex we both enjoy so much.

The bit is rubber-covered, and thick enough that when the young woman takes it in between her teeth she cannot close her lips around it. The rings stick out at the corners of her mouth and the reins loop down from these. The straps go around her head and there are blinkers on them, just as if she were a real horse. The bridle is buckled firmly in place and now she is ready, a harnessed mount there to do her Mistress's bidding.

"You know what this does to me," I whisper to Cleo. My fingers run up and down my swollen labia. I have backed off from my clit; I want this to last as long as possible.

Cleo smiles knowingly at me. "It gets even better," she says. I quickly find out what she means. Up until now, the Mistress has been wearing high-heeled, red leather shoes. But now she steps off screen, and when she comes back, she has boots in her hand. Not just any boots, but proper riding boots, black with brown leather tops, and around the ankles, secured with chrome chains, are spurs.

I can't help it. I rub across my clit until I almost come, and then back off and try to calm down. They are English-style spurs, chrome wishbones that end in rounded nubs. They don't cut flesh the way Western-style rowel spurs do, but they leave vicious, horrific small bruises. On the boots of an expert Mistress they can also leave long, ghastly red scrapes that are painful for weeks.

She puts on the boots and stands before her mount, gesturing at the boots with her riding crop. The blond woman gets down on her forearms, close to the floor, and licks them. My own tongue sticks out of my mouth as I long to clean them too. She licks them lovingly, kisses them. The fact that it is extremely difficult, almost impossible with the bit between her teeth doesn't seem to matter to her at all. I can imagine that her tongue must be stretched to the limit and it must be painful, but she has been commanded to do this and she will carry out that order. She takes the nubs of the spurs into her mouth and slowly fellates them, as best she can since she cannot completely close her lips. I can see her saliva on the bright chrome and it turns me on. I look over at Cleo; her fingers are working furiously between her legs. Obviously this tape isn't just for me.

When the boots are clean and shiny, the mount is allowed to get back up on her hands and knees. Very slowly, the Mistress arranges the reins on her mount's neck, checks the saddle, caresses the naked ass with the tip of the riding crop, and then climbs into that delicious leather seat.

I can almost feel the weight on my spine. The blonde woman gasps a little, for it can be a very trying thing, to have a girth buckled tight around your ribs and a leather saddle held in place, and then to have the weight of a Mistress added to that. Even a very small woman puts quite a strain on one's back, but that is all part of it. It is not an easy scene for a submissive to go through, but once she does, she realizes just how satisfying and wonderful it really is.

The Mistress uses the reins, the shift of her weight, taps of the riding crop to let her mount know exactly what she wants. The young blond woman moves away. Cleo and I gasp as we realize that she is carrying the black woman on her hands and knees over that horribly hard tile floor. How that must ache! But what a feeling it must be to go through such hardship to please a beloved Mistress!

They move slowly about the room and the camera makes a complete circle of them as they do. Each angle presents a new and delightful scene for both of us, and our hands are working our cunts furiously. From the front, we can see how the slave cannot close her lips, how the bit pushes her teeth apart. The rings pull at the corners of her mouth as the Mistress uses the reins to guide her. The blinders keep her from seeing anything that isn't directly in front of her, and once the camera moves away from her face she can't possibly know what is being photographed next.

It moves alongside the pair, and the blonde woman's hair is a thick equine mane over her neck. Now we can see how the saddle chafes at her, for the Mistress has not bothered with a blanket underneath and this is not a gentle saddle that comes with sheepskin under it. This is raw leather against naked skin, and I know that when the saddle is finally removed from the sweaty flesh, there will be a red, rashy place where it rubbed against her. The sound on the film is very good and we can even hear the delightful squeak of the leather as they move around the room.

Now we see the way the Mistress rides her. Her smooth leather clothes slide effortlessly on the saddle as the submissive's jerky motions cause her to move slightly in the saddle. The shot of her ass against the polished brown leather is amazing. I wish I could be allowed to pleasure that.

From behind the view is sinful. The submissive's blonde cunt, looking almost hairless, is soaking wet and it gleams in the film lights. Her tight asshole is visible and her buttocks are firm, moving against each other as she struggles to move across the hard floor.

Now the Mistress wants her to speed up, and this is what we have both been waiting for. The Mistress turns her mount's head horribly hard with the reins and the young woman gasps with the agony. The riding crop smacks hard once, twice, thrice across her ass, and the camera zooms in on the hot red welts left behind by the leather whip. I sigh. I have felt those hot stripes on my ass many times and still can never get enough of them.

Despite the punishment to her buttocks, the mount still does not move quickly enough for her Mistress. And now, as Cleo and I moan with desire, the Mistress lifts her feet and rakes those vicious spurs across the young blonde woman's flanks.

My clit is so swollen that I can feel it grow under my fingers. The blond woman cries out and rushes forward. The Mistress rakes her again and again with the spurs. Her horse is all but galloping around the room, and it is obvious that speed is no longer her intention. These cruel gashes are for the love of putting a metal nub into a slave's ribs. How I would love to feel them against my own bones.

This Mistress is expert. The scrapes are oozing blood, they are long strata of agony. The blond woman tries to plead through the thick bit and is whipped and spurred again for her attempt. She speeds up. Her skin is soaked with sweat and the leather is dark where it touches her. She is gasping for breath through the bit and I can tell that it is difficult to breathe with the girth pulled so tight. Finally, as the Mistress goads her again, she falls below her to the floor, unable to continue.

"Useless whore!" the Mistress shouts. She jumped free when her mount collapsed and now stands over her. The spotless boots push at the panting woman on the floor, who is unable to get up. The Mistress beats her mercilessly with the riding crop across her spur-raked flanks and then, finally, stops, breathing hard herself with the exertion.

This is too much for both of us. Gasping, crying out, our hands flying over our soaking slits, we come within a moment of each other. My whole body trembles with my orgasm and it takes a long time to calm down.

The scene ends and Cleo clicks off the television. I don't think I could have mustered enough strength to do that; coming has left me weak and relaxed. She holds me close and I bask in the circle of her arms.

"That was amazing," I manage to gasp. "You really know the buttons to push on me, don't you?"

"You looked like you needed some serious cheering up." She smiles and kisses my forehead protectively. "That's what friends are for."

"Consider me cheered," I smile, and still somewhat shaky, I reach for my glass of wine.

She sips from hers. "As for your dilemma," she says, "do you think that your present Mistress will ever strap a saddle on you and ride you around the room like that?"

That's all I need to make up my mind. Later that night, when I am absently looking through a pile of magazines on Cleo's table, I come across a catalogue of devices. It is an offering of gentle things for the curious but uninitiated.

I leaf through it, fascinated by the photographs and the descriptions. There are softly padded blindfolds that fasten with Velcro, wrist and ankle restraints lined with fur. Snaps are quick release, chains are small. The catalogue only lists two whips and one paddle and all of them are made of soft material, guaranteed to make a lot of noise but produce little pain and no marks.

They are devices that I would normally scoff at; they are substitutes for the agonizing toys that I crave, and they do not usually excite me. Now, however, I have a use for them.

Cleo sees me looking and she clicks in right away. "You can have that," she says. "I don't even know why I ordered it."

"I think it was destiny," I smile, and I tuck the book into my bag. In the morning I slip it into an envelope and address it to Lyla with no return name on it. When the post office opens I am first in line, and when I see it stamped and dropped into the box my heart, ever so quickly, skips a beat.

Chapter *Eight*

"I think you know something about this," Lyla smiles. I know what she's reaching for even before she picks up her bag.

Fortunately, the restaurant isn't quite full and we are alone in the corner. She takes the items out in the open with no fear of prying eyes.

Of course I'm right. One is the catalogue I sent to her, with its provocative photos of women modeling the fur-lined wrist restraints and the padded blindfolds as they kneel before other, dominant women. One dominatrix unfortunately isn't visible in the picture on the cover, but her delicious, high-heeled leather boots are, and even though the gentle devices are too tame for my liking, those boots excite me beyond belief.

The other is a copy of a book I mailed to her the following day. I wasn't too sure about doing it; I had misgivings about it even after I had dropped it through the mail slot, and I hoped that it would be received in the spirit in which I had sent it. It was a copy of *Provincetown Summer*, a book of short stories about lesbian sex, several of which featured domination. It seemed to me that the catalogue, while somewhat explicit, would be much more useful if it was accompanied by an "owner's manual."

"I sent them," I admit. I do not refer to her as "Mistress" here in the restaurant because I know that while the seed has been planted and has germinated, it hasn't quite flowered. Lyla isn't completely into her new role yet and so far I have only used the term when we are actually having sex. Using it in other, more mundane situations will undoubtedly come in time, I am sure.

My stomach is churning even as I tell her that I sent the books, and I take a quick sip of my drink to cover my nervousness. I can't read her expression and I hope I haven't taken liberties that will undo everything I have done so far.

"I read both of them," she says. "I found them very interesting." She looks around, and then lowers her voice and says the words that thrill me to my core. "I found them very exciting."

I can feel my eyes burn, but these are tears of joy. I knew right from the beginning that I had guessed correctly, that Lyla was a dominant woman who could be made aware of it, but I didn't know that it would all happen so quickly.

"There is still so much I don't understand, though," she continues. "I can't really comprehend why anyone would want to tolerate the kind of abuse that these women hand out to their submissives. Maybe I never will. The motives of the submissives are still difficult for me. But I do understand why a woman would want to dominate another. That appeals to me very much."

"Do you think," I ask quietly, "that you might one day feel a need to do this, rather than just a curious desire?"

"I think," she smiles, "that I would call it more than just a curious desire right now." She reaches into her bag again and pulls out a small pink plastic bag. "I couldn't resist. I bought you a present. Well, you might call it a present for both of us."

I take the bag across the table. Heart pounding, I open it up and peek inside. The item is wrapped in tissue paper, and with my fingers trembling I push the paper aside. It is a pair of the fur-lined restraints.

I look up at her, my eyes wide. When they were just photos in the catalogue, they were boring and commonplace. Handed to me across the table by the woman I adore, they set my pussy on fire. If she had shown me a full-body harness with studs and rings, I don't think it would have excited me more.

"In those stories, it was obvious that the roles are pretty well cut and dried," she says. "I noticed right away that the Mistress gives her orders, and the submissive obeys them, and that is that. But those women are very experienced, and I am not. If it is all right with you, I may need a little instruction in their use."

"Of course," I manage to say.

"But," she continues, smiling, obviously getting

into this as she goes on, "instruction that is given respectfully."

"Yes," I continue, my mouth open. I am sure I look dumbfounded, but then, I am watching a transformation right before my eyes.

Then she smiles again at me, a very knowing smile. It is not the look of a novice but rather, of a woman who is in command and is only now beginning to realize it. "It seems," she says, "that we should begin with the proper form of address."

My cunt throbs as I whisper, "Yes, Mistress." I am giddy as the words escape my lips, and at that moment I know that the lines have been irrevocably drawn. At the office or when we are in the company of those who do not know, she will be Lyla Kirk, my friend, my co-worker, and my equal. But that, and not this, will be the charade. This, a Mistress and her lowly submissive, is the reality. From this moment on I know that I am property to be ordered about at will—the will of this woman.

Our lunch arrives. It is excellent food, for this is one of the finest restaurants in the city, but I hardly notice what I am putting in my mouth. The plastic bag containing the restraints sits on the chair beside me, touching my leg. It seems to feel hot against my skin. My belly is tight with unrelieved want and it almost seems that my clit has swollen to a size where it is thrusting past my wet pussylips. I squirm on the chair and savor the thrill that goes through me. Lyla, however, is obviously enjoying her sauced fish immensely. Although a novice, it seems that she has all but mastered the cool detachment that makes a Mistress so arousing for me. I wonder if her labia is as needy and as soaking wet as mine is right now. I am thankful that today I wore panties under my skirt; it seems as if I am going to soak the chair with my thick, fragrant nectar if I sit there much longer.

Lunch takes an agonizingly long time, and after a while it dawns on me that Lyla isn't always this slow. She lingers over every bite and takes only the tiniest sips from her glass of red wine. My plate is clean while she is only half-finished. When I look up at her, she winks. She has obviously read the book well. Surely she knows that as every moment passes, I come closer and closer to the edge. If we were not in a public place, I would fall at her feet right now.

Afternoon coffee isn't usual for Lyla, but this time she accepts not one but two cups. I can hardly stand it, and she is more than aware of it. As she lingers—ordering a liqueur to go with it when she sees my impatience—she nonchalantly describes the domination stories in the book I sent to her.

"I really enjoyed it when the one woman got spanked," she says. "It was only when I read it that I really thought about doing something like that, and you know, it turned me on. I'd love to put you over my knee and have your little white ass there for me to spank."

My head spins. Turned over Mistress Lyla's knee and spanked! I can picture it even now, feel the blows on my buttocks. Silently I pray that she will hurry up and finish her coffee. I want her to bruise my ass so that I can't sit down for a week.

"I like the idea of doing it with a paddle, too," she continues. "I would imagine that spanking gets kind of hard on the hands after a while. And you can only spank so hard. But I think that a paddle would hurt for days, wouldn't it?"

"Yes, Mistress," I whisper. I have hurt for days after a paddling, and now I look forward to that exquisite discomfort all over again. I cross my legs, using my thighs to put pressure on my clit. It feels huge and hot.

"I think I would like to have a paddle," she says absently, and finally finishes the last of her coffee. It takes an agonizingly long time for the bill to be settled, but finally, we are out in the parking lot. I have the bag in my hand, holding it tightly.

We walk to her car and I stand beside the door. Like the restaurant, the parking lot is empty and there is no one to overhear us. I decide that a little lesson might be in order when Lyla gets behind the wheel.

I do not touch the door. Puzzled, she puts down the window beside me and asks, "Aren't you coming with me?"

"Please, Mistress," I say, "you haven't given me permission to enter, or told me where I am to sit."

She is taken aback for just a moment, and then slips into her role much more easily than I would have imagined. "I think," she says, "that sitting up front with your superior is just a little too forward, don't you?"

"Yes, Mistress," I say gratefully, and open the back door to slip inside. Normally I would expect to be forced to the floor, as my own Mistress Laura does, but all things will come in time. It is daylight, and there is always the danger that a pedestrian might see inside the car when we are stopped at a light. When we travel at night I will definitely suggest this lowly position is to my newfound dominatrix.

There is another advantage to sitting in the back seat. As the gates to Mistress Lyla's driveway come into view, I am filled with a sense of wonder and contentment when we pass through them. I am now looking at the house through a slave's eyes, and it is the most beautiful sight I could possibly imagine. I am coming home to a Southern mansion, in my rightful place behind my Mistress, as her property, as her plaything. I don't think I could ask for much more than that.

All of it is as new to me as if I were visiting the house for the first time. The awesome huge portico makes me feel small and insignificant. The doors swing open silently, beckoning me into the graciously cool interior. When they close behind me, I am trapped inside my Mistress's domain. My everyday persona is left outside. Within these walls I am nothing more than chattel.

We are still only steps inside the door when Mistress Lyla turns to me. "You are wearing too much," she says.

"I am sorry, Mistress," I reply, and strip off my dress as quickly as I can. It feels so right to be standing here before her, completely naked. She nods her head, and I fall into my favorite position, on my knees in front of her. As I lean back on my heels, I can feel the soaking heat of my pussy on my leg. Looking down I see that my nipples are rock-hard and pointing straight out.

She takes one of these between her fingers and strokes it gently. Then, without warning, she twists it swiftly, cruelly. It hurts, but my cry is more surprise than anything. I wasn't expecting it.

"That felt very good," she muses, and seems genuinely amazed to find that she enjoyed doing it to me. She twists the other nipple, even harder, and I hold my breath and bite my tongue. This is luscious agony and I drink it in.

"I think we should go to the bedroom," she continues. "I will walk there. But you—Jennifer, I think that you should crawl there, on your hands and knees."

"Yes, Mistress," I say joyfully, and I follow her. I realize then that this will entail climbing that huge antebellum staircase. But while that might have been a nasty and tedious command from Mistress Laura, it is music to my ears when it comes from Mistress Lyla's lips. It is very difficult and halfway up the stairs I don't know if I can continue; my breathing is hard and my knees are sore.

Mistress Lyla, who is at the top of the stairs waiting, sees my difficulty. She comes back down to the level I am at, and stands behind me. For a moment I think that she is going to relent and allow me to walk up the rest of the stairs properly.

Thwack! Her hand across my naked ass is harder than I would ever have thought. It startles me more than anything, and I cry out and find the strength to hurtle up the stairs. She hits me again, hard, and my skin tingles with the blow. Only when I am at the top of the stairs, panting for breath, do I realize that this is the first time she has struck me.

She realizes it too, and she looks at my bare ass approvingly. "Your cheeks are all red," she says. "I think I like the way that looks."

I follow her down the hallway to the familiar room, but somehow it looks completely different to me now. I am seeing everything through new eyes. I feel reborn; from Lyla's equal, I am now Mistress Lyla's slave.

I crawl into the huge room and she closes the door behind me. "Over there," she indicates, and I crawl to the foot of the bed and wait there on my knees.

She is now performing just for me. Slowly she

removes her suit jacket and lays it aside. Then it is time for the buttons on her white silk shirt. They open agonizingly slowly under her fingers, but once they are open, I gasp.

Under it she is wearing an outfit no doubt purchased for this occasion. The bra is made of satin, crimson red with black straps. When she removes her skirt I see that the matching panties are also that delectable fire red, and the black edges hug her sweet pale skin. Then she goes over to the closet and slips on a pair of black leather shoes with very high heels that leave me weak and wet.

She has brought the pink bag upstairs with her, and now she takes out the restraints from their tissue-paper wrapping. They were thrilling in the restaurant, but now, held by my Mistress in the confines of her bedroom, they are inflammatory. I long to kiss and lick them.

She puts them around my wrists and buckles them. The fur is soft and warm against my skin, but their gentle edge doesn't matter now at all. The fact is that Mistress Lyla has put them on me to discipline me. That makes them as cruelly sweet as if they were raw leather with pointed studs.

There is a ring on each one of them and Mistress Lyla has a snap to join them together. I am ordered to hold my arms out in front of me, the wrists together, so that she may do this. When I am thus restrained, she looks at my wrists carefully and notices that the link is quite long. If I bent my wrists I could use my thumb to snap it open.

"That doesn't look very secure," she says. "You could get out of that."

I smile. "Mistress Lyla," I say to her, "I know that

you aren't really familiar with submissives yet. I could get out of this easily if I wanted to. The fact is that there's a lot more than these cuffs holding me here. If you ordered me to just hold my wrists together, without any restraints, I would do it. Your command is enough for me."

"That's all?" she asks.

"That is how much I long to obey you," I say. "Of course, if you put me in restraints that I can't possibly get out of, that just adds to the pleasure."

"I will remember that," she says. "A full-body harness with cuffs on the waist might be exciting for me too." I stare at her in wonder. She smiles mischievously, winks, and says, "I'm capable of finding catalogues on my own too, you know."

My whole body warms with a tremor that goes from my pussy to the ends of my fingertips. Without a doubt, I know that I have finally found the Mistress of my dreams.

"Now," she says, walking around me in those delightful high heels, "I suppose the next thing is for me to think of something to punish you for. I'm sure I'll get much better at this as time goes on. For now, I think that sending me that catalogue and book without my permission is good enough."

She walks across the room and sits on the antique chair by her vanity. "I will have you over here now," she says, and I hurry to obey on my hands and knees.

"Now up here," she says, indicating her bare knees and the lap that is just barely covered by the red panties. I almost fall over myself in my haste to do her bidding. She hauls me up by the gentle cuffs. I am surprised to find that even though they are soft, they still pull hard on my wrists.

She is stronger than I have expected and this thrills me. Now I am over her knees, my belly against those delicious red panties. My ass is in the air and ready for her. My head is down and I experience that momentary giddiness as the blood rushes there. There is the sweet, dreamy sensation of almost losing consciousness and then the abrupt snap back to reality.

My arms are out in front of me and I look at them. They are bound together in restraints put there by Mistress Lyla's hands! They are gorgeous, but not as wonderful as the feel of her firm thighs against my stomach.

Now her fingers are tracing graceful, gentle patterns on my naked asscheeks. I hold my breath and dare not look around. I don't know if this is her way of softening me up for my punishment, or if she is still unsure about striking another woman and is getting up the courage to bring her hand down hard on my flesh. Surely this is different from the quick blows that hurried me up the stairs. This spanking, if I receive it, will be a carefully constructed punishment for no other reason than the satisfaction of domination and submission between two hot women. When I can't hold it any longer, I sigh and then breathe deeply, holding it. This continues for several minutes and soon I am relaxed. Her fingers feel so good on my skin. I moan ever so softly. My cunt is on fire.

Then I realize just what is happening here. I am unsure of what my Mistress's next move will be, and I am lying here across her knees in confusion. Part of me dreads the punishment and part of me longs for it, but I do not know if I will receive it or not. This is the mental torture that I longed for, the stunning contrast to Mistress Laura's endless routines. This is why I chose Mistress Lyla. This is everything I wanted.

The realization goes through me like a firm sexual shudder. I bask in it and lose my concentration for a moment. That is when she strikes.

Crack! It surprises more than hurts, but still leaves a sweet tingle in my buttocks. I gasp and tense up.

"Did it hurt?" Mistress Lyla asks. I can hear a touch of concern in her voice.

"Yes, Mistress," I say to her. She doesn't answer for a long time, and I wonder what is going through her mind. Then, slowly, as if she is savoring the word, she says, "Good."

Her hand smacks down three more times, and then she pauses again. "Your skin is going red," she observes.

"Thank you, Mistress," I reply. She waits for a moment and I decide it is time. "Mistress," I say to her quietly, "I am able to take much more than that."

"I thought you would," she says. Then she begins in earnest. The rain of blows is unbelievable. She is using her strength now, the same power that she used to pull me up and over her lap. My ass burns with each strike. She spanks first one asscheek and then the other, occasionally stretching her hand to cover both. When she slaps the tops of my thighs I gasp.

I can't help it. The tears course down my cheeks and I draw my breath in gasping, ragged sobs. Still she continues. And then, when it seems that I can take no more, she pushes me hard to the floor.

My hands bound in front of me, I fall heavily on my side. I look up at her. The look in her eyes is unmistakable; she is as hot as I am. She spreads her legs and pulls the panty away from her pussy. It is shiny with her juice and her clit is swollen and huge. "Lick me now!" she orders.

It is agony to kneel, for when my bruised buttocks touch my legs, it feels like a fresh blow. I bask in it. I thank her and put my face between her thighs. Her perfume is all around me and I drink it in.

I always thought a cold woman, one who could seemingly ignore a tongue-lashing on her sensitive clit, was the only type who could be a Mistress. The idea of an excited woman moaning and sighing over her sexual buildup seemed so unlike a Mistress that I could not imagine it.

Yet here was Mistress Lyla on the chair in front of me, behaving as she always did when I pleasured her cunt. Rather than making her seem less authoritarian, it spurred me on to lick her even faster and harder.

"Spanking you made me so wet!" she gasps, as I run my tongue along the grooves beside her clit and suck that swollen nub in between my lips. "Your ass went so red—ooooh!—and you squirmed on my legs just so! I want to spank you over and over, Jennifer, I want to make you cry at my hands! Lick me harder, lick me harder. Fuck me with your tongue. Make me come!"

She is moving all over the chair in the way I know so well. Following her is difficult because each shift of my body brings pressure on my raw ass. It is agony to have that battered skin touched, but it is exquisite torment. I relive each blow through the sharp pain even as I relish the hot, salty taste of her pussy on my tongue.

My experience tells me that she is about to come. Her hands are on my head now, pushing me deep into her folds. My tongue is moving faster than I can imagine. I wish I could get right into that soaked hole. She comes, crying, trembling, squirming on the chair. When she finally lets me go, she falls back on the chair, weak with satisfaction.

"That was very good," she says, smiling at me. "Thank you, Mistress," I say. I lick the juice from my wet lips. She sighs again, and trembles as a final thrill goes through her.

"Yes, that was very good," she repeats, and then adds, "slave."

I can hardly believe my ears. I bow low before her, still kneeling on the floor. "Thank you, Mistress," I say. "You can't imagine how long I have waited to hear that."

"I like the sound of it," Mistress Lyla says. I smile at her.

"I thought you might, Mistress," I say. And then I remember something, and my smile fades quickly.

"What's wrong?" she asks.

I can hardly find the words. "Mistress," I say to her, "I must confess to you. You knew, even before we began this, that I already had a Mistress. But now I know that you are the only Mistress I will ever want."

"So what's the problem?" She may have called me slave, she may have tanned my backside raw, but she is still new to all of this, and she is puzzled.

"The problem is that I belong to her, Mistress," I say.

"So can't you break off the relationship? Just tell her that you're seeing someone new?"

"It isn't that easy, Mistress," I say. "She owns me. I was sold to her."

"Sold?" Mistress Lyla is shocked to hear the word, and for a moment she is chummy again, my equal instead of my superior. But I am heartened when she regains her composure and her attitude almost immediately. I know that she will not do this again often.

"Yes, Mistress, sold like property," I say, and I tell her the story of how my former Mistress bartered me for a suitcase and some books to Mistress Laura. "I told you that this was a lifestyle, Mistress, and it's much more than just sex. I am a submissive and as such, I am just chattel. If someone sells me because I am their property, then I have to respect that. I can't be a submissive—I can never know true satisfaction—unless I accept all of it. And the reality here is that my Mistress Laura bought me and she owns me.

"I'm already in serious trouble because I am with you. If she finds out then I don't know what she'll do to me. And Mistress Lyla, I honestly don't know what to do!" In spite of myself I can feel tears welling up in my eyes and running down my cheeks. I can hardly swallow. I love Mistress Lyla so much! And yet I am owned by someone else!

"Well, don't cry," Mistress Lyla says crisply. "Have you forgotten that money matters are my specialty?"

"No, Mistress," I sniffle. "I haven't forgotten, but I don't know how that will help." She reaches down to wipe my tears away, as if I were a child. The protective gesture touches me so much that fresh ones spring to my eyes again.

"You say the reality is that you are owned by someone else," she says. As she speaks, I can hear her voice gaining authority and I know that she is slipping deeper and deeper into her role. "That may be reality, but it isn't carved in stone. The fact is that everyone has their price."

"Mistress?"

"As I'm sure your Mistress Laura does," she continues. "I will simply have to buy you from her."

"But what if she doesn't want to sell me, Mistress?"

"I don't think you heard me," Mistress Lyla says. "Everyone has their price. Now, how do I go about contacting this Mistress of yours?"

"Well," I say, sniffling again but more in control of my emotions now, "I think I may have a solution to that, Mistress. My friend Cleo is a submissive also—I told you that. She has told me that her Mistress knows a very powerful dominatrix who often acts as a 'broker' when submissives are bought and sold."

"So she would provide a neutral meeting place and be the mediator for the deal?"

"Yes, that is my understanding, Mistress."

"Well," Mistress Lyla says confidently, "that is certainly familiar territory. Will you ask Cleo about the details?"

I swallow hard and realize that a subtle lesson is in order. "Mistress, may I speak freely?" I ask.

"Of course," she says. I have never asked for permission to speak before, and I can see that she likes being asked.

"Mistress, our roles are very clear-cut, as you said before," I say. "If I may be so bold as to point it out to you—respectfully, please understand!—a Mistress doesn't request that a slave do something. A question always poses the remote possibility of refusal. But a command could not be refused under any circumstances."

"Then it is definitely the better method," she says. "Very well, then, I command you to speak with Cleo, and set this thing up as quickly as possible. I will expect to hear from you shortly with positive news."

"Yes, Mistress!" I say happily, and I am so ecstatic that I don't see her hand raise until she has cuffed me hard on the side of the head. With my hands still cuffed, I cannot keep my balance. The blow knocks me to the floor and I remain there, dazed and confused, my ear ringing.

"That was necessary," she says. "Your suggestion is valid and I am taking it, but I still can't let you get away with the fact that you told me what to do."

"Yes, Mistress," I whisper. "I am terribly sorry, and I beg your forgiveness." This is better than I could have dreamed.

"There is one thing," she says. "You have a Mistress, one who purchased you and paid goods for you. And yet you found yourself a new Mistress, one who is now in the position of having to put out money to buy you. After I go to all this trouble and expense, what guarantee do I have that you won't go out and find yourself yet another Mistress? You say that your Mistress Laura will be upset with you, and that is most understandable. I would be furious."

"Please understand, Mistress!" I say quickly. "I did not choose Mistress Laura; I was simply sold to her. That doesn't mean that I have not served her faithfully and well. But she does not do the things you do, Mistress, even though she has been a dominatrix for many years and you are still new to it. She does not offer the suspense that you do, she is not inventive as you are. I respect her and I have always obeyed her, but I do not love her. Mistress, I love you."

"Well," Mistress Lyla says, "I suppose other dominatrixes have taken a chance on less."

"Thank you, Mistress," I say happily.

"And now," she says, sitting back in her chair, "I

think that one orgasm is not enough. Slut, get over here and pleasure me!"

"Yes, Mistress!" I whisper, and as she pulls back the red panties again to show me the hot, sweet cunt I so desire, I know that heaven is well within my grasp.

Chapter *Nine*

To say that I am nervous is a laughable understatement. As I walk along the sidewalk, my heart is beating in my throat and my palms feel wet. Several times I almost consider turning around and returning home. But then I think about Lyla—Mistress Lyla!—and it gives me the courage to continue. I would do anything for her.

The house I am looking for is one of the old estates, not quite as opulent as Mistress Lyla's mansion, but stunningly old-world and imposing nevertheless. I walk up to the front door, under the portico. There is an iron lamp hanging from a chain and I feel like I am on display as I stand under it. From the street any passerby would see a woman in the pool of yellow light, moderately attired in a light blue dress, standing in the doorway as anyone else would, waiting for someone to answer the door. But I am a submissive, and I am on the doorstep of a Mistress. A very powerful Mistress, one I have never met before, one who now holds the power to decide whether I am to stay with Mistress Laura or be sold to the woman I adore, Mistress Lyla. Standing here, I feel as if I am wearing nothing at all, my breasts held forth, my legs spread wide, so that the whole world can see me.

My hand trembles just a bit as I ring the doorbell. There is movement inside, and then a young woman opens the door for me.

"Are you Miss Julia Radoff?" I ask her, unsure of myself.

She looks at me and seems slightly amused by the question. "No," she says. "Are you Jennifer Dobson?"

"I am," I reply.

"Then," she says, "please come inside. Mistress Julia is waiting for you."

She opens the door wider for me, and at that moment I wonder how I could not have noticed. She wears a simple, short dress. Now, inside of the folds, I can clearly see the leather collar that encircles her neck. Looking down, I see that she wears a thin leather strap about one ankle, buckled there with a ring alongside the closure. I know the setup well. A chain can quickly be attached from the collar to the ankle cuff, and depending upon its length and thickness, it can either be a thin gold adornment that falls in graceful loops, or a heavy cruel steel link that allows a submissive to walk and carry out her Mistress's commands, but prevents her from standing upright as she does.

"Wait here," the young woman says, disappearing into the house. I look around at the vestibule I am in is luxuriously furnished. Then I catch my breath and my whole body tingles. On the massive oak sideboard by the door, left carelessly behind, is a shiny black leather riding crop. The collared young woman aside, there is no doubt now that this is the correct address.

The young submissive returns shortly. "Follow me," she says, and we walk down the long hallway. It ends at what was once a formal parlor in the antebellum days. That tradition has continued, for the stunning decor suggests that this is the room where only the most favored guests would be asked to take their leave.

"Right there, Melissa," says a voice from behind me. At that moment I close my eyes and say a quick prayer under my breath, thanking all of my Mistresses for their training. Anyone else would have spun around to find out who was there. A submissive should only wait until she is given permission to do so, and fortunately I did not investigate without such consent.

"Thank you, Mistress," the young woman says. I am between her and the woman who has spoken behind me, and I can see the look on Melissa's face as she replies. It is the look I am sure I so often wear: a combination of respect, complete adoration, and a tinge of fear that perhaps the very next thing she does will displease the woman she has just obeyed. In this case, that does not happen. Melissa bows low, then leaves the room.

"So," the woman behind me says, "you are the chattel we are here to disperse."

My heart thumps in my chest. I do not know this Mistress's pleasures at all, and I am completely unsure of what to do. Perhaps she waits for a reply; perhaps she is speaking to herself and will resent an answer on my part. There is no time to think, and I make a flash decision when I do not speak at all. When there is no cruel remark or a well-placed blow, I close my eyes in thankfulness, for it seems that I have made the right decision. Of course, the next time it might be entirely different, and that is one of the joys of my servitude.

"Turn around," the voice says, and I do. I catch my breath in my throat.

The woman speaking to me sits in a chair, watching me. She is tall, ample-breasted, dark-haired, drop-dead gorgeous. She is wearing a black leather corset that laces up tightly around her body and garters that hold up shiny black stockings. She wears tall, black leather boots and black leather gauntlets. She holds a whip like a badge of office, sliding it slowly between her fingers. I automatically drop to my knees before her.

"Well, I see that someone has taken the time to train you," she says. "I am Mistress Julia, which I suppose you have gathered. Your Mistress should be arriving soon. I don't wish to hear from you until then. However, I think I would like to have you take off your clothes. We're selling you, not your dress."

I almost say, "Yes, Mistress," for it is an automatic response when a command is given. Again, at the last moment, my training takes over. I have been told not to speak, and I will not until a counter-order is given. I adore being on my knees at the feet of this beautiful Mistress, but I have little desire to feel the stripes of that whip across my back. I do not know what kind of punishments this Mistress hands out; to judge from her appearance, they are not lenient.

I slip the dress off. I wore nothing under it, and this fact seems to please this Mistress a little. Strangely, I feel no shame at being unclothed in front of a woman I do not know and have only met a minute ago. She is a dominatrix, I am a slave. It is as natural as breathing.

My own Mistress Laura follows the slave Melissa into the room a little while later. Of course I knew she would be here, but when she is announced by the young collared servant, I go cold throughout my entire body. I have betrayed her, and all of us in this room know that so well. I am afraid to look at her, for it is the first time I have seen her since she has been told of my desire to be sold.

For that reason I do not see the blow when it comes. She catches me on the side of the head, hard enough to knock me to the floor. My ears ring and I feel dizzy enough to pass out. Then I groan as the toe of her boot meets my ribs, again and again. I dare not roll over to escape the blows, but lie there meekly as she kicks me mercilessly.

Through the haze I can hear Mistress Julia's voice, suggesting that my Mistress try to hold her temper. At first I think that she is concerned for me, but then I realize it is not so. "If you damage your goods, you stand to receive much less for it," she says, and slowly my Mistress, in that thin, quiet voice that I know means she is raging within, finally agrees. She gives me permission to get back to my knees. Shakily, I do so. My ribs are horribly bruised and when I draw a ragged breath, the pain almost splits my side. I hope that my ribs are not broken.

"Look at me," my Mistress says, and I raise my

eyes slowly and fearfully. She is fully dressed, but by the hint of lace I can see at her shirtfront I know she is wearing her favorite outfit, a red corset that I know makes her feel most like a Mistress. I knew she would wear it, and the knowledge—no surprises here—gives me the final reason for wanting Mistress Lyla so badly.

Slowly I look up at her face. I can tell that she is furious, seething at me. She speaks calmly as she always does when she is angry. "I did more for you than any Mistress ever should, you worthless little shit," she says. "This is how you reward me, by sneaking off when my back is turned and finding someone else? You betrayed me! Well, I'll be glad to be rid of you now. I only hope that this Lyla doesn't change her mind and leave me stuck with you."

I do not reply, for I am still under the command of Mistress Julia, and Mistress Laura for all of her punishment did not give me permission to reply to her. My silence infuriates her and once again she strikes me, this time a hard slap across my cheek. It is not as powerful as the last blow, however, and while my head snaps sideways I manage to stay on my knees this time.

"I told her I didn't want to hear from her," Mistress Julia says idly. "Of course, she's still your slave, you can order her to do whatever you want. There's a whip here if need be. But I think you might want to take my advice and not mark her up too much. After all, you wouldn't scratch the paint on a car you were trying to sell."

"You're right," my Mistress agrees, and I can see that she is making an effort to relax. Glasses of wine brought by another one of Mistress Julia's submissives—the second woman I have seen in this house under her command, and I wonder just how many she has—and a seat on the beautiful white sofa help to improve her mood.

About half an hour later Melissa comes to the doorway, bows low, and waits for permission to speak. When it is given, she informs her Mistress that Lyla has arrived.

"About time," Mistress Laura says coldly, almost under her breath.

"Actually, she's right on time," Mistress Julia says. It's obvious that she's becoming annoyed by my Mistress, who is behaving far from professionally about this. "Keep your head. It always makes for better bargaining, and of course, you want the most you can possibly get for this slut."

When Mistress Lyla walks in, I am so proud of her that my heart feels full. She is immaculately dressed in an expensive suit, and she appears calm and in control. Inwardly I know that she must be as nervous as I am, a relative novice in the presence of my own Mistress and this most powerful liaison. But on the outside she is as cool and haughty as they, and I could not imagine anyone who would not believe that she had been in control of submissives for years.

Introductions are made, and a glass of wine is brought for Mistress Lyla. There is small talk, about the weather and the furniture in the room, and a bit of history as Mistress Julia and Mistress Lyla compare the lineage of their antebellum houses. Like a scornful child I take a bit of vindictive cheer in the fact that my Mistress Laura, living in a brand-new house, can only marginally enter this discussion. This is replaced again by pride when Mistress Lyla graciously changes the subject of conversation for the sake of etiquette.

Against her smooth composure and fine manners, Mistress Laura seems almost ill-bred and low.

This goes on for another forty minutes or so. My legs are cramped under me and my knees ache, but I would not have missed such a scene for the world. All three of them ignore me. I am only chattel, of no more consequence than the ottoman or the table. They will get to me in due time.

That time does happen, when Mistress Julia sets down her glass. "Ladies, we are here for a reason," she says. "Why don't we get our business out of the way? Then we can enjoy a fresh drink and some more conversation."

The other two agree. Now it is time for Mistress Julia to stand up and take over, and I quickly sneak a glance at her gorgeous legs in those tight black boots. I envy the women who serve her, until I sneak another glance, this time at Mistress Lyla. There is only one woman here for me.

"Get up," Mistress Julia says, and with difficulty I do so, for my legs are stiff and my ribs ache horribly. I stand before the three of them, naked. They look at me with the same bored expressions that might be used to assess livestock at an auction.

"So," my Mistress Laura says, "I understand that you want to buy this worthless slave."

"If you think her so worthless," Mistress Lyla replies, "then perhaps I can get a bargain."

Ooooh! All the way here I worried for Mistress Lyla. She is still new to this and has barely flexed her dominatrix muscles, and I feared that the other two women might chew her up right in front of me. No fear! My heart leaps. I believe now that she will hold her own.

"What is your offer?" Mistress Julia asks of Mistress Lyla.

"I do not plan on paying a lot for her," Mistress Lyla says. "It is my understanding that you didn't pay much for her yourself, when you got her."

"How do you know that?" my Mistress Laura asks, angry now, and very defensive.

"She told me," Mistress Lyla replies. My own Mistress is furious again. "The slave lies!"

"That may be so," Mistress Lyla says. "If so, then I believe an untrustworthy slave is worth considerably less."

For a moment both of the other women are taken aback. They know that Mistress Lyla is a novice and both expected that this would be quick and easy, with the scales tipped heavily in Mistress Laura's favor.

In this I am much more enlightened than they are, for I know that this is not Mistress Lyla dealing with them now. This is Lyla Kirk, in charge of protecting the accounts of one of the state's largest manufacturing firms. There is not an executive in the country who can bargain her down or pull one over on her. She handles millions of dollars a week flawlessly; bargaining for one submissive who originally sold for a suitcase and a handful of books is nothing.

Of course there is another understanding in this room, that this is an elaborate scene which is being played out for the benefit of all, and I can tell that all three of them are enjoying it immensely. I wonder if Mistress Lyla is soaking wet under that beautifully tailored suit. My mouth waters at the thought of being able to suck those pussy hairs dry.

"What will you offer, then?" Mistress Julia repeats.

"I will offer you what you paid for her," Mistress

Lyla says. "A suitcase and some books. Of course you have trained her well and your efforts can't go unrewarded. For your work I offer a crystal bowl. It's Baccarat, and very nice; I am sure you will like it."

Despite themselves, both Mistresses gasp ever so slightly. The magnitude of Mistress Lyla's offer is overwhelming.

My Mistress Laura, regaining herself, takes on a cocky attitude to hide her momentary lapse. "I thought you said you didn't plan on paying much," she says.

"I don't," Mistress Lyla replies. This is the same cool cunning I have seen played out in the head office boardroom a number of times. She has a poker face and a razor-sharp mind that has been the envy and the downfall of many an executive or banker. "I told you that I am offering you what you paid for the slave: a suitcase and some books. That is certainly not much. The crystal is not payment for the slave and I think that you misunderstand me. I am offering that for the trouble you have taken over the years to train her. I think that it is a fair amount for the work you have done."

"She has a good point," Mistress Julia says. "If you went to the trouble of training a slave then you should receive something for your time."

"Of course," Mistress Laura says, haughtily, to let Mistress Lyla know that her offer had never been misconstrued. She stands and seems to think about the offer, but I know her well enough. The deal is closed in her mind. The posturing is because Mistress Lyla has the upper hand here and my Mistress Laura is no longer in control of the situation. She is saving face by giving the impression that she might still turn down this extremely generous offer. Finally, slowly, she says, "I would like to see the goods first."

"I expected nothing less," Mistress Lyla says, and she turns to Mistress Julia. The haughty, corseted woman goes to the doorway and smacks her whip against it once. Melissa appears almost instantaneously, and then rushes to obey her command.

The young submissive returns shortly with a suitcase. I immediately recognize the leather handle and patterned cloth that identifies it as Louis Vuitton. The other two Mistresses know it too, and their eyes open wide. This is even more valuable than the crystal that so impressed them.

The bowl is wrapped in a cloth inside the suitcase and my Mistress Laura examines it carefully, and then passes it to Mistress Julia, as mediator, to look over herself. I have to suppress a smile when I notice that the books are cheap paperbacks, two of them obviously well used. Neither of the two women mention this, even as they pick them up and look at them.

Mistress Laura takes so long examining everything that it seems to me she is trying even Mistress Julia's patience. Finally, she says, "It's an acceptable offer. The worthless slave is yours."

I don't know how I stay motionless. I want to leap with joy, kneel before my new Mistress, and beg to wear her collar. Instead, I stand in place, waiting for instructions. They are not long in coming, for Mistress Lyla orders me to dress myself.

"Will you stay for more wine?" Mistress Julia asks.

"Thank you, but no," Mistress Lyla replies. "I have an engagement later on, and I want to drop this slave off at my house and put a collar on her before I go. Perhaps next time."

"Next time, then," Mistress Julia says, and she shakes my new Mistress's hand in parting.

Mistress Laura also shakes hands and can't resist a parting shot when she says, "I thought you didn't want to overspend."

Mistress Lyla stops at the doorway, motions for me to stop, and turns and smiles at her. She is obviously enjoying herself as she says, "I didn't."

We follow Melissa down the long hallway to the front door. Mistress Lyla's car is at the curb. She indicates the back door with a nod of her head, and I know that this is my command. I wait there for her, until she gets in and the locks click open. I sit down and look at the back of her head.

My mind is spinning. I am once again embarking on a new journey and I know instinctively that this is the first step. In all aspects she is now Mistress Lyla, my owner, and everything that we had is behind us now. I do not speak to her, for I have not been given permission to do so. I sit in silence as she drives.

She takes me to her house. I sit and watch as the garage doors flip open automatically and she drives the huge car inside. The doors close behind us and we sit in the half-lit garage. She sits in the front seat for a long time, looking ahead. I long to ask what she is thinking, but that is forbidden. She is now my owner, and I am now her property.

Finally she opens the door and gets out. She walks around the car and the door beside me is opened. But instead of waiting for me to get out, she gets into the car, forcing me on to the floor with a touch of her hand.

She sits on the seat and pulls up her skirt. She wears nothing underneath and the rich smell of her cunt perfume fills the car. I can see the wetness on the lips of her pussy.

"Now," she says, "I want to find out if I got just what I paid for."

Chapter *Ten*

"You know," Mistress Lyla says, "one of the real joys of going on these trips is when you do get a little time to yourself, you can do some shopping."

It is late Wednesday afternoon, and we are in Toronto. That by itself would be new to me, for it is the first time I have done a trade show in this largest Canadian city. What makes it even fresher for me is that once again, Cleo and I are accompanied by the accounting department's Lyla Kirk—my Mistress Lyla.

As always, Cleo and I were first into the convention center, making sure our booth was set up and everything ready to go for the customary just-after-dawn push that always put us ahead of the competition. Now that everything was in order, we had a few hours to relax.

This time our rooms were in one of the finest hotels in the city, and I wondered how much leverage Mistress Lyla had used when they were chosen. As soon as Cleo saw the huge bathtub with its whirlpool jets, she decided that a hot, bubbly bath was definitely more interesting than going shopping before dinner. We decided on a time and place to meet for our evening meal, and then at Mistress Lyla's demand, she and I set out to see the sights.

The downtown streets were crowded and for this reason, Mistress Lyla quietly gave me permission to address her without the respectful title. Just as respectfully, I thanked her. She had given me similar permission while we were in the airport, on the plane, and inside the convention center. Of course, during this trip her permission was just a formality, for we were "on the job" at this point and calling her Mistress would definitely have been the wrong thing to do in front of others at the show.

But that was not the point. Everything depended on the fact that Mistress Lyla gave me the command to dispense with the title. By doing this, I was still under her orders. Tomorrow, I know that she will give me such a command before we leave to work the grueling hours of the trade show. At times, when we are presenting our line of fasteners to prospective clients, it will sometimes appear that Cleo and I are her superiors within our company. But once we are back in the hotel and I go back to her room with her, the charade will be over.

Before we left the hotel we stopped by Cleo's room

to invite her along, but she begged off, citing the whirlpool. "We will see you at dinner, then," my dominatrix said.

"Yes," Cleo replied, and then added, "Mistress," before she closed the door.

Mistress Lyla was puzzled as we walked down the hall together. "Why did she call me that?" she asked.

"Because you are a dominatrix, Mistress," I replied. Permission to dispense with the title was not given when we were alone in the hotel, when others could not hear us, and I was glad to use the term again.

"But I am not her superior," Mistress Lyla said. "She belongs to someone else, doesn't she?"

"She does, Mistress," I replied, as I pushed the button to summon the elevator. "But as submissives, we are inferior to all dominatrixes, whether they directly control us or not. It is a term of respect. From now on, whenever you meet a submissive and she knows that you are a dominatrix, she will address you as 'Mistress.' She risks both your wrath and the anger of her own superior if she does not."

"My wrath?"

"Mistress," I said, "dominatrixes don't take another's slave without her permission, or abuse another's slave enough to cause serious injury, or give a command that counters one already given by the owner. At least, they usually don't. But if you met another dominatrix's slave and that slave was rude to you, what would you do?"

"Well," Mistress Lyla said, thinking about it, "I would probably get very angry."

"Wouldn't you be inclined to teach her a lesson? Perhaps a good slap across the face?"

"That would probably be my immediate reaction," my Mistress said.

"And," I continued, "there is not a dominatrix in the world who would not expect you to do that. Of course, once you had done that, you would probably be invited to help that dominatrix beat the shit out of the slave, just to make sure the lesson was learned."

Mistress Lyla said nothing more, for the elevator had arrived, but all the way down to the lobby I could see that the idea had definitely taken root.

And now we are out on the street, walking up the sidewalk and looking over this fascinating city. It has a "gay village" and before long it becomes obvious that we are in the center of it. When I see two women holding hands I am elated, and the more I look around, the more lesbians I see. My trained eyes don't take long to see the dominatrixes walking with their submissives a few respectful steps behind them, and I hope desperately that people will recognize us. I am so proud of my Mistress that I wish I was walking in chains, led by her with a leash.

There are stores here that sell leather goods and erotic books, and it puzzles me that my Mistress does not stop in them. Instead, I notice that she has a piece of paper in her hand and that she is looking intently at the street signs.

"Forgive me," I say—although I am sure I could use the term Mistress here, in this friendly place, I am under command not to use it and so I obey—"but are you looking for something specific?"

"I am," my Mistress says, and when she does not elaborate I ask no more, but follow her as she looks up and down the street. Finally she stops a police officer waiting on the corner and asks; she directs us down a side street and then up another street that is small enough to be just an alley.

"Are you sure this is correct?" I ask. It seems like we are lost, until my Mistress notices the small sign hanging over a doorway up ahead. It is this that she is searching for.

I breathe deeply as soon as we walk through the door into the store. It is the smell of hundreds of pieces of leather and it is intoxicating.

The weather here, while not as stifling as the summer heat back in our Southern home, is still in the low eighties, and the store is not air conditioned. The leather scent is almost overwhelming and I smile. It is a musk that I would happily drown in. It is the smell of both submission and domination at the same time.

There is a lovely woman at the cash register, dressed simply in a tank top and shorts; she assesses us instantly and immediately gives all of her attention to my Mistress. For me there is not even a glance, and I know that my status is obvious.

"Is there something I can help you with?" she asks.

"There certainly is," Mistress Lyla smiles. "I will be honest with you; I am new at this, and I own practically nothing. I have come here to rectify that."

The woman smiles, and I notice that it is the smile of solidarity. Submissives fight for the right to grovel at her feet, I am sure. "We have everything you will ever need," she says.

This is obvious. The store seems small, but I soon realize that there are rooms behind the one we are in. This first one is filled with shoes of every description. Most of them have shockingly high heels, all of them stiletto-thin. Their heels look razor-sharp and I long to see them on Mistress Lyla's feet, with those heels in my mouth, my Mistress ordering me to clean them, to fellate them.

In one small section near the bottom are shoes that fascinate me, for I have not seen anything like these before. Segregated from the powerful high-heeled shoes, they are obviously for slaves only. Black, ugly, heavy, there is a whole range of them and all of them look terribly uncomfortable. Several pairs of them have rings set into the leather, meant for hobbling. One of them, when I dare to peek into it, has hideous, sharp studs inside to tear into a submissive's feet once she stands in them. I shudder and hope that Mistress Lyla doesn't take a liking to these.

A little further into the room is a collection of harnesses, all of them tacked onto the wall with the prices beside them. Some are for the men who cower at the feet of dominant men or women: cockrings, ball harnesses, belts with studded pouches. Others are for women, and these intrigue me. There are leather bras with buckles to squeeze the tits into painful points. There are chastity belts that lock around a cunt. There are harnesses and blindfolds, wrist and ankle cuffs, and even a horrible leather hood with a zipper across the mouth. I shudder. I have seen all of these items before and have worn some of them, but seeing them all displayed on the wall at once gives me a delicious chill.

My Mistress is now in another room and I hurry to follow her. This room is mostly clothing for dominatrixes, and she is going through the racks as the clerk points out particularly interesting items. Their selection is stunning. I can see everything from suits that outfit from head to toe in leather, to costumes made up of only a few well-placed straps.

In the middle of everything is a large, square glass-fronted counter. The clerk and my Mistress are busy and ignoring me, so I move over to the counter for a look. It takes my breath away.

One side of the counter is dedicated to whips. They have every description here, lovingly laid out on a bed of white satin to show off the shining black leather. There are riding crops, bullwhips, small personal sticks, and in one corner, a majestic cat-o'-nine-tails, its cruel plumage streaming out over the white satin. There is even a whip with a tiny metal barb set into the end of it. That makes my blood run cold when I think of the damage it would do.

Another side is gags and blindfolds, ball gags of every size, goggles, eye covers and full-face masks in leather, cotton, and shiny rubber.

The third side is gloves: long leather gauntlets, satin gloves with eight buttons up the arms, fingerless leather gloves, gloves with studs over the knuckles. There is even a chain-mesh glove, such as the type that butchers wear, and I shudder to think about how it might be used.

The fourth side is an assortment of items. There are buttplugs in all sizes and dildos, by themselves or on leather harnesses. There are ben-wah balls, vibrators, condoms, lubricants. There are all sorts of rings to be worn in pierced nipples, labia and foreskins. And in one corner, all by itself, is a small item that at first I do not recognize. When I get closer I notice that it is a tiny branding iron. The sweat that breaks out on my forehead isn't from the heat.

"Jennifer!" The voice breaks me out of my daze and I hurry over to where my Mistress is waiting with the clerk. That young woman has a tape measure in her hands.

I am measured, completely. The thin dress I am

wearing is no impediment and shortly the clerk is jotting down my bust size, my waist size, my height. "Now I'm sure there are other things you'd like to look at in the store," my Mistress says, and I take the not-so-subtle hint and walk back into the first room, where the shoes are. I catch another glimpse of those slave hobble boots and I am thankful that my shoe size was not included in the measurements.

When we leave, my Mistress hands me the large bag to carry. It is heavy and I long to peek inside, but I know better. I can only think about it as we find our way back to the crowded main street. I am thrilled to see that we are walking back to the hotel.

In the lobby, we only get quick glances from the staff and other guests as we walk in, but I feel as if all eyes are upon me. Surely they notice that I am a step behind her! And they have to know what kind of merchandise is in this bag! I can't believe that the whole world doesn't know that we are Mistress and slave, on our way upstairs together.

In the elevator we are alone. "Is the bag heavy?" she asks me.

"Oh, no, Mistress," I say to her.

"Fine," she says, but there is a coldness to her voice. I shudder, half in fear and half in elation. I am amazed at how quickly she is turning into a wickedly cunning dominatrix.

We reach the door to our suite. Only one room has been reserved for both of us. I still don't know what the sleeping arrangements will be, and I do not dare ask, but I do know that there is only one king-sized bed. I highly doubt that I will be asked to take it or even to share it.

Mistress Lyla opens the door and stands back. I

step through it, but before I am even over the threshold, she pushes me so hard from behind that I fall to my knees on the carpet. The bag flies off and lands beside a chair.

"Mistress?" I cry out. My knees are on fire from sliding across the rug and my wrists hurt from the fall.

She closes the door quietly behind her. "That's exactly it," she says. "I'm supposed to punish you when you don't do what you're told—isn't that correct?"

"Yes, Mistress," I say to her.

"And you were told to call me Lyla, were you not?"

"Yes, Mistress, I was," I say.

"But in the elevator," she says, as she slips off her shoes, "you called me Mistress."

"I thought," I say, "that since we were alone, it would be respectful of me to use that term. I thought I had permission."

"You are correct; it would be respectful," she admits, "and from here on, you are to use it again, until we are in a situation where it would not be discreet. But even though it was respectful, you had not been given permission to use it. Permission is not an automatic thing, Jennifer."

I drop my eyes. "I am sorry, Mistress," I say. "Please forgive me."

"Well, there will be forgiveness, but I will have to punish you first," Mistress Lyla says. Then, just for a moment, the dominatrix is gone and she is just Lyla Kirk, still new to everything, still feeling the newfound power of her position. "That's right, isn't it?" she asks. "I'm supposed to think of things to punish you for, aren't I?"

"Mistress," I say, "this is everything I dreamed it would be."

She regains her haughty composure almost immediately. She amazes me every time I see her, and I know that I will see very few of these momentary lapses from now on.

"Then I think you will hand me that bag," she says. "No, wait. I think I would rather have it brought in your mouth, like a dog would fetch it."

I start toward the bag, but my Mistress adds, "Naked, please," and so I stop and slip off my clothes before I continue. The carpet, chosen to be long-wearing, is rough and burns my already sore knees.

The plastic bag has fallen so that the handles are flat on the floor and it is very difficult to pick it up between my teeth. For just a moment I consider lifting it with my hand, for my Mistress is behind me and she wouldn't be able to see it. But that would be contrary to my orders, and so I struggle to catch it between my teeth. When I finally lift it, it is heavy and the plastic slips out of my mouth. I have to bend down and go through the whole routine again, but this time I make sure that I have a firm hold on it.

"Good doggie!" my Mistress crows. Once again I am heartened by how quickly she falls into the role. I sit on my haunches before her, with the bag still in my mouth. She takes it from my hands.

"I bought some presents for you," she continues, as she opens the bag. "You know, I've always liked dogs. They're good companions and they can be a lot of fun. That's why I thought I might like to have one here with me, on this trip."

The first item that comes out is a leather collar. It is heavy, chrome-studded, with a large buckle and a ring for a leash. "Come here," she says.

I move forward, happily, on my hands and knees.

When she drops her hand I know it to be a command that I am to sit, which I do. She reaches down and buckles the collar about my throat. It is very loose and hangs down on my chest.

"Mistress, may I speak freely?" I ask, hesitantly.

"You may," she says.

I take a deep breath. "If I may be so bold," I say, "I believe that you underestimate how much punishment I am capable of taking. We have a prearranged signal, the one we discussed, which I am to show you if I can't tolerate the level we reach."

"I know that," she says.

"I have not given you the signal, Mistress," I say, bowing respectfully. "I am nowhere near that plateau."

"I understand," she says. I am happy. Prior to this, she might have dropped her composure and asked me what she should do. But this time, she accepts it all as taken, as a Mistress receiving a deferential comment from her slave.

She unbuckles the collar and tightens it around my throat. Now I can feel the leather against my skin and I feel complete within the its circle. I love it when a Mistress places a collar around my neck. When it is Mistress Lyla I am giddy with joy.

"Of course," she adds, "I will now have to punish you for suggesting that."

"Thank you, Mistress," I say. Punishment is exactly what I am looking forward to.

Next out of the bag is a leash. This is snapped on to the ring on my collar. "I suppose that since you haven't had a walk today, you'll need one," she says, and she starts to walk.

The room is very large and Mistress Lyla goes all around it. Her stride is long and it is difficult for me to keep up with her. At first she slows down when I start to drop behind, but soon she is tugging hard on the leash to make me hurry. It pulls on my neck and I struggle to move faster. At one point she almost drags me. I am joyous.

Then we stop, and she loops the leash around the arm of a chair. "Stay," she says, as she might to a dog. Then she picks up the bag and walks into the other room. I sit, obediently, wondering what is coming next. My pussy is sopping and throbbing so much that I can hardly stand it. I wish I had the nerve, while under a Mistress's command, to touch it and possibly relieve some of the pressure. But I am too well trained and my hand won't move even close to that swollen, sex-starved nubbin.

She takes so long that I can hardly stand to wait. But wait I do, and I will wait all night if that is how long it takes her to come out. I have not been given permission to rise.

When she finally comes out I bow down on the carpet before her, whispering, "Mistress!" It is an automatic reaction when I see the goddess that stands before me.

She has purchased the outfit I caught a glimpse of on the way out. It is made up completely of thin leather straps, joined with heavy chromed rings and decorated with thin chrome chains. One strap goes around her chest, attached to straps that go on either side of her delicious breasts to form an open bra. Straps weave down her belly and slip between her legs to cover that wonderful pussy. The chains circle her waist and attach to the straps at her back. On her feet she has a pair of impossibly high, stiletto-heeled shoes in shiny black patent leather. On her hands are fingerless gloves, the ones with chrome studs across the knuckles. She wears a black leather cap and her dark hair flows luxuriously out from under it.

"You like my outfit, yes?" she says, as she stands and models it. I have never seen anything so stunning in my life and I am sure my eyes are still huge. I can't get enough of the sight of her in it. My pussy aches and my mouth waters at the sight of her cunt, covered by that strip of thin black leather. I long to lick those shoes and have those stiletto heels push hard against my tongue.

She walks over and stands right by me, so close that I can see the moisture on her cunt hairs and smell the rich perfume. "You want that, don't you?" she says.

"Yes, Mistress," I whisper. She brings herself so close that my tongue, stretched out to reach her, just misses the hot folds. Then she spins about and walks away. I sigh heavily, until I realize that she has picked up another purchase, a heavy black leather paddle.

"Spanking is nice," she says, "but I just couldn't resist this." She slaps it gently against her hand, but even that light blow results in a hefty smacking sound. I can almost feel it against my asscheeks. I want it so badly, so badly, and she walks toward me with it in her hand...

...and then, just as quickly, she looks at her watch and puts the paddle down. "We're going to be late for dinner," she says, and abruptly she walks back into the other room.

I feel tears in my eyes. She was just steps away with that paddle, and now I have to wait. When she comes back she is fully dressed, but at the last moment she opens a button on her shirt. The leather harness is under it and I sigh with longing.

Now she unbuckles the collar and orders me to stand up. My throat feels naked without it. She leaves the collar on the table, but she takes the leash and ties it tightly around my waist. "Now dress," she says, and I slip on my clothes over the leather restraint.

I can feel it, as hot as wanting, as we walk down the hallway. Cleo is already in the dining room when we arrive, and she respectfully stands when Mistress Lyla comes into the room. She only sits down when my Mistress nods slightly to her, and it is obvious that my Mistress appreciates this treatment. It seems that she molds more into her role minute by minute.

Mistress Lyla puts her bag on the floor between my chair and hers. At one point, when I am reaching for my cocktail, I happen to glance down and go first cold and then searing hot right through. The handle of the paddle is sticking out of the top of it. Throughout the whole meal I sneak quick peeks at it, and Mistress Lyla notices and smiles.

Dinner takes forever, and the discussions about the trade show and how we are going to approach the customers tomorrow seem so far away for me. What do I care about clients, when my Mistress Lyla sits beside me wearing leathers and chains? How can I concentrate when I can feel the leather leash that she has wrapped around my waist? Who cares about product lines when there is a paddle beside me, a paddle that I know will be used later to tan my ass?

Once again Mistress Lyla makes me sit in a restaurant, almost overcome with longing, while she takes her time. The conversation flows only because she continues to talk about work and our role at the trade show. Cleo and I are professional about what we do, and in the past we have been able to talk easily about it even through cocktail parties, boring clients, and all-night emergency meetings. I am thankful now for that. I feel like someone else is talking and only when I listen to myself do I realize it is me. My whole being concentrates on my pussy.

Finally Mistress Lyla says, "It's getting late and we have an early start. If you will excuse me, Cleo, I would like to return to my room."

"Not at all," Cleo replies, and I hear the unspoken "Mistress" at the end of it. "It's time for me to turn in as well." She is grateful, for I know she is tired and there is no way she would ever suggest calling an end to the evening when a Mistress present in the room had not already done so. Such is the training we receive!

The elevator ride seems impossibly long and while we are in the small cubicle Cleo keeps silent, her eyes on the floor. When we stop, she turns to go to her room.

"Good night, Cleo," my Mistress says. Cleo looks around for a moment and sees that no one else is in the hallway. "Good night," she says, and then adds quietly, "Mistress."

I can't help but notice Mistress Lyla's smile at the word. I feel sorry for Cleo as she walks down the hallway to her room, by herself. I know that she has at least one video in her suitcase and there is a player in her room. But that is just a tape, and I have a real live Mistress here with me, taking me back to her room.

Mistress Lyla opens the door to the room. I follow her inside and stand, unsure, with no commands to follow.

"Undress," Mistress Lyla says, disappearing into the other room. When she comes back, her no-

nonsense suit and her sensible shoes are gone. She is once again clad only in the spider's-web weaving of leather and chains, those shiny black leather shoes on her feet.

I have left the leash around my waist. Mistress Lyla grabs the end of it and uses it to pull me forcefully to the floor. She buckles the collar back around my throat, then unwraps the leash and puts it back in its rightful place. She uses this to walk me, like a dog, into the bedroom.

The bed is huge and inviting, but I am not asked to get on to it. Instead, she ties the leash to a chair so that I can get close to the bed but can't quite touch it.

"On the chair," she says, and pushes me—not quite a kick—with the toe of one shoe when I don't understand what she means. Finally I understand and hurry to obey. I am now lying across the chair with my ass in the air. It is the same position I took when she spanked me.

This time there is not the mercy of a bare hand. Instead, I close my eyes and wait, for I know what is coming. When it does, it sucks the breath right out of me.

Wham! The paddle comes down hard on my skin and I cry out. It really hurts. She smacks again, twice more, once on each cheek, then stands back to examine her work.

"Very nice," she says appraisingly. "That clerk was right, this is much better than just a spanking." She touches my burning buttocks with her hand; her touch is cool and comforting on my skin. "You should see this, Jennifer. It's all a nice mottled red. Well, I think I can do better than that."

She does. The paddle cracks down over and over on my battered flesh. Tears course down my cheeks and I sob. Finally I cry out, "Mercy, please, Mistress!"

"Is that a signal for clemency?" she asks, the paddle raised to strike again.

"No, Mistress!" I sob. "It is a plea from your slave for mercy!"

"Then it is of no interest to me," she says, and brings the paddle down hard. My ass is on fire, and my pussy is as well. She knows this and she rubs the handle of the paddle against my slit. I moan as the hot chills go through me, and almost involuntarily I push my cunt hard against it. She pulls the paddle away. "This is for my pleasure, not yours," she says. She grabs my collar and pulls me to the floor. I cry out when my pummeled cheeks hit the carpet. It is as if I am sitting on live coals.

"This," she continues, "is for my pleasure also." She makes sure I am watching as she reaches into her bag and brings out a large, battery-powered vibrator.

"The paddling," she says, "is because you called me Mistress when you were told not to. I also told you that I would have to punish you for suggesting that I tighten the collar. That is what this is for."

I am confused; the vibrator is something I use for pleasure, not punishment. But her reasoning is immediately apparent when she pushes the leather strap away from her wet pussy and turns the dial that makes the vibrator buzz.

"I know how much you enjoy licking me," she says, as she sits down on the edge of the bed facing me. The vibrator buzzes up against her swollen, delightful lips. "I know that you like to put your tongue on me and taste my juice. I know that you like to suck my clit and push your tongue into my hole. You do, don't you?"

"Yes, Mistress," I whisper. My tongue is licking my lips now, wishing it were those other hairy lips that my eyes are glued to.

"It would give you such gratification to be able to pleasure me," she continues. The vibrator has pushed apart her pussylips and I can see the sweet pink edge of her clit. I can all but taste its salty heat in my mouth. "You want this cunt. You want to taste it, lick it, fuck it. But you can't. I'm going to get my pleasure from this vibrator, and you can only sit there and watch."

This is a cruel and cunning punishment indeed. I would give anything to be there between her legs. When she trembles, I want to be sending those chills up her spine. I want to suck on her nipples and work my way down to her hairy recess. Instead, I am tied to the chair, my ass blistered, forced to watch as my Mistress casts me aside in favor of an electrical device.

She is as noisy and as exuberant as always and when she comes I moan aloud, but this time in agony instead of ecstasy. She makes me kiss the vibrator and I savor it, licking her thick, wine-rich juices off the warm plastic surface.

"It's time for bed," she says, as she slips the leather straps off in preparation. "That wake-up call comes very early." She will sleep naked, obviously in the bed, and I wonder where I will be permitted to sleep.

It doesn't take long to find out. She takes the leash and makes me crawl to the foot of the bed, where she ties the leash around the post. I will sleep on the floor, but as long as I am alongside my sleeping Mistress I am happy.

I am afraid, however, that I underestimate the latent cruelty I have helped to awaken. She has one more trick in her bag, one that is so original it takes my breath away.

"You recognize these, of course," she says, as she stands over me, holding them.

Of course I do. They are tie-wraps, thin plastic straps with a loop at one end. They are used to neatly tie electrical wires together; once the loose end is inserted into the loop, they can be tightened to any circumference. The loop is one-way; the wrap can always be tightened further, but it will not loosen. Our company sells them and they are our number-one product. They are the main reason why Cleo and I attend trade show after trade show, selling clients on their quality.

Up until now I had never thought of them as having any uses other than the industrial ones. But now, as Mistress Lyla makes me lie on my side on the carpet, the familiar little devices are as nasty and heartless as any item I have seen in SM catalogues.

She puts one around each ankle, not so tight that it would leave marks, but enough that I can feel it. Then one goes around each wrist, and I am ordered to curl into a ball. Now she takes one more, and uses it to bind all four together.

My arms and wrists are joined as one, and I cannot move. I long to stretch out my legs, but they will not move. My spine is curved, doubled over, and my arms are out straight. The position is uncomfortable right from the start, but Mistress Lyla has put me in it, and I will suffer it uncomplaining all night. I love her so much!

I can't look up, and I imagine how she looks, so beautiful in her nakedness as she stands before the mirror and brushes out her long hair. I hear the sheets rustle as she gets into bed. "Jennifer," she says, "you can't imagine how soft this bed is! And the pillows are so comfortable. I'm going to sleep like a baby."

Then the lights go out, and I can hear her breathing become deep and regular as she goes to sleep. My arms are numb and my legs ache. My bruised buttocks throb uncontrollably and my poor pussy is about to burst with unrelieved pressure. My throat is encircled with a leather collar and I am lying on my side on the floor. I have never been happier in my life.

Chapter *Eleven*

"Sure is hot," the woman says as she passes on the street. "It is," I reply. It's only the type of pleasantry strangers exchange when they meet, but today it's a very accurate one. I'm back in the land of Southern hospitality and the thermometer is snaking very close to the top on this stifling, humid day.

I am also back with my Southern Mistress, who has called me and told me to come to her house. It is the first time I have seen her since we came back from Toronto, six days ago. The first sound of her voice on the phone made me weak.

How I remember that trip! As tired as I was, there

was little sleep for me that first night. My arms and legs alternated between cramps and numbness, firmly attached to each other by the plastic straps.

I would force myself to calm down, listening to my Mistress's slow, even breathing as she lay in the comfortable bed above me. After a while I would doze off, but it would either be a light, twilight sleep from which I easily awoke or a deeper sleep with frightening dreams that would rouse me. The first time I came out of a dream, I momentarily forgot where I was, and I thrashed about until I realized why I could not move. The straps cut painfully into my wrists and ankles.

I was powerless to even roll over onto my other side, and my ribs and hips began to ache from lying on the floor. No carpet, no matter how thick, can protect a slave when her superior decides that the floor will make an adequate bed.

I believe at one point I began to sob, but only part of it was because of my agony. It felt so fulfilling to be there, under my Mistress's command. It was something my former Mistress Laura would never have thought of, and it made me so much happier to know that my decision about my co-worker Lyla Kirk had been the right one.

Halfway through the night, something happened that made me think about it even more. Waking up from yet another dream, I pulled hard against the plastic straps, which did not give.

I realized then that, for the first time, my Mistress had put me into bonds that I could not possibly escape from. Our company makes these tie-wraps to be the best and strongest on the market, and they are. The plastic straps can be broken, but only by someone with much, much more strength than I, and my wrists would probably snap before the restraints would.

Up until that point, my Mistress had doled out punishments that I had to choose to accept as they were handed out: I could have unbuckled the wrist cuffs or walked away from the paddle, if I had chosen to do so. But from this torture there was no escape. I was completely in her control. She could get up in the morning, get dressed and depart, leaving me completely helpless to be found by the maid. I would not be able to leave this room, stand up or even stretch my limbs unless my Mistress cut the straps.

That filled my heart until I thought it would burst, and it was the revelation I needed. I loved her so much at that point I could hardly wait until morning just to see her face. Sleep still did not come easily, but I spent the rest of the night contented.

The morning at the trade show was another story. It was some time before my cramped legs would even hold me up, and I hurt right through to my bones. Fortunately my Mistress allowed me the pleasure of a long, hot shower—providing I licked her pussy, which took no urging at all—and I stood under the steaming water until my muscles loosened. Struggling in the straps had left dark marks on my wrists and ankles, and I was thankful that I had included a long-sleeved shirt in my suitcase.

Cleo noticed right away. "What happened to you?" she asked, as soon as we were alone together. I was still walking stiffly and this, combined with the shirt, caught her attention.

I told her everything that had happened, and vicariously she drank it all in. I could imagine how wet her pussy was getting as I recounted the story, for I knew just how soaked mine was getting! I forgot my discomfort momentarily when we got busy at the booth, but whenever there was a lull, I relaxed long enough to notice just how sore I really was.

Mistress Lyla spent much of the day going around to other booths to see how they were set up and how their representatives worked with the clients. Occasionally she would come back to our booth, often with coffee for both of us, and when she looked at me I thought I would melt. I slept on the floor every night after that, in different configurations. One night she put the leather cuffs on me and snapped them together, so that I could move my legs but had to keep my wrists together. Another night I had one wrist shackled to one ankle. Each morning, Cleo looked at my stiff walk and sighed longingly.

The bag from the leather shop remained by my Mistress's suitcase, obviously still containing items that I had not seen. My whole being strained to open the top and look inside, but I dared not, and I still do not know what else was inside.

There are two trucks in Mistress Lyla's driveway, both with the name of a well-known contractor painted on the side. As I walk up to the house I hear hammering and turn to see men working at the garage.

They look at me, appraising me. They are good-looking men, well tanned and muscled from working in the sun, but they do not interest me. I am here for one reason only, and that is my Mistress Lyla. The men go back to work, carrying items into the large garage, and I continue on to the house.

"You look hot," my Mistress says, as she opens the door for me. "It is very warm outside, Mistress," I say. I feel sodden. My dress is wet and my hair is limp, and the cool air of her house is as refreshing as a tall drink. She is impeccable, fresh and crisp in her linen dress, and I feel grimy next to her.

"It must be hot working in that garage," she says, as she looks out the front door to see what is progressing. "Well, I'm paying to have it renovated, and the weather is not my problem." She closes the door behind us. I wonder if the men working out there could have any clue as to the special relationship that will be played out in this house.

"Naked, please," she says almost absently. It is the way she prefers me to be, and indeed it is the way I prefer it myself. I have taken to wearing nothing but thin dresses with nothing underneath, so that I can shed my clothes almost immediately. I do this now and stand before her, completely naked. I marvel that she practically ignores the fact that a nude woman is before her, ready for her commands. I know that I could never be a Mistress; this haughty, elegant, necessary detachment would be beyond me. She, instead, has grown into it and has made it a second skin.

She, on the other hand, wears a gorgeous set of silk lounging pajamas, obviously expensive and very suited to her. She has an iced coffee in one hand, and it thrills me to see her like this. She is my Southern plantation owner, my Mistress, my superior. She lives the life of leisure, and I am her property, bound to obey her commands.

"It occurred to me," she says, "that the fact that you like to be ordered to do things could prove useful to me."

"Mistress?" I ask.

"Well," she says, "I have been doing a bit of

research and I've discovered that domination doesn't always have to be directly sexual. Am I correct?"

"Absolutely, Mistress," I reply. How else can I explain it? Everything I do for my Mistress is done for sex and for love of her, even if it doesn't always involve tongues, pussies, fingers, and toys!

"I thought so," she says. "So I thought, why on earth am I paying a maid to come in and clean this house? I can save my money and just order my slave to do it."

"Mistress," I sigh, "tell me where the broom is." She is obviously delighted with this aspect of our roles as she points out the bucket, the mop, the dusters. "I don't expect you require constant supervision," she says.

"Mistress, you have commanded me to clean this house," I tell her. I know that my love for her shines in my eyes. "It will be spotless. As your submissive I can do no less."

"Then I have better things to do with my time than watch you sweep," she says, and she leaves the room. I breathe deeply, catching the last whiff of her cologne as she exits. I can hear her open the front door and as I glance down the hall, I see her looking out from the porch. She is obviously watching the men at work on her garage. I wonder idly what could possibly be done to renovate a garage; for a moment I imagine that she is thinking how nice it would be if she could simply order them to do their work just for the love of being commanded!

I only realize just how big this house is when I start to clean it. The kitchen floor is immense, all beautiful, cool, terra-cotta tile, and it doesn't take me long to mop it all down. But then I move through the long halls, into the enormous rooms, all of them done in hardwood floors with mats or small carpets on them. Three hours later, I have only done half of the main floor and there is still the floor above. Occasionally I can hear my Mistress, either her footsteps in the hallway above me or her voice coming from her chair on the porch as she talks on the phone. She does not come in, which makes me even more determined to do a perfect job. I feel a need to prove to her that I don't need her standing over me in order to have her commands carried out.

I am almost finished in the living room when I notice an unruly pile of books and papers on one table. I go to straighten it up and stop right in my tracks when I see what is on top.

It is a novel about submission, one of my favorites. I remember so well the night Cleo and I read it aloud to each other, stopping every chapter to relieve the pressure in our aching pussies. Now everything makes sense.

I open the book and thumb the pages I know so well. Sure enough, in chapter eight, the dominatrix orders her submissive to clean the house for her, since it doesn't make sense to pay a housekeeper. The submissive, ordered to remove her clothes, cleans the house in the nude. The book even contains the line my Mistress used—"I have better things to do with my time than watch you sweep!" No wonder it sounded so familiar!

I feel completely satisfied and almost subconsciously I hold the book to my chest. My Mistress has gone to the trouble of locating and reading books about domination and is using them like textbooks in order to learn exactly what she should do. She wants this just as much as I do.

I tidy the books, leaving them in the order they were in. Then, the room finished, I go back to the long hallway. The staircase rises majestically in front of me, but right now, all I can think about is how many risers there are to clean.

There is only one way to do them, and that is on my hands and knees, wiping each one down with oil soap. I am halfway up them when my Mistress's voice comes from behind me, saying, "You don't have to wax them, Jennifer. They're too slippery if you do."

"Thank you, Mistress," I say. I am very grateful for this. I am thrilled to be doing this under my Mistress's command, but to be truthful, I really don't enjoy housecleaning at all, and I have a maid service to come in regularly to keep my own home in order. The only time I actually mop and vacuum is when I am naked, under command from my superior.

"I think," she says, "I will have you finish those stairs, and then I have other plans for you. The top floor can wait for another day."

"Thank you, Mistress," I reply again. Although the house is comfortably air conditioned, I am sweaty and tired from the work. I look forward to finishing the stairs, but not only because it means my task will be over. No, it also means that Mistress Lyla has something else in store.

I finish the top stair with a silent sigh of relief, and take the bucket and sponge back to the closet under Mistress Lyla's watchful eye. Once they are put away, I return to her, kneeling in front of her on the hardwood floor of the hallway. My knees are bruised from the cleaning, but I don't even feel the discomfort. All I know is that I am at the feet of the woman I love.

"You will remember," Mistress Lyla says, "that

there were quite a few things in that bag we brought from Toronto."

I say nothing, looking at the floor. How well I did remember the difficulty I had picking it up from the rug with my teeth, and how heavy it was, heavy enough that it slipped out of my mouth again. But so far I had only seen her chain and leather outfit, and the collar, leash, and paddle that were used on me in the hotel room. The bag obviously contained much more than that.

"I bought a lot of merchandise there," she continues. "Of course I am eager to try it all out, but I still don't seem to have the feel for spontaneous punishment for no reason at all. I am sure that will come in time. For now, I am satisfied to discipline you whenever I feel you have done something to deserve it."

"Mistress," I say, "surely you aren't dissatisfied with my housework. I did everything you told me to, Mistress!"

She glares at me for my sudden outburst, and I can see she is thinking about slapping me, but then she stands back, calmly, cooly. This hauteur terrifies me and I tremble.

"You were supposed to tidy the living room," she says. "If you will come with me, I will show you where my dissatisfaction lies."

Obediently, I follow a few steps behind her. My mind races, trying to remember what I did wrong. I straightened everything up, dusted every knickknack, washed the floors, and vacuumed the carpets. What could be wrong?

Mistress Lyla points to the pile of books and papers, the one with the domination novel on top. It is unruly, scattered about. "I would hardly call that tidy," she says.

I am almost in tears. "Mistress, please!" I cry. "I did tidy that pile, I did! I straightened everything up…" I stop suddenly, for something has clicked for me. Of course! It is yet another scene from the novel on top, and it tumbles through my mind: the submissive doing everything correctly, the dominatrix messing it up in order to punish her. I am silent. I am trapped, and no words will get me out of this.

"I believe," she says, "that you are saying I am wrong."

"Oh, no, Mistress! I'm not saying that at all!" I fall to my knees in front of her. I have lost, and my only hope is acquiescence. "You are correct, I neglected to tidy that pile. I am terribly sorry."

"Sorry," she says, "is not enough." Up until now the scene has proceeded almost as it did in the book, but at that moment Mistress Lyla takes over. My scalp is on fire, and I scream. She has grabbed a handful of my long hair and is dragging me by it.

I can only scramble on my hands and knees to try and keep up with her. She is very strong and I have no doubt that she can pull me around the entire house in this manner. When she heads for the stairs I shriek. She walks up them, her hands still in my hair, and I try my best to follow her. The stairs bang hard against my body. Half crawling, half dragged, I finally find myself at the top of that upper hallway.

Still I am pulled, right to the bedroom at the far end of the house. Here I am thrown violently to the carpet, and I can only gasp and sob. She casually discards a clump of my hair from her hand, and tears roll down my cheeks.

"Over the chair," she says, and miserably I throw myself stomach-first on it, so that my back is exposed.

Then I watch as she reaches into a top drawer.

The item she pulls out is a scourge, and my eyes widen in terror. It is only a small whip, less than two feet long, but it has a thick handle that tapers down to a cruelly braided leather end.

"Now," she whispers, "I will discover the joy of making a slave scream!"

She brings it down on my back and I gasp. It is as if white-hot coals have been dropped on my flesh. She brings her arm up again and again, and the scourge licks fire across my back.

Four times it falls across my spine, and then she says, "Turn over!" I do and the chair presses hard against the welts the whip has raised. I whimper miserably.

Her target now is my upper thighs, and this is far worse. I struggle to hold my shoulders up, for relaxing them would mean bending my spine painfully to the contour of the chair. Now I can see the whip as it rises up. Mistress Lyla's expression is surprisingly calm, but in her eyes I can see the sexual excitement that I know so well. I realize that under those brightly colored pajamas is a burning, wet, needy pussy.

My legs hurt even before the whip comes down, and my eyes follow its swift curve. Five times it strikes me. Now I can feel slithering heat, and I see that it has drawn thin lines of blood across my thighs. They are horribly red against my pale skin.

The sixth and seventh lashes crisscross these red lines and I cry. With her eighth strike she gets her wish. I can control myself no longer and I scream my agony. Her cruel smile beams.

"It is everything they said," she says contentedly, and now the sexual excitement is evident. Still holding the whip, she comes to straddle my leg.

The blood stains her pajamas, but she doesn't care. I hold my arms backwards against the floor, trembling with the strain to keep my shoulders up.

She rubs hard against my flogged skin and I scream with this new agony. I can feel the heat of her cunt right through the silk as she grinds her pussy on my leg. She rides me like a horse, back and forth on my battered flesh with that needy slit.

She thrusts the handle of that whip into my face. "Suck it!" she orders, and I do. The leather is hot, sweaty, musty. I lick it and suck it deep into my mouth. Her crazed movement on my leg thrusts it hard against my tongue and I gag. This excites her even more.

Now her free hand is pinching my nipple, but I hardly feel this new torment. My leg burns and my mouth is filled with the leather device. Her hair swings wildly against my chest as she fucks my leg and my own cunt is throbbing.

When she comes, it is as explosive as ever. She all but screams with the orgasm as it rips through her and she rides my leg until every tremor is finished. Then she gets up, takes the whip from my mouth, and leaves me there. I am starved for air and I gasp, trying to catch my breath.

"Adequate," she says. "Now get up, I don't want you dripping blood on the floor. You'll lick it up if you do."

It is almost impossible to rise, but I get up, all of my body shaking. I look down at my leg; it is smeared with blood and with the pussyjuice that soaked through her silk pajamas. The rusty taste of blood is in my mouth and every muscle in my body aches. But I am thrilled. "Thank you, Mistress," I whisper.

She is busy taking off her pajamas, and I marvel again at her beautiful body. "Put these in to soak, before they are permanently stained," she orders, and I rush to comply.

When I come back she has changed into a loose-fitting robe. She looks wonderful, and I am ashamed by my appearance. It obviously annoys her also, for she says, "You are a mess."

"I am sorry, Mistress," I say.

"Well, come and clean up," she says, and I follow her. We go right down to the first floor where there is a bathroom used mostly by guests. I know that her own private, ensuite bath will never be open to me again, unless it is for me to clean. A slave's soil can never contaminate a Mistress's private chamber.

She starts the shower and orders me inside. The water is icy cold, and I hesitate. She slaps me hard on the thigh, the one that she rode so furiously, and I cry out with the pain. "Inside," she orders.

No matter how hot the weather, I enjoy my showers very warm and this is agony. Still, I have been ordered inside and that is enough for me to comply. I wash my hair and soap myself. The water causes the welts to ooze blood, which runs down my leg. Finally the bleeding stops, and I assess the damage. My leg is crisscrossed with cruel red welts. I know they will disappear in time, but it will be most painful for me until they do.

Mistress Lyla has a special salve for this, and once I have dried off—using a small, thin towel, not the luxurious thick bath sheet that I spy hanging on the wall and covet so much—she sits me down and holds the jar out to me. The medicine is thick, brown, and smells hideously like turpentine. It burns like a mineral spirit too, and I moan and try to concentrate on something else to keep my nausea at bay. This obviously delights Mistress Lyla, and she takes the jar from me and slathers the ointment on the stripes she has laid across my back. They burn just as horribly and I know that the flogging must have drawn blood there too.

"Now come with me," she says, and stiffly I follow her. The stripes on my leg burn fresh with each movement. She takes me back upstairs to the bedroom where I received the punishment. I look at the chair and marvel at the Mistress that Lyla Kirk has become.

"Stand there," she orders, pointing to a spot beside another chair, and I do so. Now she comes back with another item, a leather harness, but with something on it that I can't immediately identify.

She holds it up to show me, and I am struck by the originality of it. It is a paging device, the kind used to reach executives on the run. During the trade shows I wear them almost constantly.

Mistress Lyla indicates that I should hold out my hand, and she lays it in my palm while pushing a button on the side of it. It vibrates hard; it is a silent pager.

The harness it is attached to is a leather device, most commonly used to hold dildos when women fuck other women. The pager is attached to the leather piece where the plastic penis usually goes.

Now she sits on the chair and this harness is fitted to my waist, and I understand why the clerk measured me so carefully. The straps fit perfectly and when the buckle is tightened, the pager just rubs up against the top of my clit. I understand completely. The small plastic box will be hidden by a skirt and if I sit carefully it will not interfere with my normal activities.

"You are going to leave now," Mistress Lyla says. "I will call you on the telephone and actually speak to you when I want you. This pager is not an indication that you are to call me."

As she adjusts the leather straps one more time, it all makes sense to me. This pager, which vibrates so strongly, just touches that most sensitive place in my slit.

"You will wear this until I tell you otherwise," she continues. "You will take it off to wash and whenever you need to use the toilet, but once you are finished you will put it right back on, in exactly the same way I have adjusted it here. Do you understand?"

"Yes, Mistress," I say.

"Then dress and leave," she says simply. It is difficult to walk down the long staircase with my injured leg and my stiff back, but much easier than the way I went up the first time, my Mistress's hands in my hair. I collect my dress in the hallway and slip it over my head. Fortunately the skirt falls below my knee and covers the horrible marks left by the flogging.

Mistress Lyla stands at the top of the staircase, and I turn before I leave. "Jennifer," she says, "I will say that you did an excellent job of cleaning the house."

"Thank you, Mistress!" I sigh, and I long to be able to run up the stairs and kneel before her. I love her so! But permission to do so is not given, and I am under orders to leave. When I swing the front door open, the outside heat is like a blast furnace.

"Jennifer?" I turn in the open door. "Yes, Mistress?" She smiles at me. "I understand it now," she says. Then she turns and walks away from me, down the hall, to the bedroom. I can't control my smile.

The men working on the garage stop to watch me

as I walk by. It is difficult and I put everything into walking as normally as possible, even though my body screams with agony. I pray that my wounds will not open again and stain my leg crimson. Eventually they lose interest and go back to their work, all of which is taking place inside the former slaves' quarters.

The straps of my harness rub on my skin, which is already sweaty from the heat, and I know that they will eventually make marks of their own. The pager is smooth and hard against my clit. I wonder how long it will be before she calls. I wonder just how I will be able to wait.

Chapter *Twelve*

The first call comes at two o'clock. It wakes me up gradually out of my deep sleep and at first I think I am in the middle of a grand erotic dream. Only at the last moment do I sit up straight, just as the electronic pager stops vibrating against my clit.

As my Mistress had ordered, I was wearing the leather harness to bed. For two days it had done nothing, just touched the top of my clit until I almost forgot it was there. Now, at this early hour, it comes to life.

I turn on the light and look down at the black leather straps that encircle my waist and run between my legs. The small pager is tight against my mound.

It goes off again less than a minute later. I sigh; it is a strong, pulsating movement and it massages my clit like a lover's tongue. It stops all too quickly and I gasp, wanting more.

Three more times it goes off, the impulses coming less than thirty seconds apart. It is just enough to get me close to coming, and then it shuts off. I almost sob with frustration. I turn it in my hands as far as the harness will allow, but I can find no phone number printed on it anywhere. The tiny screen, which would normally display the message, has been painted over with thick black paint and I can't scrape it off. What I wouldn't give to be able to call it over and over, and keep up that joyous buzzing on my cunt!

I touch the tip of my finger to my swollen clit and breathe heavily as the chills go through me. I am so excited that I can hardly stand it. I have to come, I have to come!

Then the telephone rings on my bedside table and I scurry to pick it up. "Mistress!" I say, breathlessly, and then suddenly I go cold. It was an automatic reaction and I pray that it is her; how would I explain myself to someone else?

"I see you know how to greet me," her silken voice says, and I relax. "I also see that you are wearing your harness."

"Mistress, you ordered me to wear it," I say. "I have no choice but to obey you."

"Then," she says, "I trust that you will carry out the order I am about to give you. I know that you are touching yourself; I would too, if something had me that excited. But under no circumstances are you to put your hand anywhere near your pussy. Is that understood?"

"Yes, Mistress," I reply, somewhat dejected. How am I going to stand this constant state of arousal, if I am denied the ability to relieve it? But it has been ordered, and I will obey!

"Nothing will come near that little pink gash of yours," she says. "No vibrator, no toys, nothing. That pussy belongs to me and me alone. Is this clear?"

"Absolutely, Mistress," I reply, and then I am left looking at the telephone receiver: She has hung up the phone.

Four more times the little black box comes to life against my pussy, until I can hardly think straight. My body reacts automatically and with a shock I realize that my hand is now on my thigh, my fingers about to reach for my clit. I snatch my hand back, breathing hard, terrified to think that I almost didn't obey my Mistress's command. Her hold on me is so strong that even when she has no way of knowing if I have obeyed or not, I can do nothing but comply.

The hardest part of all of this is waiting for the pager to vibrate again. My whole body is tuned to it, waiting for it, and I realize that this is the fine point of this exercise. Not the sexual buildup with no chance of release, even if that is a particularly cruel circumstance. No, the idea is that my Mistress is now constantly on my mind as I wait for her to dial the number and start that little box tantalizing my clit. Even when the pager is motionless I am now continually concentrating on it.

I don't even remember falling asleep; I wake up with the rays of morning sunlight coming through the curtains. Fortunately it is Saturday and I don't have to go to work. Instead, I call Cleo and see if she is available for a late breakfast. We agree to meet in an hour.

As I hang up, the pager vibrates against my slit. I wait and wait, hardly daring to breathe, but after ten minutes it still does not vibrate again.

I take the harness off and shower quickly, not wanting to be a second longer than necessary without it. It gives me a feeling of completeness when I buckle it back around my waist. One hip has an abrasion on it where the leather has rubbed during the last two nights and I slip a bandage on my skin to protect it.

I also rub a bit of lotion into my legs. The welts are still fiery red and they have crusted over with long, thin scabs where the whip drew its allotment of blood from my flesh. It hurts terribly to touch them, but the pain coursing through my legs brings back that magical moment all over again. With the tips of my fingers I manage to rub lotion into the ridges carved into my back by the whip. These ache as well, reminding me of what my Mistress has become. It has been a welcome and wonderful transformation.

I slip on a cool, simple dress, checking in the mirror to be sure that neither my flogged leg nor the bulge of the pager shows. The vibrations have not been set off since that one call just as I was phoning Cleo.

When I get into the car, the softly padded seat pushes the pager up against my pussy. I squirm on it, enjoying the smoothly rounded corner of the device against me. Then, my face going hot, I stop immediately. Mistress Lyla warned me that there was to be no sexual satisfaction for me, and I must obey!

"You're wearing a what?" Cleo asks, as she sips at her coffee. I long to be able to pull up my skirt and show her the delightful harness with its unorthodox attachment, but we are in a restaurant and so I can only describe the arrangement. Cleo listens intently; at one point she licks her lips, as if eying a tempting sweet.

When I am finished, she leans back in her chair, and I can see that she is excited also. "You know how envious I am right now," she says, and I nod. She belongs to a Mistress also, a beautiful, haughty woman well known for both her creativity and her cruelness, but my dominatrix's use of this everyday item is unique.

"The waiting is everything," I say to her, as I drink my own coffee. "Cleo, you can't imagine what it's like to wake up and have that thing go off and bring you so close. And then nothing until my Mistress decides to call me again. I don't know if that call will come in twenty seconds, or twenty minutes, or if it will come at all! I can't do anything else but lie there and wait for it. There's no use trying to read or watch television, because I'm not concentrating on that. I'm just thinking about the next time that pager's going to go off."

"And not let you go off as well," Cleo smiles, and we both laugh at her pun.

Our plates arrive. There are biscuits and gravy for Cleo—decidedly unhealthy, she admits, but one of her prime weaknesses—and an equally gooey and rich serving of eggs Benedict for me. I savor that first bite; I love the texture and the combination of salty meat, warm egg, and thick sauce.

"Almost as good as sex, right?" Cleo smiles. She knows how much I enjoy this occasional treat.

"Well, when they're from this place, they're often better," I reply, sinking my teeth into my second bite. Cleo chuckles. Given the choice between breakfast or serving a Mistress...well, I know why she laughs.

Suddenly I drop my fork, and it clatters against my plate. "It went off," I gasp.

The eggs are forgotten. The pager vibrates hard against my clit, which swells almost immediately. I can feel it growing and I can almost imagine it wrapping its hot pinkness around the plastic corner that presses against it. I shudder as the thrills go through my spine. Then, all too quickly, it is finished, and I slump in my seat.

Cleo watches me intently but I do not sit up. The pager is motionless against me once again. I wait, my mouth slightly open, breathing hard, but my Mistress has not dialed the number again. I silently pray for that stimulation again, but it does not come and I could all but sob for want of it.

We sit for several minutes. "Finish your breakfast, then," Cleo urges. "I'm sure she'll call again. She just wants to really build you up."

"Well, she does a good job of it," I say, and I take up my fork. The eggs are still just as delicious but I hardly taste them. How can I, when every fiber of my being is waiting for the pager to awaken my cunt again?

The waiter takes our plates when we are finished and brings us more coffee. I almost drop my cup when the pager vibrates again, and Cleo sighs. She knows what is happening, and I know that she longs for this long-distance control that my special dominatrix holds over me.

Three more times it goes off. In the middle of a busy restaurant, out in the open, I am so close to coming! I try to control my breathing and my excitement, but it is almost impossible. I am sure that everyone in the room knows what is going on. I can feel how wet my cunt is and I hope the back of my dress isn't soaked.

I am so excited, so attuned to my Mistress's control of my emotions, that I don't notice the waiter at the table until Cleo touches my arm.

"Excuse me, are you Jennifer Dobson?" he asks.

"I am," I say, confused, wondering how he knows this. By the look on Cleo's face it is a surprise to her too, and none of her doing.

He presents a small cordless telephone. "There is a call for you," he says, holding out the tray it is on.

I look questioningly at Cleo, who shrugs. No one knows I am here. I pick up the receiver.

"I wish to see you," my Mistress says, and I almost drop the phone in my surprise. "You will walk here from where you are. Ask Cleo to take your car home with her, I know she took a taxi. I will expect you at one this afternoon." Then there is a click, and the dial tone takes over from her voice.

"Your Mistress?" Cleo asks.

"How did you know?"

"The expression on your face," my friend replies. "It isn't hard to tell."

I realize I'm still staring at the phone, which I slowly put down on the table. "I can't imagine how she knew I was here," I say. "I didn't tell anyone."

"I guess that's why they are Mistresses, and we are their submissives," Cleo says. "I've always wondered how they can second-guess us the way they do, and know exactly what we're doing and what we're thinking. It must be an amazing talent to have. I'm just thankful that I can benefit from it."

"I'm supposed to walk to her house from here," I say. "She wants you to take my car."

"Well, I can live with that," Cleo says; she enjoys driving my convertible. "Jen, I'm envious of your pager, but I don't think I'd want to be under a command like that today. It must be a hundred degrees out there and that's a good four miles, isn't it?"

"That's a conservative estimate," I say, and I feel limp and sweaty already. "But I'm sure she has her reasons."

"Of course she does," Cleo says. "Just like we have ours." I have a long walk ahead of me, so we quickly call for the check.

Outside, the heat and the bright sunshine are stifling, and reluctantly I hand my keys over to my friend. Of course, Cleo isn't really bound by my command to accept them, but she does. Partly she does so because she would rather drive than wait for a taxi. Moreso, she does it because we are both submissives, both sisters in our sexual preference. Taking the car completes my commandment and so she does it for me, just as she knows I would do it for her.

The trees overhead, hanging romantically with Spanish moss, provide some shade as I walk along, but the heat is still like a furnace around me. My skin is hot and soaked where the leather straps are firmly buckled around my waist and across my cunt. I can feel the pager move with each step against my slippery, sweaty skin.

It goes off ten minutes into my walk, and I stop and savor the sensation. I don't care if people stare at me, standing on the sidewalk smiling and trembling. My Mistress is controlling me even here!

The pager goes off almost regularly, and after the first three times, I check it against my watch. Every ninety seconds. I keep one eye on that second hand as I walk along, and just as the sweep moves up to twelve, I stop, drinking in the delicious quivering on my pussy.

But my new Mistress is as unpredictable as my old Mistress was firmly into her routines. The ninety-second interval is gone. Now the pager goes off after thirty seconds, after two minutes. When it stays motionless for six minutes, I am almost beside myself waiting for it. I am in a sexual frenzy over this device strapped to my cunt.

The heat is so intense that I feel almost dizzy when the overhead canopy of trees ends and I have to walk in the sun. Normally I would have worn a hat, but I had not anticipated this when I went to the restaurant. Of course, going home first to pick one up would have been unthinkable, for Mistress Lyla had told me specifically to give my keys to Cleo and walk all this way by myself.

I reach the gates of my Mistress's house ten minutes early, and I walk up the long driveway. The workmen at the garage give me curious but lazy glances; the sun is high overhead and they are hot. I wonder why they haven't opened the big garage doors to let in some fresh air, for only the one small door at the end is agape.

I am still early and I don't dare ring the bell until exactly the stroke of one o'clock. It wouldn't do any harm, so I start walking over to the garage to see exactly what is going on.

Mmmmmmmm! The vibrator goes off just as I cross the driveway, and I stop, oblivious to the stare that one of the workmen gives me. Well, there's no possibility of going over to the garage now, for I am just too attuned to my Mistress and her pager at this moment. I go back to the walkway and continue up to the house. I long for the pager to go off again, and I sigh. I wonder if my Mistress is watching me from the window. The call might have been a warning to stay away from the garage, and I decide at that moment that Mistress's renovations are none of my business. I will leave the workmen alone, now and in the future.

The men walk back and forth from their trucks occasionally to get tools or lumber and I don't want them to look up at the house and see me waiting by the door. Instead, I walk up the side of the house, in the shade, by Mistress Lyla's water garden. I have only caught a glimpse of this area before and now I can't help but enjoy all of it. A small fountain sends a bubble of water up from the surface of the pond, making the water lilies bob gently. Heavy, brightly colored blossoms bloom along the edge and reflect in the water. A couple of weeds poke up between the flowers and I reach down and pull them out. I have no doubt that one day soon this will become my job as well.

There is a small bench, placed so that one can sit and enjoy the pond and its flowers, but I dare not sit down. This is my Mistress's garden and I am positive it is not intended to be a resting place for a submissive! Instead, I stand, longing to take my weight off my tired legs. Even so, it is comforting to be in this beautifully landscaped place.

It is so pleasant that I forget the time, and when I look at my watch I go cold. Two minutes past one! My hand at my mouth, my mind racing, I rush for the front door and push the button for the doorbell. I curse the workmen, for I want to be on my knees when Mistress Lyla opens the door and yet I dare not, for they might see me. As it is, I bow my head and hold up my palms in a gesture of capitulation.

I hear the door open, but I do not dare raise my head. Her voice is cold. "I believe there is something wrong with your watch," she says.

"Please, Mistress," I say, my voice trembling, "I was in your garden because I was early. I lost track of the time—"

"I also don't believe I asked for an excuse," she says. "Come inside. I'm not air conditioning the whole state."

I step through the door. I can feel tears overflowing my eyes, for I am truly sorry that I kept my Mistress waiting. I only hope that she realizes how sincere I am.

"Well," she says, and I am still too nervous to look up at her, "I was going to try punishing you for nothing at all, just because I haven't done that yet. But it seems that you've given me a reason after all." I can hear her reach for something on the table by the wall. "Look up at me."

I do. My heart swells with love for her, and with shame at myself for having kept her waiting. She is resplendent in a flowing, saffron-colored robe. In her hand she has my leather dog collar, which she fastens around my throat. It is loose enough that she can put her hand through it and lead me around, and this is what she does.

To my surprise, though, she isn't cruel. I expected her to roughly haul me around with it, perhaps once again up those stairs, scrambling on my hands and knees. Instead, she uses it merely as a guide. We cross the hallway and go up to the second floor. The pager, motionless, bumps against my clit with every step.

This time we go not to her bedroom, but to another room at the other end of the hall. I saw this one once before, when she showed me around the house, but at that time it was furnished as a spare bedroom. Now the furniture has been moved around, and it looks more like a television studio.

The bed is now in the middle of the room, freshly made. Opposite it, on a heavy tripod, is a video camera, pointing at those inviting sheets. There is another camera behind the bed. On a stand beside the first camera are two television monitors. Their tubes are visible from the bed and they are turned on; I can see the bed in color on the screen. Between the two cameras and the two monitors, I can see everything that might happen on the bed, both from behind and in front.

Mistress Lyla walks me to a spot beside the bed, and I can see myself on the screens. "Undress," she says, and obediently I slip off my dress.

I have never watched myself filmed on television before and I can't take my eyes away. My body is pale white, offsetting the black straps of the harness with the pager held to my pussy. The quality is excellent and I can clearly see myself from front and back. The red welts on my legs and my back are visible.

Mistress Lyla sits on the bed beside me and slowly unbuckles the harness. "You kept this on at all times, as I ordered?" she asks.

"Yes, Mistress," I reply. "With only the exceptions that you mentioned, to wash and to use the toilet."

She smiles. "Excellent," she says. "It is a lovely device, isn't it?"

"Mistress," I sigh, "I have never been kept on edge like that before."

"Good," she says. "Now on the floor. I have work for you." I sit before her on the hardwood floor, while she takes the pager off the harness. She drops the leather device at my feet, and walks over to a dresser. There is a jar on top of it with a rag, and she hands these to me. "That's been worn by a slave," she says. "I want every trace of you cleaned off it."

The jar contains saddle soap, and I hurry to clean the leather harness completely. Mistress Lyla leaves the room while I am doing this, and I glance up every so often to see myself on the television screen. The picture is of a small, naked slave, wearing a dark collar around her throat, cleaning her torture device with a rag. It is a beautiful sight.

I finish up just as she comes back. She is magnificent. She wears a leather corset that holds up her delicious breasts, but her dark nipples peek out over the top of it. It comes to just above her waist, leaving her mound dark and invitingly visible to me. In one hand she carries a riding crop and in the other, an item that she keeps hidden from me. I wonder what it is.

"Give me that," she says, and I hand up the leather harness to her. The hidden item fits into the hole placed there for it, in the spot where the pager was inserted before. It is a huge, black plastic penis.

I shudder, but I can't avert my eyes as Mistress Lyla straps the familiar harness about her own loins. Outfitted now, she is sadistically threatening. The black penis stands out from her mound. The head is huge, the shaft decorated with realistic veins. As I stare at them, they almost seem to throb.

"Sit on the bed," she orders, and I perch on the very edge of it. I can see myself on the television screen. "Now suck my dick!"

I take the head into my mouth. It has a plastic, chemical taste that is completely at odds with the rich, delicious smell of her pussy, so close to my face.

She is not gentle. I gag as she pushes the dildo into my mouth, but the sound of her voice excites me.

"You love sucking cock, don't you?" she whispers. Her own excitement is evident. "You take it so nicely into your mouth. I'll bet you've sucked lots of women's dicks, haven't you? Haven't you?"

I can't answer, for my mouth is filled with this plastic prick, but I moan affirmatively and nod my head as best I can. "I thought so," she says. "You eat my prick so nicely. That feels so good."

The black cock shines with my saliva as I take it in and out of my mouth. Then Mistress Lyla moves, and her actions are so quick that I am taken by surprise.

She uses her superior strength and speed to grab my collar, lift me up, and spin me about. Her knee pushes into my back and I am knocked onto my stomach on the bed. Instinctively I try to rise and am rewarded by a smart crack of the riding crop across my shoulders.

"I've always liked the sight of a cock fucking a cunt," she says. "I love to see it pounding in. But why should men have all the fun? Now I have a slave of my own, and a cock of my own to go with it!"

I can feel the huge head of that plastic dick against my pussylips, and as I lift my head, I can see it as well on the television monitor. The camera behind the bed captures the sight of that black member against my pink slit. Mistress Lyla's naked ass, the black leather strap snaking in between her buttocks, is poised high, ready to strike.

She slams the cock into me, and I cry out. It isn't lubricated and it enters me roughly. Mistress Lyla is completely taken with this scene and she pulls it almost all the way out and then slams it back in.

I watch her fuck me, from in front and behind, on

the screens. She is watching them too. When she is pounding into me, as quickly and firmly as a jackhammer, she lifts the riding crop and smacks me four times hard across the shoulders. Then, using it like a horse's bit, she holds it with both hands across my lips and forces it between my teeth. She uses this makeshift bridle to control me as her hips push forward and jam that huge black cock into my hole.

She is wild as she pulls the cock out of me, and on the screen I can see it, standing out straight from her mound, shiny with my pussyjuice. She takes the whip out of my teeth and lays it on the bed beside me. Then she uses her hands to grab my asscheeks and pull them apart.

Her intentions hit me like a sledgehammer. "No, Mistress!" I scream, but I am immediately rewarded when she picks up the crop and slams it against the red scourge welts on my back. I bite my tongue hard.

"It's not your place," she hisses, "to decide what your punishment will be!"

"I am sorry, Mistress!" I cry, and then I brace myself for what I know is coming next. I should try to relax, but when your pussy is throbbing, your shoulders and back are rent with welts, a whip has been thrust in your mouth, and you know you are about to be bum-fucked, there is simply no way to relax!

I feel the huge head against the tight opening of my ass. Mercifully, my Mistress enters me slowly, but that doesn't mean it isn't difficult. I have never been violated in this way before and tears stream down my cheeks.

I feel as if the black dildo will split me in half. I swallow hard, fighting nausea, and for just a half a second I consider using the signal for clemency.

But then I look at the television screen and I like what I see: My Mistress, the leather harness around her hips, the dildo sticking out like a cock of her own, pushing herself into my ass as I lie spread before her, waiting for her to enter. She controls me as I have never been controlled before, by any Mistress. At that moment, I welcome the pain. I want to do this for my Mistress, and I want her to do it to me.

The cock is smeared with my pussyjuices and it slides into that tightest forbidden place. She sets up a regular rhythm with it, fucking me slowly, speeding up gradually. My asscheeks feel like they are spread a foot apart.

Now she screws me as hard as she did in my pussy and I gasp with every thrust. I am sobbing and this drives her wild. "You love my cock in your ass, you slut, don't you?" she cries.

"Yes, Mistress!"

"Say it!"

"I love it! I love your cock in my ass, Mistress, I love it so!" She pushes deep and now I can feel her mound right against my asscheeks. I can see on the television screen that she's got that cock as deep in my rectum as it can possibly go. "Faster, slut, you want it faster!" she moans.

"Please, faster, deeper, Mistress!" I hardly know what I'm saying, but it feels so good to say it. "Fuck me harder, Mistress! Come deep inside my ass!"

I look at the screen. She has her hand on her pussy and she's fingering her clit hard and fast even as she fucks me. Her moans get louder as her fingers work on that wet place that I love to lick so much.

"I want to come in you," she moans, and I can see her hand is soaked. "I want to shoot my load inside your ass. It'll be so hot and wet, Jen, it'll just fill you up—oooh!"

She thrusts hard and deep as she comes, and her hand stays on her clit until her trembling and her moans finally calm down. I have never experienced such a scene before and I am completely satisfied. Truly, this is a submissive's dream!

Slowly she pulls the huge black cock out of my ass. There is thin, watery blood mixed with my pussyjuice on it. As the head leaves me, I feel a huge sense of relief, followed by an almost overwhelming urge to shit. This gradually passes, but the pain doesn't, and I wonder how long it will be before my overstretched and overworked ass ceases this throbbing and aching.

Breathing heavily, still shaky from her massive orgasm, Mistress Lyla unbuckles the harness and lets it drop to the floor. "Clean that," she says, and without a second glance she walks out of the room.

I'm unsure of how to do it, for she has not given me permission to go to the bathroom to use the faucet. Instead, I use the rag that I cleaned the leather with. When the dildo is cleaned and dry I place it respectfully on the bed and wait for Mistress Lyla to return.

She takes the better part of an hour, and I sit and wait for her, watching myself on the television monitors. When she comes back, she goes straight to the cameras and turns them off. Then, to my surprise, she opens the door of the stand that the televisions sit on. Inside is a video cassette machine, and when she pushes a button it ejects a tape.

"This will certainly make for some interesting viewing later on," she says. She notices my expression and adds, "You can rest assured that this will go no further than this house. This is for my personal pleasure only."

I breathe a sigh of relief. "Thank you, Mistress," I say.

"Of course," she smiles, "I might just wrap a copy up for you at Christmas."

I smile back at her and thank her. Suddenly I have an overwhelming desire to watch the scene over and over, to see myself degraded by this extraordinary Mistress who only a short time ago didn't even know that such scenes could ever take place.

I am allowed to shower in the downstairs bathroom, once again in the icy water that I detest so much. Then I dress and am told by my Mistress that she will call me when she wants me again.

The workmen are still busy on the garage and they look at me as I pass. I try to walk naturally, but it's difficult, for my ass throbs painfully. It seems I spend half my time trying to look like nothing's happened, just for the benefit of these contractors.

This time I wear no pager; my Mistress has no material hold on me right now. But I am a submissive, and she is my dominatrix. An electrical device isn't necessary to keep her on my mind. I will not stop thinking about her for even a minute.

Chapter *Thirteen*

My Mistress doesn't call me for almost two weeks. During that time, my ass finally stops its constant throbbing, and the stripes on my back and legs slowly fade. Just because they're gone, though, doesn't mean the memory has faded in the slightest, and my mind constantly takes me back to that room and my Mistress jamming her huge black cock into first my pussy and then that tight forbidden rosebud.

During that time I am commanded into her presence once, but not by her; rather, it comes to me through a call to my desk from her secretary. Normally I don't go up to the floor where her office is, for I have no business that takes me there. Still, it's enough to know that she is in the same building with me, even if I don't see her at all during my working day.

I go upstairs, and the secretary tells me to go into my Mistress's office. I have never been in it before; it is huge, opulently furnished with mahogany desks and chairs, a thick carpet, and windows that look out over the city.

My Mistress stands behind her desk, and I want to throw myself to the floor in front of her. But then I realize that there is a man sitting in the chair opposite her desk. He gets up as I walk in.

"George, I would like you to meet Jennifer Dobson. Jennifer, George Murphy," my Mistress says, and almost numb, I shake his hand.

"Pleased to meet you," he says, and sits down once I fall into the chair my Mistress indicates.

"Likewise," I say, and it seems like I am listening to someone else's voice speaking. I am so hot I can hardly stand it. I want to call her Mistress, I want to obey her. I want to be thrown over that desk and violated again. Instead, I must sit here, controlling my simmering emotions, and be polite to a stranger!

"Jennifer is the woman I was telling you about, George," my Mistress continues. "She is our top producer, bar none, and she can work a trade show like you wouldn't believe. We send her out with another woman, Cleo Ames, and when they come back we have to go on double time to fill all the orders they generate."

George smiles at me. "I certainly wish we had someone like you in our organization," he says. "Lyla has nothing but praise for you and your work."

"Thank you," I say slowly; my mouth feels frozen.

I almost want to laugh. Praise for me! He should see me as I really am, naked at her feet, being called a slut, having a whip lay my skin open, begging to lick her pussy!

There is a little more small talk, and then Mistress Lyla tactfully says, "Jennifer, I know you're busy, I hope we didn't take up too much of your time." Taking the hint immediately, I shake George's hand in parting and hurry out of the office to the elevator.

My hands are shaking so badly I can hardly push the button. I don't go back to my own office but right down to the cafeteria, where I get a cup of coffee and sit at a table in the corner, trying to gather myself.

Mistress Lyla is cunning beyond anything I ever expected of her. There was no need to call me into her office; meeting George was completely unnecessary. It was only done so that I would be in Mistress Lyla's presence, unable to serve her but just to sit and drink her all in before being summarily dismissed. This brief meeting will only serve to heighten my need to see her again, but I have no way of knowing when that will be.

I finish my coffee and slowly walk back to the elevator. I pass by Cleo's office and nod at her. She has been in a state of sexual excitement all week herself, and I know she is under her Mistress's orders as well. I long to hear about it, just to share her pleasure. "Lunch?" I ask.

She shakes her head, but her smile is huge. "I have to meet—you know," she says.

I feel so happy for her. "You want me to cover for you, in case you don't come back for the rest of the day?"

"Would you?" she asks gratefully. "Thanks so much."

"Enjoy yourself," I say, and walk on to my own office.

I go inside, close the door, and wonder how long it will be before I am summoned again, but without anyone else there to get in our way.

I find out as I am getting ready for bed. The phone rings right on the stroke of midnight, and my heart stops for a moment. No one else ever calls this late!

"I want you here in half an hour," she says simply, and before I can reply I hear the familiar click and then the dial tone.

That doesn't leave me enough time to walk there, and so I take my car—gratefully, as it turns out, for the night is oppressively hot and humid. The streets are deserted at this hour and I feel like I am all alone, making my solitary way through the darkness to obey my command.

The lights are burning in their carriage lanterns on top of the posts as I drive through the gates. Small floodlights burn and illuminate the house as I come up the long driveway, and I shudder with a cool chill. The huge antebellum house, with its trees hanging with moss and its large, manicured lawn makes me feel as if I have driven back a century and a half in time. I almost expect Scarlett O'Hara to come out on the porch and wave to me.

I slam on the brakes suddenly and rub my eyes. There is a woman on the porch, in a long, wide hoop skirt, with a bonnet on her head.

It takes me a moment until I realize that it is Mistress Lyla, dressed in the style of our Southern heritage, waiting for me on that huge expanse.

I stop the car right where it is; it would spoil the mood to drive right up to the house. I get out, surprised by how still the night is. Set so far back from the road and protected by trees, the estate gets none of the city noise. All I can hear are crickets, making the scene complete. I can also smell wood smoke, and I wonder who would be foolish enough to light their fireplace on a steamy night like this.

I walk up to the foot of the steps, for I know instinctively that permission will be required before I am allowed onto the porch. I wait, my head down, my palms lifted, trying to seem as humble as possible.

"So," my Mistress says coldly, "you decided to come back."

I am confused. "Mistress," I say, "you told me to be here."

"Quiet!" she hisses, and I obey. She pauses for a moment. "Look at me," she says.

I do. She is resplendent in the ornate, lacy dress, and the oversized bonnet, tied under her chin, frames her face deliciously. At long last I feel like I am finally owned as a slave by a Southern gentlewoman, and it warms me throughout.

"I thought you had run away," she continues, and it immediately becomes clear to me that she is defining our roles for this scene. "When I came home you were not here. I considered setting out the dogs to find you, but then I knew that you are nothing more than an ignorant slave, far too stupid to make it on your own. I knew you would come back, with your tail between your legs, begging forgiveness."

"Please, Mistress," I say, "I want to come back. I want to be yours."

"You are mine," she says curtly. "The problem is that you don't always remember it. Well, I think it's time that we solved that problem completely."

She throws something down at me. "Pick that up and put it on," she says, and when I bend down I find it is my leather dog collar. I put it around my throat, buckling it at the back of my neck, and she smiles at the sight.

"Now," she says, "undress." I hesitate. I know we are within the privacy of her estate, but this is something I have never done before.

What a mistake! She is down the steps in an instant, and before I can even cringe she brings back her arm and delivers a smashing blow to my cheek. It knocks me to my knees on the grass, and my face burns where her hand connected.

"I am sorry, Mistress!" I sob, and I tear off a button in my haste to remove my garments. In an instant I am before her, naked except for the collar. In that instant I realize that this is how I have always longed to be, and instead of being frightened by my nudity out in the open I am thrilled.

Now she grabs my collar with her hand and pulls me behind her. We walk down the long driveway. The sharp stones cut and bruise my bare feet but I have no choice; I have to follow. We are walking away from the house and I wonder where we are going.

My heart is in my throat as we walk down the driveway closer and closer to the road. But I trust my Mistress, and I know that she would never put us in danger of being seen; after all, how would you explain a hoop-skirted Southern belle leading a naked woman by a dog collar? Any passersby would call the police. But to me, it is the most natural thing in the world.

Then we veer off the driveway, and I see where we are going. The garage is there, a brilliant white building in the darkness. It is then that I notice there is a chimney on it, with smoke lazily curling out of it. This is the source of the wood smoke I smelled earlier, and my curiosity peaks.

She opens the small door and thrusts me inside by my collar. Normally she would order me to my knees, as she often does. But this time, she allows me to stand there, staring, my eyes wide, my mouth open. I simply do not believe what I see.

The clock turns back a hundred and fifty years. The garage has been transformed back into slaves' quarters, back to its original appearance. It is so realistic that I can't believe it was ever anything else.

The walls are finished in rough, weathered logs, chinked with plaster. The concrete floor has been replaced with dirt, packed down hard, cool against my bare feet.

There are windows, small ones, with ragged cloth curtains hung up to keep out the elements. There is nothing but a solid wall behind them, for no one can look in on this fantastic scene, but they are so well constructed that I feel that if I were to pull back one of the torn sheets I would see nothing but acres and acres of cotton and corn, tended by those people owned by the Mistress of this estate.

On one wall the fireplace crackles, making the whole building unbelievably hot and close. The hearth is made of stones and the fire burns directly on the floor of the firebox. There is a swinging hook with an iron kettle on it for cooking, and brushes and pokers beside a small pile of wood. This fire, and a couple of candles, provide the only illumination in this room. The dancing flames cast strange, unworldly shadows on the log walls.

The furniture is shabby, sparse. A rough-hewn pine

table sits close to the fire and there is one complete bed. It is an old-fashioned rope bed, with a criss-cross of ropes through the frame to support the mattress. That mattress consists of a wool bag stuffed with straw. My skin itches just looking at it.

"Mistress!" I am finally able to gasp.

"It is impressive, isn't it?" she smiles. "It was difficult explaining to them that I wanted to turn this back into an authentic slave home, but if you're willing to pay the price you can get those contractors to do anything."

Now my eyes, adjusting completely to the firelight, stop in the middle of the room. As hot as the room is, I go cold. There is another rope bed, but without its protective straw-stuffed mattress. Beside it, on a small weathered table, is the cat-o'-nine-tails that so impressed me in the leather shop we visited in Toronto.

Once I have seen them, Mistress Lyla is back into her role. "I can't believe that you actually wandered away," she says. "You know that will never be tolerated."

She cuffs me down to my knees on the hard-packed dirt floor, but holds up my chin so that I am watching her. She unties the bonnet and takes it off her head, laying it on the large table. Then she unbuttons her dress and slips it off.

Her undergarments are just as authentic. She wears a Southern-style whalebone corset, made of dazzling white cotton eyelet fabric. It squeezes her waist and blossoms out under her beautiful breasts, which peek above the fabric creamy smooth, the nipples pink and luscious. Unlike most corsets, though, this one doesn't go between her legs. Her dark pussy looks delicious in the firelight.

She pulls me toward the rope bed, the one without

the comfort of a mattress. As I get closer I realize that each of the four posts has a short chain around it, and each chain ends in a leather cuff. These are not the fur-lined ones, the gentle restraints that my Mistress started off with. These are chrome-studded, the leather raw and unfinished on the inside. These will hurt.

She pushes me roughly onto the bed on my stomach. The rope is thick and rough, knotted in a grid pattern. It is like lying on wire mesh. It presses painfully against my tits and bites hard into my skin. I can see my flesh protruding from between the ropes in grotesque pale squares.

My Mistress takes her time lashing me to the bed. She tickles my feet when my ankles are tied, until I sob for mercy. There is no laughter. This is torture.

She pulls my arms up roughly and shackles them to the bedposts. The bed is wide enough that my arms and legs are pulled straight out and my muscles stiffen very quickly. My body is shiny with sweat, for the room is stifling from the fire. Her skin glows also and the effect of the red, flickering flames on her body makes her look even more menacing.

She walks all around me, surveying me. At one point she slips her fingers in between my legs and brushes her hand over my swollen clit. I moan and buck my hips automatically, which earns me a good swat across my asscheeks. It feels so good and I go limp when she finally takes her hand away.

Walking over to the hearth, she puts four more logs on the fire. Slowly they catch and the flames roar up. The room is hot now and I wonder why she has done this. But she is a Mistress, and I am a slave. She need offer no reason for her actions.

"Now," she says coldly, calmly, quietly, "we shall

discover what happens to slaves who try to run away."

For a second my whole back goes ice cold. Then the burning agony sets in, almost before I hear the crack of the whip. The nine tails of the cat lick across my spine, leaving destruction in their path.

"Oh, this is nice!" my Mistress croons, as she lifts the whip again. I watch as the tails stream down in a graceful arc, and a split second later my mind explodes as the pain whips through my whole body.

She strikes again and again. The tails go dark with my sweat. By the warmth oozing down slowly down my sides, I expect that my blood has darkened them too. I can't believe how much it hurts.

"Will you—run away—again?" my Mistress demands. Her words are punctuated by cracks of the whip across my spine.

"No, Mistress!" I scream. Tears flow copiously down my cheeks. I sob, I cry, I flail in my bonds, but there is no escape. My back is hers, to punish as she wishes.

"You know your place is here!" she says. The tails fall twice more. "This is your home, you are my property!"

"Yes, Mistress!" I sob. I almost see stars. Twice the whip strikes across my asscheeks and this newly battered flesh burns hot and red.

"Say it!"

"I belong here, Mistress! Here with you!" It's almost impossible to get my breath. "I'll never run away again, Mistress! Never!"

Breathing hard, she throws the cat against the rough log wall. Its nine tails tangle and it lies there, shiny in the flickering firelight. I have never feared or respected anything the way I do this whip.

She walks to each corner of the bed, unbuckling the cuffs from my arms and legs. My skin is raw where I have struggled in the bonds and the leather has rubbed on me. I do not get up, for I have not been given permission. Instead, I lie there, my back on fire, my front bruised by the grid of ropes. I am thrilled.

"On your back," Mistress Lyla orders, and I gasp. When I do not move quickly enough, she grabs my wrist and all but flips me over.

I scream. The ropes grind against my flogged skin. For a moment my head goes light and I almost lose consciousness.

"Is it painful, slave?" my Mistress asks.

"Horribly, Mistress," I am finally able to gasp. For just a moment she looks concerned, and then she switches back to that cold, haughty smile. "Good," she says.

Once again my wrists and ankles are cuffed, so that I lie spread-eagle on the rope bed. My whole body bears the dark red marks where I was pressed against the rope grid. My poor tits are swollen and the nipples are dark. A rope mark goes right across the left one.

Now my Mistress takes two soft leather straps from the table. There is a buckle at the end of each one. Smiling almost kindly, she runs her hand gently up and down my right thigh.

She takes one strap and runs it through the rope grid just above my knee, then buckles it closed on my leg. The second strap secures my leg just below my pussy. With my weight on it, the rope bed is as taut and strong as if it were made of steel wire, and I am effectively locked in place. My leg cannot move even an inch in any direction.

There are heavy leather gloves hanging from a nail

beside the hearth and my Mistress makes sure I am watching intently as she takes them down and slips them on her hands. In the firelight her nipples are so huge and dark that my mouth waters for want of sucking on them. I can see moisture on her cunt hairs and I know this isn't sweat.

The fire is so huge and burning so fiercely that she can only stand in front of it for a moment. That's long enough to reach in and take out an item. When she turns around and shows it to me I can't help myself. I scream.

It's the branding iron that I saw behind the counter. When it was there, sitting behind glass on display, it frightened me. That is nothing compared to what I see now.

Now it is in my Mistress's hands, protected from its heat by the leather gloves. The star pattern on its end is cherry red and a wisp of smoke rises from it as an ash burns away. I can smell the wood smoke on it, and I can almost feel its heat as Mistress Lyla walks across the room with it.

She brings it closer and closer, the metal glowing, the shaft in the hands of the woman who owns me, who bought me, who controls me. And now the meaning of my tightly strapped leg becomes horribly clear.

She pauses for just a moment, looking at my wide, terror-filled eyes. "I do not see the sign for clemency," she says.

I lick my lips, hardly daring to trust my voice. When I do speak it is barely more than a whisper. "You will not, Mistress," I say.

I feel the intense heat from the branding iron when it is more than a foot from my skin. My Mistress stands above me, a Southern gentlewoman marking her property, deciding just where on my thigh to place this indelible, ineradicable sign of ownership.

Instinctively I close my eyes when the brand finds its spot. My whole leg is on fire. The pain shoots up through my spine and I go dizzy. I can smell my own flesh burning. When I open my eyes, I see the small star sink into my leg, watch the smoke rising from my skin.

It only takes a few seconds but it feels like hours. Finally Mistress Lyla takes the iron away, but the pain remains. I swallow hard, blink away the tears that blur my vision and run down the sides of my face. My whole body goes limp in its bonds. I don't even notice my whipped back against the rope anymore, just the agony of having a red-hot iron bite its way into my flesh.

The branding iron drops to the dirt floor. Then Mistress Lyla is over my head, that sweet pussy against my lips, and gratefully I lick her.

She is so excited that her steamy juice runs unchecked down my cheeks. My tongue slips over her swollen clit, pushes up into her soaked hole, moves back to tickle at her ass.

She grinds her pussy onto my face until I can hardly breathe. It is complete satisfaction for me. My back ripped up by her whip, my leg carrying her brand, I pleasure her as I never have before. She is wild on my tongue, bucking back and forth and soaking me with her nectar.

She twists my nipples hard when I focus on her hot nub and I gasp and poke my tongue up in the grooves on either side. When I fuck her hole with my mouth, she reaches down to pull my pubic hair painfully. I have to pleasure her. She, in turn, needs to torment me, and both of us are thrilled in these roles.

"Lick me harder!" she gasps. "Harder, you slut, you whore, you slave! Make me come!"

Somehow I find the strength to make my tongue move even faster on her cunt. She is everywhere on me. I breathe her perfume, drink her juice, feel her fingers on my tortured body.

"Coming—coming!" she gasps, and I can feel her whole body tremble. Then she explodes, screaming out her pleasure, grinding on my face. She comes not once but twice, two explosive orgasms one right after the other, and she stays on my tongue until the very last tremor has passed through her and left her weak.

When she rises, she is shaky. She takes a moment to catch her breath, her eyes never leaving that horribly burned place on my leg. It is now swollen, fiery red, oozing a watery clear liquid. I can hardly wait for it to heal. It will be a perfect star, burned into my flesh, a symbol of my ownership to this extraordinary Mistress who controls my every thought.

"You will need that looked after," she says. She goes over to the fireplace, where the iron cooking pot sits half in the flames. There is a bundle of leaves tied into a brush on the mantle and she dips this into the pot.

The pot contains an evil-smelling, dark pitch. She brushes it with the leaves onto the wound on my leg. I scream out, for it burns almost as badly as the branding did. Once the pain subsides, though, it feels almost comforting.

"That will help it heal," she says, as she throws the branches into the fire. I watch them curl up and turn black in the flames. "It's an old slave remedy. You should become familiar with it."

"Yes, Mistress," I say, as she walks around to the

bed. She unbuckles the straps that hold my thigh immobile, and I look as my skin goes from ghostly white to red where the leather held me so tightly.

Then she loosens each ankle and wrist, and tells me to stand up. I try to, but my legs won't hold me and I fall heavily to the floor.

I am in agony. My leg is burning from the brand and my back is ripped up from my flogging with the cruel nine tails of the leather cat. My wrists and ankles are raw from the leather restraints. And yet, when I am able to get to my knees, I take my Mistress's hand and kiss it. It is all I know I will be allowed to do, but it is hardly a fraction of the love I feel for her at this moment.

"It's too hot in here," my Mistress says, as she wipes away the sweat from the back of her neck. Her white cotton corset is dark with perspiration and her hair, tied back with a ribbon, clings to her skin.

I am just as uncomfortable in the close, fire-heated room, and I long to be dragged back up that driveway and into the air-conditioned mansion. It will be so comfortable, sitting in that cool air, perhaps given a cold drink.

All of that is dashed when Mistress Lyla snaps a chain to the collar I wear around my neck. There is a heavy metal ring screwed into the log wall opposite the fireplace and it is to this ring that I am chained.

She is not completely without compassion, for she brings a wooden bucket over from beside the hearth. It contains water and a dipper for drinking, but I know that it will be as hot as soup from sitting by the fire. Still, it is given to me by my Mistress, and I am grateful for that.

The chain gives me enough room to lie down on

the hard dirt floor, but I don't know how I will be able to do that. To lie on my back will mean rubbing the floor with the open welts from the whip. To lie on my stomach will put that open brand against the dirt. On my side, my hips will ache from the unforgiving floor.

None of this is any of my Mistress's concern. She blows out the candles in their tin holders on the tables, but she pays no heed to the fire that still crackles merrily in the hearth. It will die down in time, but I know that it still has a few hours left, and the embers will remain hot until well after morning. Of course, by that time the sun will be up, beating with its intense Southern rays on the roof and bringing the temperature up again.

But none of that matters as I watch my Mistress, in her corset, as she moves about the slaves' quarters in the firelight. I would suffer anything for this woman. When she smiles at me, I know that at some time in the future I probably will.

Just before she opens the door I have to let her know. "Mistress," I say, "I love you so much, Mistress, I will serve you forever!"

She stops, framed in the rough log doorway, a Southern gentlewoman speaking to her slave. "Jennifer, I never expected anything less," she replies.

The door closes behind her, and I hear the sound of a key turning in the lock. I am a prisoner here, chained to this wall by my throat, unable to leave until such time as Mistress Lyla decides to open the door again.

None of that matters, for the lock, the collar, and the chain are all symbolic. So are the stripes on my back and the star that I will carry in my flesh for the rest of my life. My bonds to Mistress Lyla go far beyond any collar or cuff.

I settle on the hard dirt floor as best I can, and I savor the pain that still racks my body. It is an intoxicating elixir. From these rough log walls other voices speak to me. I breathe deeply, and intently, I listen.

The Masquerade Erotic Newsletter

◆◆◆◆◆◆◆◆◆◆◆◆◆◆◆◆◆◆◆

FICTION, ESSAYS, REVIEWS, PHOTOGRAPHY, INTERVIEWS, EXPOSÉS, AND MUCH MORE!

◆◆◆◆◆◆◆◆◆◆◆◆◆◆◆◆◆◆◆

"*The Masquerade Erotic Newsletter* presents some of the best articles on erotica, fetishes, sex clubs, the politics of porn and every conceivable issue of sex and sexuality." —*Factsheet Five*

"I recommend a subscription to *The Masquerade Erotic Newsletter*.... They feature short articles on "the scene"...an occasional fiction piece, and reviews of other erotic literature. Recent issues have featured intelligent prose by the likes of Trish Thomas, David Aaron Clark, Pat Califia, Laura Antoniou, Lily Burana, John Preston, and others.... it's good stuff." —*Black Sheets*

"It's always a treat to see a copy of *The Masquerade Erotic Newsletter*, for it brings a sophisticated and unexpected point of view to bear on the world of erotica, and does this with intelligence, tolerance, and compassion." —Martin Shepard, co-publisher, The Permanent Press

"Fun articles on writing porn and about the peep shows, great for those of us who will probably never step onto a strip stage or behind the glass of a booth, but love to hear about it, wicked little voyeurs that we all are, hm? Yes indeed...." —MT, California

"We always enjoy receiving your *Masquerade Newsletter* and seeing the variety of subjects covered...." —*body art*

"... a professional, insider's look at the world of erotica ..." —*SCREW*

"I recently received a copy of *The Masquerade Erotic Newsletter*. I found it to be quite informative and interesting. The intelligent writing and choice of subject matter are refreshing and stimulating. You are to be congratulated for a publication that looks at different forms of eroticism without leering or smirking." —DP, Connecticut

"I must say that the *Newsletter* is fabulous...."

—Tuppy Owens, Publisher, Author, Sex Therapist

◆◆◆◆◆◆◆◆◆◆◆◆◆◆◆◆◆◆◆

Free GIFT

WHEN YOU SUBSCRIBE TO:
The Masquerade Erotic Newsletter

Receive two **MASQUERADE** books of your choice.

Please send me Two MASQUERADE Books Free!

1. _____

2. _____

☐ I've enclosed my payment of $30.00 for a one-year subscription (six issues) to: ***THE MASQUERADE EROTIC NEWSLETTER.***

Name _____

Address _____

_____

City _____ State _____ Zip _____

Tel. (____) _____

Payment ☐ Check   ☐ Money Order   ☐ Visa   ☐ MC

Card No. _____

Exp. Date _____

Please allow 4–6 weeks delivery. No C.O.D. orders. Please make all checks payable to Masquerade Books, 801 Second Avenue, N.Y., N.Y., 10017. Payable in U.S. currency only.
Order by phone: 1-800-458-9640 or fax, 212 986-7355   **Y54L**

ROSEBUD BOOKS

SUSAN ANDERS
PINK CHAMPAGNE
Tasty, torrid tales of butch/femme couplings—from a writer more than capable of describing the special fire ignited when opposites collide. Tough as nails or soft as silk, these women seek out their antitheses, intent on working out the details of their own personal theory of difference. $5.95/282-5

LAVENDER ROSE
Anonymous
A classic collection of lesbian literature: From the writings of Sappho, Queen of the island Lesbos, to the turn-of-the-century *Black Book of Lesbianism*; from *Tips to Maidens* to *Crimson Hairs*, a recent lesbian saga—here are the great but little-known lesbian writings and revelations. $4.95/208-6

EDITED BY LAURA ANTONIOU
LEATHERWOMEN II
A follow-up volume to the incredibly popular and controversial *Leatherwomen*. Laura Antoniou turns an editor's discerning eye to the writing of women on the edge—resulting in a second collection sure to ignite libidinal flames in any reader. Leave taboos behind, and be ready to speak the unspeakable— because these Leatherwomen know no limits.... $4.95/229-9

LEATHERWOMEN
A groundbreaking anthology. These fantasies, from the pens of new or emerging authors, break every rule imposed on women's fantasies, telling stories of the secret extremes so many dream of. The hottest stories from some of today's newest and most outrageous writers make this an unforgettable exploration of the female libido. $4.95/3095-4

LESLIE CAMERON
THE WHISPER OF FANS
"Just looking into her eyes, she felt that she knew a lot about this woman. She could see strength, boldness, a fresh sense of aliveness that rocked her to the core. In turn she felt open, revealed under the woman's gaze—all her secrets already told. No need of shame or artifice...." $5.95/259-0

AARONA GRIFFIN
PASSAGE AND OTHER STORIES
An S/M romance. Lovely Nina is frightened by her lesbian passions until she finds herself infatuated with a woman she spots at a local café. One night Nina follows her and finds herself enmeshed in an endless maze leading to a mysterious world where women test the edges of sexuality and power. Exploring forbidden sexual territory with rare confidence and scalding detail, Griffin's riveting tale is an uncompromising exploration of the many erotic flavors available to the modern woman... $4.95/3057-1

VALENTINA CILESCU
THE ROSEBUD SUTRA
"Women are hardly ever known in their true light, though they may love others, or become indifferent towards them, may give them delight, or abandon them, or may extract from them all the wealth that they possess." So says *The Rosebud Sutra*—a volume that promises to teach women's secrets. A young woman learns to use these secrets in her licentious quest for pleasure with a succession of lady loves.... $4.95/242-6

ROSEBUD BOOKS

THE HAVEN
The shocking story of a dangerous woman on the run—and the innocents she takes with her on a trip to Hell. J craves domination, and her perverse appetites lead her to the Haven: the isolated sanctuary Ros and Annie call home. Soon J forces her way into the couple's world, bringing unspeakable lust and cruelty into their lives. The Dominatrix Who Came to Dinner! $4.95/165-9

MISTRESS MINE
Sophia Cranleigh sits in prison, accused of authoring the "obscene" *Mistress Mine*. For Sophia has led no ordinary life, but has slaved and suffered—deliciously—under the hand of the notorious Mistress Malin. How long had she languished under the dominance of this incredible beauty—and how many times had she been driven to ecstasy by her cruel attentions? $4.95/109-8

LINDSAY WELSH

NECESSARY EVIL
What's a girl to do? When her Mistress proves too systematic, too by-the-book, one lovely submissive takes the ultimate chance—choosing and creating a Mistress who'll fulfill her heart's desire. Little did she know how difficult it would be—and, in the end, rewarding.... $5.95/277-9

A CIRCLE OF FRIENDS
The author of the nationally best-selling *Provincetown Summer* returns with the story of a remarkable group of women. Slowly, the women pair off to explore all the possibilities of lesbian passion, until finally it seems that there is nothing—and no one—they have not dabbled in. Desire is explored with abandon in this torrid, touching volume. $4.95/250-7

A VICTORIAN ROMANCE
Lust-letters from the road. A young Englishwoman realizes her dream—a trip abroad under the guidance of her eccentric maiden aunt. Soon Elaine comes to discover her own sexual potential, as a hot-blooded Parisian named Madelaine takes her Sapphic education in hand. $4.95/175-6

PRIVATE LESSONS
A high voltage tale of life at The Whitfield Academy for Young Women—where cruel headmistress Devon Whitfield presides over the in-depth education of only the most talented and delicious of maidens. Elizabeth Dunn arrives at the Academy, where it becomes clear that she has much to learn—to the delight of Devon Whitfield and her randy staff of Mistresses! $4.95/116-0

BAD HABITS
What does one do with a poorly trained slave? Break her of her bad habits, of course! *Bad Habits* was an immediate favorite with women nationwide. "Talk about passing the wet test!... If you like hot, lesbian erotica, run —don't walk...and pick up a copy of *Bad Habits*."—*Lambda Book Report* $4.95/3068-7

ANNABELLE BARKER

MOROCCO
A luscious young woman stands to inherit a fortune—if she can only withstand the ministrations of her cruel guardian until her twentieth birthday. With two months left, Lila makes a bold bid for freedom, only to find that liberty has its own excruciating and delicious price. $4.95/148-9

A.L. REINE

DISTANT LOVE & OTHER STORIES
In the title story, Leah Michaels and her lover Ranelle have had four years of blissful, smoldering passion together. One night, when Ranelle is out of town, Leah records an audio "Valentine," a cassette filled with erotic reminiscences....Tales to warm the heart—and other vital organs! $4.95/3056-3

RHINOCEROS BOOKS

EDITED BY LAURA ANTONIOU

SOME WOMEN
Over forty essays written by women actively involved in consensual dominance and submission. Professional mistresses, lifestyle leatherdykes, whipmakers, titleholders—women from every conceivable walk of life lay bare their true feelings about about issues as explosive as feminism, abuse, pleasures and public image. $6.95/300-7

BY HER SUBDUED
Stories of women who get what they want. The tales in this collection all involve women in control—of their lives, their loves, their men. So much in control, in fact, that they can remorselessly break rules to become the powerful goddesses of the men who sacrifice all to worship at their feet. $6.95/281-7

JEAN STINE

SEASON OF THE WITCH
"A future in which it is technically possible to transfer the total mind... of a rapist killer into the brain dead but physically living body of his female victim. Remarkable for intense psychological technique. There is eroticism but it is necessary to mark the differences between the sexes and the subtle altering of a man into a woman." —*The Science Fiction Critic* $6.95/268-X

JOHN WARREN

THE LOVING DOMINANT
Everything you need to know about an infamous sexual variation—and an unspoken type of love. Mentor—a longtime player in the dominance/submission scene—guides readers through this world and reveals the too-often hidden basis of the D/S relationship: care, trust and love. $6.95/218-3

GRANT ANTREWS

SUBMISSIONS
Once again, Antrews portrays the very special elements of the dominant/submissive relationship...with restraint—this time with the story of a lonely man, a winning lottery ticket, and a demanding dominatrix. One of erotica's most discerning writers. $6.95/207-8

MY DARLING DOMINATRIX
When a man and a woman fall in love it's supposed to be simple, uncomplicated, easy—unless that woman happens to be a dominatrix. Curiosity gives way to unblushing desire in this story of one man's awakening to the joys to be experienced as the willing slave of a powerful woman. $6.95/3055-5

SARA ADAMSON

THE SLAVE
The second volume in the "Marketplace" trilogy. *The Slave* covers the experience of one exceptionally talented submissive who longs to join the ranks of those who have proven themselves worthy of entry into the Marketplace. But the price, while delicious, is staggeringly high.... Adamson's plot thickens, as her trilogy moves to a conclusion in the forthcoming *The Trainer*. $6.95/173-X

THE MARKETPLACE
"Merchandise does not come easily to the Marketplace.... They haunt the clubs and the organizations.... Some of them are so ripe that they intimidate the poseurs, the weekend sadists and the furtive dilettantes who are so endemic to that world. And they never stop asking where we may be found...." A compelling tale of the ultimate training academy, where only the finest are accepted $6.95/3096-2

RHINOCEROS BOOKS

THE CATALYST
After viewing a controversial, explicitly kinky film full of images of bondage and submission, several audience members find themselves deeply moved by the erotic suggestions they've seen on the screen. Each inspired coupling explores their every imagined extreme, as long-denied urges explode! $4.95/3015-6

DAVID AARON CLARK

SISTER RADIANCE
From the author of the acclaimed *The Wet Forever*, comes a chronicle of obsession, rife with Clark's trademark vivisections of contemporary desires, sacred and profane. The vicissitudes of lust and romance are examined against a backdrop of urban decay and shallow fashionability in this testament to the allure—and inevitability—of the forbidden. $6.95/215-9

THE WET FOREVER
The story of Janus and Madchen, a small-time hood and a beautiful sex worker, *The Wet Forever* examines themes of loyalty, sacrifice, redemption and obsession amidst Manhattan's sex parlors and underground S/M clubs. Its combination of sex and suspense led Terence Sellers to proclaim it "evocative and poetic." $6.95/117-9

ALICE JOANOU

BLACK TONGUE
Praise for Alice Joanou:
"Joanou has created a series of sumptuous, brooding, dark visions of sexual obsession and is undoubtedly a name to look out for in the future." —*Redeemer*

Another mysterious, seductive book of dreams from the author of the acclaimed *Tourniquet*. Exploring lust at its most florid and unsparing, *Black Tongue* is a trove of baroque fantasies—each redolent of the forbidden and inexpressible. A young writer already at the height of her powers, Joanou creates some of erotica's most intoxicating and unforgettable characters.

$6.95/258-2

TOURNIQUET
A heady collection of stories and effusions from the pen of one our most dazzling young writers. Strange tales abound, from the story of the mysterious and cruel Cybele, to an encounter with the sadistic entertainment of a bizarre after-hours cafe. By turns lush and austere, Joanou's intoxicating command of language and image makes *Tourniquet* a sumptuous feast for all the senses. Strong stuff from a writer at the beginning of her career. $6.95/3060-1

CANNIBAL FLOWER
"She is waiting in her darkened bedroom, as she has waited throughout history, to seduce the men who are foolish enough to be blinded by her irresistible charms. She is Salome, Lucrezia Borgia, Delilah—endlessly alluring, the fulfillment of your every desire.... She is the goddess of sexuality, and *Cannibal Flower* is her haunting siren song."—Michael Perkins $4.95/72-6

MICHAEL PERKINS

EVIL COMPANIONS
A handsome edition of this cult classic that includes a new preface by Samuel R. Delany on the creation of this brutal novel. Set in New York City during the tumultuous waning years of the Sixties, *Evil Companions* has been hailed as "a frightening classic." A young couple explores the nether reaches of the erotic unconscious in a shocking confrontation with the extremes of passion.
$6.95/3067-9

RHINOCEROS BOOKS

AN ANTHOLOGY OF CLASSIC ANONYMOUS EROTIC WRITING

Michael Perkins, acclaimed authority on erotic literature, has collected the very best passages from the world's erotic writing—especially for Rhino*ceros* readers. "Anonymous" is one of the most infamous bylines in publishing history—and these steamy excerpts show why! Masterpieces of an underground genre. $6.95/140-3

THE SECRET RECORD: Modern Erotic Literature

Michael Perkins, a renowned author and critic of sexually explicit fiction, surveys the field with authority and unique insight. Updated and revised to include the latest trends, tastes, and developments in this misunderstood and maligned genre. An important volume for every erotic reader and fan of high quality adult fiction. $6.95/3039-3

HELEN HENLEY

ENTER WITH TRUMPETS

Helen Henley was told that woman just don't write about sex—much less the taboos she was so interested in exploring. So Henley did it alone, flying in the face of "tradition" by producing *Enter With Trumpets*, a touching tale of arousal and devotion in one couple's kinky relationship. $6.95/197-7

PHILIP JOSE FARMER

A FEAST UNKNOWN

"Sprawling, brawling, shocking, suspenseful, hilarious..."
—Theodore Sturgeon

Farmer's supreme anti-hero returns. *A Feast Unknown* begins in 1968, with Lord Grandrith's stunning statement: "I was conceived and born in 1888." Slowly, Lord Grandrith—armed with the belief that he is the son of Jack the Ripper—tells the story of his remarkable and unbridled life. Beginning with his discovery of the secret of immortality, Grandrith's tale proves him no raving lunatic—but something far more bizarre.... $6.95/276-0

THE IMAGE OF THE BEAST

Herald Childe has seen Hell, glimpsed its horror in an act of sexual mutilation. Childe must now find and destroy an inhuman predator through the streets of a polluted and decadent Los Angeles of the future. One clue after another leads Childe to an inescapable realization about the nature of sex and evil.... $6.95/166-7

SAMUEL R. DELANY

EQUINOX

The *Scorpion* has sailed the seas in a quest for every possible pleasure. Her crew is a collection of the young, the twisted, the insatiable. A drifter comes into their midst, and is taken on a fantastic journey to the darkest, most dangerous sexual extremes—until he is finally a victim to their boundless appetites. A reprint of Delany's classic *The Tides of Lust*, now appearing under the author's original title. $6.95/157-8

ANDREI CODRESCU

THE REPENTANCE OF LORRAINE

An aspiring writer, a professor's wife, a secretary, gold anklets, Maoists, Roman harlots—and more—swirl through this spicy tale of a harried quest for a mythic artifact. Written when the author was a young man, this lusty yarn was inspired by the heady—and hot—days and nights of the Sixties. $6.95/124-1

RHINOCEROS BOOKS

DAVID MELTZER
ORF
He is the ultimate musician-hero—the idol of thousands, the fevered dream of many more. And like many musicians before him, he is misunderstood, misused—and totally out of control. From agony to lust, every last drop of feeling is squeezed from a modern-day troubadour and his lady love on their relentless descent into hell. A haunting tale from an acclaimed poet, and the author of the legendary *Agency* trilogy (now available from Kasak Books).
$6.95/110-1

LEOPOLD VON SACHER-MASOCH
VENUS IN FURS
This classic 19th century novel is the first uncompromising exploration of the dominant/submissive relationship in literature. The alliance of Severin and Wanda epitomizes Sacher-Masoch's dark obsession with a cruel, controlling goddess and the urges that drive the man held in her thrall. The letters exchanged between Sacher-Masoch and Emilie Mataja—an aspiring writer he sought as the avatar of his forbidden desires—are also included in this new edition of a book that changed sexual writing forever. $6.95/3089-X

SOPHIE GALLEYMORE BIRD
MANEATER
Through a bizarre act of creation, a man attains the "perfect" lover—by all appearances a beautiful, sensuous woman but in reality something far darker. Once brought to life she will accept no mate, seeking instead the prey that will sate her hunger for vengeance. A biting take on the war of the sexes, this stunning debut goes for the jugular of the "perfect woman" myth. An incredible debut novel from one of the most original and assured writers to come along in years. $6.95/103-9

TUPPY OWENS
SENSATIONS
A piece of porn history. Tuppy Owens tells the unexpurgated story of the making of *Sensations*—the first big-budget sex flick. Originally commissioned to appear in book form after the release of the film in 1975, *Sensations* is finally released under Masquerade's stylish Rhino*ceros* imprint. $6.95/3081-4

DANIEL VIAN
ILLUSIONS
Two disturbing tales of danger and desire in Berlin on the eve of WWII. From private homes to lurid cafés to decaying streets, passion is explored, exposed, and placed in stark contrast to the brutal violence of the time. $6.95/3074-1
PERSUASIONS
"The stockings are drawn tight by the suspender belt, tight enough to be stretched to the limit just above the middle part of her thighs..." A double novel, including the classics *Adagio* and *Gabriela and the General*, this volume traces desire around the globe. International lust! $6.95/183-7

LIESEL KULIG
LOVE IN WARTIME
An uncompromising look at the politics, perils and pleasures of sexual power. Madeleine knew that the handsome SS officer was a dangerous man. But she was just a cabaret singer in Nazi-occupied Paris, trying to survive in a perilous time. When Josef fell in love with her, he discovered that a beautiful and amoral woman can sometimes be wildly dangerous. $6.95/3044-X

MASQUERADE BOOKS

JULIETTE II: Vengeance on the Lord *David Aaron Clark*
The Marquis de Sade's infamous Juliette returns—and at the hand of David Aaron Clark, she emerges as the most powerful, perverse and destructive nightstalker modern New York will ever know. Under this domina's tutelage, two women come to know torture's bizarre attractions, as they grapple with the price of Juliette's promise of immortality.

Praise for Dave Clark's *The Wet Forever*:
"David Aaron Clark has delved into one of the most sensationalistically taboo aspects of eros, sadomasochism, and produced a novel of unmistakable literary imagination and artistic value." —Carlo McCormick, *Paper* $5.95/240-X

THE PARLOR *N.T. Morley*
It was a rainy New Year's Day when Kathryn entered bondage. Lovely Kathryn gives in to the ultimate temptation. The mysterious John and Sarah ask her to be their slave—an idea that turns Kathryn on so much that she can't refuse! But who are these two mysterious strangers? Little by little, Kathryn comes to know the inner secrets of her stunning keepers. $5.95/291-4

NADIA *Anonymous*
"Nadia married General the Count Gregorio Stenoff—a gentleman of noble pedigree it is true, but one of the most reckless dissipated rascals in Russia..." Follow the delicious but neglected Nadia as she works to wring every drop of pleasure out of life—despite an unhappy marriage. Another classic Anonymous title providing a peek into the secret sexual lives of another time and place. $5.95/267-1

THE STORY OF A VICTORIAN MAID *Nigel McParr*
What were the Victorians really like? Chances are, no one believes they were as stuffy as their Queen, but who would have imagined such unbridled libertines! One maid is followed from exploit to smutty exploit, as all secrets are finally revealed! $5.95/241-8

CARRIE'S STORY *Molly Weatherfield*
"I had been Jonathan's slave for about a year when he told me he wanted to sell me at an auction. I wasn't in any condition to respond when he told me this..." Desire and depravity run rampant in this story of uncompromising mastery and irrevocable submission. Mind-boggling excess makes *Carrie's Story* one of the hottest novels ever published. $5.95/228-0

CHARLY'S GAME *Bren Flemming*
Charly's a no-nonsense private detective facing the fight of her life. A rich woman's gullible daughter has run off with one of the toughest leather dykes in town—and Charly's hired to lure the girl back. One by one, wise and wicked women ensnare one another in their lusty nets! $4.95/221-3

ANDREA AT THE CENTER *J.P. Kansas*
"You're going to be part of a special community for a few months. You'll be treated well here at the center. It's going to be the most enlightening experience of your life. When it's over, you'll be returned to where you come from." Kidnapped! Lithe and lovely young Andrea is, without warning, whisked away to a distant retreat. Gradually, she is introduced to the ways of the Center, and soon becomes quite friendly with its other inhabitants—all of whom are learning to abandon all restraint in their pursuit of the deepest sexual satisfaction. $4.95/206-X

ASK ISADORA *Isadora Alman*
An essential volume, collecting six years' worth of Isadora Alman's syndicated columns on sex and relationships. Alman's been called a "hip Dr. Ruth," and a "sexy Dear Abby," based upon the wit and pertinence of her advice. Today's world is more perplexing than ever—and Isadora Alman is just the expert to help untangle the most personal of knots. $4.95/61-0

MASQUERADE BOOKS

LESSONS AND LOVERS — *Elaine Platero*
"Hettie felt like a kind of sex-doll for the other two, a living breathing female body to demonstrate the responses and vulnerabilities of womankind to a young man who was hungry for knowledge...." When a repressed widow, her all-too-willing manservant, a voluptuous doctor and an anxious neophyte take a country weekend together, crucial lessons are learned by all! $4.95/196-9

THE SLAVES OF SHOANNA — *Mercedes Kelly*
Shoanna, the cruel and magnificent, takes four maidens under her wing—and teaches them the ins and outs of pleasure and discipline. Trained in every imaginable way: from simple fleshly joys to techniques for the handling of unimaginable instruments, these students go to the head of the class! $4.95/164-0

LOVE & SURRENDER — *Marlene Darcy*
"Madeline saw Harry looking at her legs and she blushed as she remembered what he wanted to do.... She casually pulled the skirt of her dress back to uncover her knees and the lower part of her thighs. What did he want now? Did he want more? She tugged at her skirt again, pulled it back far enough so almost all of her thighs were exposed...." $4.95/3082-2

THE COMPLETE *PLAYGIRL* FANTASIES — *Editors of Playgirl*
The best women's fantasies are collected here, fresh from the pages of *Playgirl*. These knockouts from the infamous "Reader's Fantasy Forum" prove, once again, that truth can indeed be hotter, wilder, and *better* than fiction. $4.95/3075-X

STASI SLUT — *Anthony Bobarzynski*
Adina lives in East Germany, far from the sexually liberated, uninhibited debauchery of the West. She meets a group of ruthless and corrupt STASI agents who use her as a pawn in their political chess game as well as for their own perverse gratification—until she uses her talents and attractions in a final bid for total freedom! $4.95/3050-4

BLUE TANGO — *Hilary Manning*
Ripe and tempting Julie is haunted by the sounds of extraordinary passion beyond her bedroom wall. Alone, she fantasizes about taking part in the amorous dramas of her hosts, Claire and Edward. When she finds a way to watch the nightly debauch, her curiosity turns to full-blown lust! $4.95/3037-7

LOUISE BELHAVEL

FRAGRANT ABUSES
The saga of Clara and Iris continues as the now-experienced girls enjoy themselves with a new circle of worldly friends whose imaginations match their own. Polymorphous perversity follows the lusty ladies around the globe! $4.95/88-2

DEPRAVED ANGELS
The final installment in the incredible adventures of Clara and Iris. Together with their friends, lovers, and worldly acquaintances, Clara and Iris explore the frontiers of depravity at home and abroad. $4.95/92-0

TITIAN BERESFORD

CINDERELLA
Beresford triumphs again with this intoxicating tale, filled with castle dungeons and tightly corseted ladies-in-waiting, naughty viscounts and impossibly cruel masturbatrixes—nearly every conceivable method of erotic torture is explored and described in lush, vivid detail. $4.95/305-8

JUDITH BOSTON
Young Edward would have been lucky to get the stodgy old companion he thought his parents had hired for him. Instead, an exquisite woman arrives at his door, and Edward finds his compulsively lewd behavior never goes unpunished by the unflinchingly severe Judith Boston! $4.95/273-6

MASQUERADE BOOKS

NINA FOXTON
An aristocrat finds herself bored by amusements for "ladies of good breeding." Instead of taking tea with proper gentlemen, Nina invents a contraption to "milk" them of their most private essences. No man ever says "No" to Nina! $4.95/145-4

A TITIAN BERESFORD READER
A captivating collection! Beresford's fanciful settings and outrageous fetishism have established his reputation as one of modern erotica's most imaginative and spirited writers. Wild dominatrixes, deliciously perverse masochists, and mesmerizing detail are the hallmarks of the Beresford tale. $4.95/114-4

CHINA BLUE
KUNG FU NUNS
"When I could stand the pleasure no longer, she lifted me out of the chair and sat me down on top of the table. She then lifted her skirt. The sight of her perfect legs clad in white stockings and a petite garter belt further mesmerized me. I lean particularly towards white garter belts." The infamous China Blue returns!
$4.95/3031-8

HARRIET DAIMLER
DARLING • INNOCENCE
In *Darling*, a virgin is raped by a mugger. Driven by her urge for revenge, she searches New York in a furious sexual hunt that leads to rape and murder. In *Innocence*, a young invalid determines to experience sex through her voluptuous nurse. Two critically acclaimed novels in one volume! $4.95/3047-4

AKBAR DEL PIOMBO
SKIRTS
Randy Mr. Edward Champdick enters high society—and a whole lot more—in his quest for ultimate satisfaction. For it seems that once Mr. Champdick rises to the occasion, nothing can bring him down. Rampant ravishment follows this libertine wherever he goes! $4.95/115-2

DUKE COSIMO
A kinky romp played out against the boudoirs, bathrooms and ballrooms of the European nobility, who seem to do nothing all day except each other. The lifestyles of the rich and licentious are revealed in all their glory. $4.95/3052-0

A CRUMBLING FAÇADE
The return of that rogue, Henry Pike, who continues his pursuit of sex, fair or otherwise, in the most elegant homes of the most irreproachable and debauched aristocrats. No one can resist the irrepressible Pike! $4.95/3043-1

PAULA
"How bad do you want me?" she asked, her voice husky, breathy. I shrank back, for my desire for her was swelling to unspeakable proportions. "Turn around," she said, and I obeyed....This canny seductress tests the mettle of every man who comes under her spell—and every man does! $4.95/3036-9

ROBERT DESMOND
PROFESSIONAL CHARMER
A gigolo lives a parasitical life of luxury by providing his sexual services to the rich and bored. Traveling in the most exclusive circles, this gun-for-hire will gratify the lewdest and most vulgar sexual cravings! $4.95/3003-2

THE SWEETEST FRUIT
Connie is determined to seduce and destroy Father Chadcroft. She corrupts the unsuspecting priest into forsaking all that he holds sacred, destroys his parish, and slyly manipulates him with her smoldering looks and hypnotic aura. The last word in erotic manipulation. $4.95/95-5

MASQUERADE BOOKS

MICHAEL DRAX
SILK AND STEEL
"He stood tall and strong in the shadows of her room... Akemi knew what he was there for. He let his robe fall to the floor. She could offer no resistance as the shadowy figure knelt before her, gazing down upon her. Why would she resist? This was what she wanted all along...." A stunning tale of lustful surrender. $4.95/3032-6

OBSESSIONS
Victoria is determined to become a model by sexually ensnaring the powerful people who control the fashion industry: Paige, who finds herself compelled to watch Victoria's conquests; and Pietro and Alex, who take turns and then join in for a sizzling threesome. $4.95/3012-1

LIZBETH DUSSEAU
TRINKETS
"Her bottom danced on the air, pert and fully round. It would take punishment well, he thought." A luscious woman submits to an eccentric artist's every whim—finally becoming the sexual trinket he had always desired.
$5.95/246-9

THE APPLICANT
"Adventuresome young woman who enjoys being submissive sought by married couple in early forties. Expect no limits." Hilary answers an ad, hoping to find someone who can meet her special needs. The beautiful Liza turns out to be a flawless mistress, and together with her husband Oliver, she trains Hilary to be the perfect servant. $4.95/306-6

SPANISH HOLIDAY
She didn't know what to make of Sam Jacobs. He was undoubtedly the most remarkable man she'd ever met.... Lauren didn't mean to fall in love with the enigmatic Sam, but a once-in-a-lifetime European vacation gives her all the evidence she needs that this hot man might be the one for her.... A tale of boundless romance and insatiable desires, this is one holiday that may never end!
$4.95/185-3

CAROLINE'S CONTRACT
After a long life of repression, Caroline goes out on a limb. On the advice of a friend, she meets with the dark and alluring Max Burton—a man more than willing to indulge her deepest fantasies of domination and discipline. Caroline soon learns to love the ministrations of Max—and agrees to a very *special* arrangement.... $4.95/122-5

MEMBER OF THE CLUB
"I wondered what would excite me.... And deep down inside, I had the most submissive thoughts: I imagined myself ... under the grip of men I hardly knew. If there were a club to join, it could take my deepest dreams and make them real. My only question was how far I'd really go?" A woman finally goes all the way in a quest to satisfy her hungers, joining a club where she *really* pays her dues—with any one of the many men who desire her! $4.95/3079-2

SARA H. FRENCH
RETURN TO TIMBERLAND
Pack your bags—it's time for a trip back to Timberland, the world's most frenzied sexual resort! Prepare for a vacation filled with delicious decadence, as each and every visitor is serviced by unimaginably talented submissives. The nubile maidens of Timberland are determined to make this the raunchiest camp-out ever! $5.95/257-4

MASQUERADE BOOKS

GWYNETH JAMES

DREAM CRUISE

Angelia has it all—a brilliant career and a beautiful face to match. But she longs to kick up her high heels and have some fun, so she takes an island vacation and vows to leave her sexual inhibitions behind. And does she ever! From the moment her plane takes off, she finds herself in one hot and steamy encounter after another—and her horny holiday doesn't end on Monday morning! $4.95/3045-8

JOYCELYN JOYCE

PRIVATE LIVES

The illicit affairs and lecherous habits of the illustrious make for a sizzling tale of French erotic life. A wealthy widow has a craving for a young busboy; he's sleeping with a rich businessman's wife; her husband is minding his sex business elsewhere! **$4.95/309-0**

CANDY LIPS

The high-powered world of publishing serves as the backdrop for one woman's pursuit of sexual satisfaction. From a fiery femme fatale to a voracious Valentino, she takes her pleasure where she can find it. Luckily for her, it's most often found between the legs of the most licentious lovers! A dazzling and ambitious woman's climb up the corporate ladder of Lust Inc.!

$4.95/182-9

KIM'S PASSION

The life of a beautiful English seductress. Kim leaves India for London, where she quickly takes upon herself the task of bedding every woman in sight! One by one, the lovely Kim's conquests accumulate, until she finds herself in the arms of gentry and commoners alike. **$4.95/162-4**

CAROUSEL

A young American woman leaves her husband when she discovers he is having an affair with their maid. She then becomes the sexual plaything of various Parisian voluptuaries. Wild sex, low morals, and ultimate decadence in the flamboyant years before the European collapse. **$4.95/3051-2**

SABINE

There is no one who can refuse her once she casts her spell; no lover can do anything less than give up his whole life for her. Great men and empires fall at her feet; but she is haughty, distracted, impervious. It is the eve of WW II, and Sabine must find a new lover equal to her talents. **$4.95/3046-6**

THREE WOMEN

A knot of sexual dependence ties three women to each other and the men who love them. Dr. Helen Webber finds that her natural authority thrills and excites her lover Aaron. Jan, is involved in an affair with a married man whose wife eases her loneliness elsewhere. **$4.95/3025-3**

THE WILD HEART

A luxury hotel is the setting for this artful web of sex, desire, and love. A newlywed sees sex as a duty, while her hungry husband tries to awaken her to its tender joys. A Parisian entertains wealthy guests for the love of money. Each episode provides a new variation in this lusty Grand Hotel! **$4.95/3007-5**

DEMON HEAT

An ancient vampire stalks the unsuspecting in the form of a beautiful and utterly irresistible woman. When her insatiable appetite has drained every last drop of juice from her victims, they hunger for more—even if it means being sucked to death! **$4.95/79-3**

MASQUERADE BOOKS

HAREM SONG
Young, sensuous Amber flees her cruel uncle and provincial village in search of a better life, but finds she is no match for the glittering light of London. Soon Amber becomes a call girl and is sold into a lusty Sultan's harem—a vocation for which she possesses more than average talent! $4.95/73-4

JADE EAST
Laura, passive and passionate, follows her husband Emilio to Hong Kong. He gives her to Wu Li, a connoisseur of sexual perversions, who passes her on to Madeleine, a flamboyant lesbian. Madeleine's friends make Laura the centerpiece in Hong Kong's underground orgies. Soon Laura becomes one of Emilio's steamy slaves for sale! $4.95/60-2

RAWHIDE LUST
Diana Beaumont, the young wife of a U.S. Marshal, is kidnapped as an act of vengeance against her husband. Jack Beaumont sets out on a long journey to get his wife back, but finally catches up with her trail only to learn that she's been sold into white slavery in Mexico. $4.95/55-6

THE JAZZ AGE
The time: the Roaring Twenties. A young attorney becomes suspicious of his mistress while his wife has an fling with a lesbian lover. *The Jazz Age* is a romp of erotic realism from the heyday of the flapper and the speakeasy.
$4.95/48-3

AMARANTHA KNIGHT

THE DARKER PASSIONS: *FRANKENSTEIN*
What if you could create a living, breathing human? What shocking acts could it be taught to perform, to desire, to love? Find out what pleasures await those who play God.... $5.95/248-5

THE DARKER PASSIONS: *DR. JEKYLL AND MR. HYDE*
It is an old story, one of incredible, frightening transformations achieved through mysterious experiments. Now, Amarantha Knight explores the steamy possibilities of a tale where no one is quite who—or what—they seem. Victorian bedrooms explode with hidden demons. $4.95/227-2

THE DARKER PASSIONS: *DRACULA*
From the realm of legend comes the grand beast of eros, the famed and dreaded defiler of innocence. His name is Dracula, and no virgin is protected from his unspeakable ravishments. He brings his victims to the ecstasy that will make them his—forever. A classic fiend recast as the ultimate voluptuary. $4.95/147-0

ALIZARIN LAKE

THE EROTIC ADVENTURES OF HARRY TEMPLE
Harry Temple's memoirs chronicle his amorous adventures from his initiation at the hands of insatiable sirens, through his stay at a house of hot repute, to his encounters with a chastity-belted nympho—and many other exuberant and over-stimulated partners. $4.95/127-6

EROTOMANIA
The bible of female sexual perversion! It's all here, everything you ever wanted to know about kinky women past and present. From simple nymphomania to the most outrageous fetishism, all secrets are revealed in this look into the forbidden rooms of feminine desire. $4.95/128-4

AN ALIZARIN LAKE READER
A selection of wicked musings from the pen of Masquerade's perennially popular author. It's all here: *Business as Usual, The Erotic Adventures of Harry Temple, Festival of Venus,* the mysterious *Instruments of the Passion,* the devilish *Miss High Heels*—and more. $4.95/106-3

MASQUERADE BOOKS

MISS HIGH HEELS
It was a delightful punishment few men dared to dream of. Who could have predicted how far it would go? Forced by his sisters to dress and behave like a proper lady, Dennis finds he enjoys life as Denise much more! $4.95/3066-0

THE INSTRUMENTS OF THE PASSION
All that remains is the diary of a young initiate, detailing the twisted rituals of a mysterious cult institution known only as "Rossiter." Behind sinister walls, a beautiful young woman performs an unending drama of pain and humiliation. Will she ever have her fill of utter degradation? $4.95/3010-5

FESTIVAL OF VENUS
Brigeen Mooney fled her home in the west of Ireland to avoid being forced into a nunnery. But the refuge she found in the city turned out to be dedicated to a very different religion. The women she met there belonged to the Old Religion, devoted to the old ways of sex and sacrifices. $4.95/37-8

PAUL LITTLE

TUTORED IN LUST
This tale of the initiation and instruction of a carnal college co-ed and her fellow students unlocks the sex secrets of the classroom. Books take a back seat to secret societies and their bizarre ceremonies in this story of students with an unquenchable thirst for knowledge! $4.95/78-5

DANGEROUS LESSONS
A compendium of corporeal punishment from the twisted mind of bestselling Paul Little. Incredibly arousing morsels abound: *Tears of the Inquisition, Lust of the Cossacks, Poor Darlings, Captive Maidens, Slave Island*, even the scandalous *The Metamorphosis of Lisette Joyaux*. $4.95/32-7

THE LUSTFUL TURK
The majestic ruler of Algiers and a modest English virgin face off—to their mutual delight. Emily Bartow is initially horrified by the unrelenting sexual tortures to be endured under the powerful Turk's hand. But soon she comes to crave her debasement—no matter what the cost! $4.95/163-2

TEARS OF THE INQUISITION
The incomparable Paul Little delivers a staggering account of pleasure and punishment. "There was a tickling inside her as her nervous system reminded her she was ready for sex. But before her was...the Inquisitor!" Wild and pleasurable penalties abound in this story set during one of histories most notorious periods. $4.95/146-2

DOUBLE NOVEL
Two of Paul Little's bestselling novels in one spellbinding volume! *The Metamorphosis of Lisette Joyaux* tells the story of an innocent young woman initiated into a new world of lesbian lusts. *The Story of Monique* reveals the sexual rituals that beckon the ripe and willing Monique. $4.95/86-6

CHINESE JUSTICE AND OTHER STORIES
The notorious Paul Little indulges his penchant for punishment in these wild tales. *Chinese Justice* is already a classic—the story of the excruciating pleasures and delicious punishments inflicted on foreigners under the tyrannical leaders of the Boxer Rebellion. One by one, each foreign woman is brought before the authorities and grilled. Scandalous tortures are inflicted upon the helpless females by their relentless, merciless captors. $4.95/153-5

SLAVES OF CAMEROON
This sordid tale is about the women who were used by German officers for salacious profit. These women were forced to become whores for the German army in this African colony. The most perverse forms of erotic gratification are depicted in this unsavory tale of women exploited in every way possible. $4.95/3026-1

MASQUERADE BOOKS

THE PRISONER
Judge Black has built a secret room below a women's penitentiary, where he sentences the prisoners to hours of exhibition and torment while his friends watch from their luxurious box seats. Judge Black's House of Corrections is a demonic and inescapable dungeon equipped with one purpose in mind: to administer his own brand of rough justice! $4.95/3011-3

ALL THE WAY
Two excruciating novels from Paul Little in one hot volume! *Going All the Way* features an unhappy man who tries to purge himself of the memory of his lover with a series of quirky and uninhibited women. *Pushover* tells the story of a serial spanker and his celebrated exploits in California. $4.95/3023-7

THE AUTOBIOGRAPHY OF A FLEA III
That incorrigible voyeur, the Flea, returns! This time Flea visit Provence to spy on the younger generation, now coming into ripe, juicy maturity. With the same eye for detail, the Flea's observations won't fail to titillate yet again! $4.95/94-7

CAPTIVE MAIDENS
Three beautiful young women find themselves powerless against the wealthy, debauched landowners of 1824 England. They are banished to a sexual slave colony where they are corrupted into participation in every imaginable perversion. Each young lovely is transformed into a raving nymphomaniac by the tantalizing torturers. $4.95/3014-8

SLAVE ISLAND
A leisure cruise is waylaid, finding itself in the domain of Lord Henry Philbrock, a sadistic genius, who has built a hidden paradise where captive females are forced into slavery. The ship's passengers are kidnapped and spirited to his island prison, where the women are trained to accommodate the most bizarre sexual cravings of the rich, the famous, the pampered and the perverted. Once in Philbrock's power, these helpless women are pushed beyond any and all civilized boundaries! Lord Philbrock's paradise has a submissive angel waiting for every man—and a life of sexual excess planned for every woman. $4.95/3006-7

MARY LOVE

THE BEST OF MARY LOVE
Mary Love leaves no coupling untried and no extreme unexplored in these scandalous selections from *Mastering Mary Sue, Ecstasy on Fire, Vice Park Place, Wanda,* and *Naughtier at Night.* $4.95/3099-7

ECSTASY ON FIRE
The inexperienced young Steven is initiated into the intense, throbbing pleasures of manhood by the worldly Melissa Staunton, a well-qualified teacher of the sensual arts. Soon he's in a position—or two—to give lessons of his own! Innocence and experience in an erotic explosion! $4.95/3080-6

NAUGHTIER AT NIGHT
"He wanted to seize her. Her buttocks under the tight suede material were absolutely succulent—carved and molded. What on earth had he done to deserve a morsel of a girl like this?" $4.95/3030-X

MASTERING MARY SUE
Mary Sue is a rich nymphomaniac whose husband is determined to pervert her, declare her mentally incompetent, and gain control of her fortune. He brings her to a castle in Europe, where, to Mary Sue's delight, they have stumbled on an unimaginably depraved sex cult! $4.95/3005-9

ANGELA
Angela's game is "look but don't touch," and she drives everyone mad with desire, dancing for their viewing pleasure but never allowing a single caress. Soon her sensual spell is cast, and only she can break it! $4.95/76-9

MASQUERADE BOOKS

RACHEL PEREZ
ODD WOMEN
These women are lots of things: sexy, smart, innocent, tough—some even say odd. But who cares, when their combined ass-ettes are so sweet! There's not a moral in sight as an assortment of Sapphic sirens proves once and for all that comely ladies come best in pairs. $4.95/123-3

AFFINITIES
"Kelsy had a liking for cool upper-class blondes, the long-legged girls from Lake Forest and Winnetka who came into the city to cruise the lesbian bars on Halsted, looking for breathless ecstasies. Kelsy thought of them as icebergs that needed melting, these girls with a quiet demeanor and so much under the surface...." $4.95/113-6

CHARLOTTE ROSE
THE DOCTOR IS IN
From the author of the acclaimed *Women at Work* comes a delectable trio of fantasies inspired by one of life's most intimate relationships. Charlotte Rose once again writes about women's forbidden desires, this time from the patient's point of view. Fast becoming a favorite among women everywhere for her frank and gutsy style, Rose is in rare form in this steamy ode to the medical profession. Open and say 'Aaaahhhh...!' $4.95/195-0

WOMEN AT WORK
Hot, uninhibited stories devoted to the working woman! From a lonesome cowgirl to a supercharged public relations exec, these uncontrollable women know how to let off steam after a tough day on the job. A wildly popular and critically acclaimed title, that includes "A Cowgirl's Passion," ranked #1 on Dr. Ruth's list of favorite erotic stories for women! $4.95/3088-1

SYDNEY ST. JAMES
THE HIGHWAYWOMAN
A young filmmaker making a documentary about the life of the notorious English highwaywoman, Bess Ambrose, becomes obsessed with her mysterious subject. It seems that Bess touched more than hearts—and plundered the treasures of every man and maiden she met on the way. $4.95/174-8

GARDEN OF DELIGHT
A vivid account of sexual awakening that follows an innocent but insatiably curious young woman's journey from the furtive, forbidden joys of dormitory life to the unabashed carnality of the wild world. Pretty Pauline blossoms with each new experiment in the sensual arts. $4.95/3058-X

ALEXANDER TROCCHI
THONGS
"Spain, perhaps more than any other country in the world, is the land of passion and of death. And in Spain, life is cheap, from that glittering tragedy in the bullring to the quick thrust of the stiletto in a narrow street in a Barcelona slum. No, this death would not have called for further comment had it not been for one striking fact. The naked woman had met her end in a way he had never seen before—a way that had enormous sexual significance. My God, she had been..." $4.95/217-5

HELEN AND DESIRE
Helen Seferis' flight from the oppressive village of her birth became a sexual tour of a harsh world. From brothels in Sydney, to opium dens in Singapore, to harems in Algiers, Helen chronicles her adventures fully in her diary. Each encounter is examined in the scorching and uncensored diary of the sensual Helen! Widely considered one of Trocchi's masterpieces. $4.95/3093-8

MASQUERADE BOOKS

THE CARNAL DAYS OF HELEN SEFERIS
Private Investigator Anthony Harvest is assigned to save Helen Seferis, a beautiful Australian who has been abducted. Following clues in Helen's explicit diary of adventures, he explores the depths of white slavery in pursuit of the ultimate sexual prize. $4.95/3086-5

WHITE THIGHS
A fantasy of obsession from a modern erotic master. This is the story of Saul and his sexual fixation on the beautiful, tormented Anna of the white thighs. Their scorching passion leads to murder and madness every time they submit to their lusty needs. Saul must possess Anna again and again. An arousing and disturbing masterpiece—and the cornerstone of Alexander Trocchi's reputation. $4.95/3009-1

SCHOOL FOR SIN
When Peggy leaves her country home behind for the bright lights of Dublin, her sensuous nature leads to her seduction by a stranger. He recruits her into a training school where no one knows what awaits them at graduation, but each student is sure to be well schooled in sex! $4.95/ 89-0

MY LIFE AND LOVES (THE 'LOST' VOLUME)
What happens when you try to fake a sequel to the most scandalous autobiography of the 20th century? If the "forgers" are two of the most important figures in modern erotica, you get a masterpiece, and THIS IS IT! One of the most thrilling forgeries in literature. $4.95/52-1

MARCUS VAN HELLER

TERROR
Another shocking exploration of lust by the author of the ever-popular *Adam & Eve*. Set in Paris during the Algerian War, *Terror* explores the place of sexual passion in a world drunk on violence. *Terror* reveals the legendary Van Heller at the top of his game. $5.95/247-7

KIDNAP
Private Investigator Harding is called in to investigate a mysterious kidnapping case involving the rich and powerful. Along the way he has the pleasure of "interrogating" an exotic dancer named Jeanne and a beautiful English reporter, as he finds himself further enmeshed in the sleazy international crime underworld. $4.95/90-4

LUSCIDIA WALLACE

KATY'S AWAKENING
Katy thinks she's been rescued after a terrible car wreck. Little does she suspect that she's been ensnared by a ring of swingers whose tastes run to domination and unimaginably depraved sex parties. With no means of escape, Katy becomes the newest initiate into this sick private club—much to her pleasure! $4.95/308-2

FOR SALE BY OWNER
Susie was overwhelmed by the lavishness of the yacht, the glamour of the guests. But she didn't know the plans they had for her. Sexual torture, training and sale into slavery! How many sweet young women were taught the pleasures of service in this floating prison? $4.95/3064-4

THE ICE MAIDEN
Edward Canton has ruthlessly seized everything he wants in life, with one exception: Rebecca Esterbrook. Frustrated by his inability to seduce her with money, he kidnaps her and whisks her away to his remote island compound, where she learns to shed her "inhibitions." Soon, Rebecca emerges as a writhing, red-hot love slave! $4.95/3001-6

MASQUERADE BOOKS

DON WINSLOW

THE MANY PLEASURES OF IRONWOOD
Meet Charli, Robin, Kitteridge, Nikki, Annie, Diane and Meredith—seven lovely young women who are employed by The Ironwood Sportsmen's club for the entertainment of gentlemen. A small and exclusive club with seven carefully selected sexual connoisseurs, Ironwood is dedicated to the relentless pursuit of sensual pleasure. This merry brotherhood of confirmed hedonists are known for their uncontrollable yen for sex! $5.95/310-4

CLAIRE'S GIRLS
You knew when she walked by that she was something special. She was one of Claire's girls, a woman carefully dressed and groomed to fill a role, to capture a look, to fit an image crafted by the sophisticated proprietress of an exclusive escort agency. High-class whores blow the roof off! $4.95/108-X

GLORIA'S INDISCRETION
"He looked up at her. Gloria stood passively, her hands loosely at her sides, her eyes still closed, a dreamy expression on her face ... She sensed his hungry eyes on her, could almost feel his burning gaze on her body...." $4.95/3094-6

THE MASQUERADE READERS

THE COMPLETE EROTIC READER
The very best in erotic writing together in a wicked collection sure to stimulate even the most jaded and "sophisticated" palates. $4.95/3063-6

THE VELVET TONGUE
An orgy of oral gratification! *The Velvet Tongue* celebrates the most mouth-watering, lip-smacking, tongue-twisting action. A feast of fellatio and *soixante-neuf* awaits readers of excellent taste at this steamy suck-fest. $4.95/3029-6

A MASQUERADE READER
Strict lessons are learned at the hand of *The English Governess*. Scandalous confessions are found in *The Diary of an Angel*, and the story of a woman whose desires drove her to the ultimate sacrifice in *Thongs* completes the collection. $4.95/84-X

EASTERN EROTICA

HOUSES OF JOY
A masterpiece of China's splendid erotic literature. This book is based on the *Ching P'ing Mei*, banned many times. Despite its frequent suppression, it has somehow managed to survive—read it and see why! $4.95/51-3

THE CLASSIC COLLECTION

MAN WITH A MAID
The adventures of Jack and Alice have delighted readers for eight decades! A classic of its genre, *Man with a Maid* tells an outrageous tale of desire, revenge, and submission. Over 200,000 copies of this scorching classic in print! $4.95/307-4

MAN WITH A MAID II
Jack's back! With the assistance of the perverse Alice, he embarks again on a trip through every erotic extreme. Jack leaves no one unsatisfied—least of all, himself, and Alice is always certain to outdo herself in her capacity to corrupt and control. An incendiary sequel! $4.95/3071-7

MAN WITH A MAID: The Conclusion
The final chapter in the epic saga of lust that has thrilled readers for decades. The adulterous woman who is corrected with enthusiasm and the clumsy maid who receives grueling guidance are just two who benefit from these lessons!
$4.95/3013-X

MASQUERADE BOOKS

Confessions of a Concubine II: HAREM SLAVE
The concubinage continues, as the true pleasures and privileges of the harem are revealed. For the first time, readers are invited behind the veils that hide uninhibited, unimaginable pleasures from the world.... The can't-miss continuation of one of erotica's hottest confessionals. $4.95/226-4

CONFESSIONS OF A CONCUBINE
What *really* happens behind the plush walls of the harem? An inexperienced woman, captured and sentenced to service the royal pleasure, tells all in an outrageously unrestrained memoir. No affairs of state could match the passions of a young woman learning to relish a life of ceaseless sexual servitude. $4.95/154-3

PROTESTS, PLEASURES AND RAPTURES
Invited for an allegedly quiet weekend at a country Vicarage, a young woman is stunned to find herself surrounded by shocking acts of sexual sadism. Her curiosity is piqued, and she begins to explore her own capacities for cruelty—leading to a search for an punishable partner. $4.95/204-3

INITIATION RITES
Every naughty detail of a young woman's breaking in! Under the thorough tutelage of the perverse Miss Clara Birchem, Julia learns her wicked lessons well. During the course of her amorous studies, the resourceful young lady is joined by an assortment of lewd characters. $4.95/120-9

TABLEAUX VIVANTS
Fifteen breathtaking tales of erotic passion. Upstanding ladies and gents soon adopt more comfortable positions, as wicked thoughts explode into sinfully scrumptious acts. Carnal extremes and explorations abound in this tribute to the spirit of Eros—the lustiest common denominator! $4.95/121-7

LADY F.
A wild and uncensored tale of Victorian passions and penalties. Master Kidrodstock suffers deliciously at the hands of the stunningly cruel and sensuous Lady Flayskin—the only woman capable of taming his wayward impulses. Pleasures are paid for dearly in this scorching diary of submission. $4.95/102-0

THE YELLOW ROOM
The "yellow room" holds the secrets of lust, lechery, and the lash. At the beginning, these secrets are excruciating, and are dealt out without mercy. After a while, even the most stubborn soul converts to the pleasures of punishment. $4.95/96-3

SACRED PASSIONS
Young Augustus comes into the heavenly sanctuary seeking protection from the enemies of his debt-ridden father. Within these walls he learns lessons he could never have imagined and soon concludes that the joys of the body far surpass those of the spirit. $4.95/21-1

CLASSIC EROTIC BIOGRAPHIES

JENNIFER AGAIN
In her dream she was naked, but there was no one on the streets to see her nakedness. Then she turned a corner, and a tall man was standing before her in the middle of the eerily empty street. She didn't know him, yet he seemed to know her: His lips formed her name: Jennifer.... One of contemporary erotica's hottest characters returns, in a sequel sure to blow you away. Once again, the insatiable Jennifer seizes the day—and extracts from it every last drop of sensual pleasure! $4.95/220-5

JENNIFER
From the bedroom of an internationally famous—and notoriously insatiable—dancer to an uninhibited ashram, *Jennifer* traces the exploits of one thoroughly modern woman. Moving beyond mere sexual experimentation, Jennifer slowly comes to a new realization of herself. $4.95/107-1

MASQUERADE BOOKS

ROSEMARY LANE J.D. Hall
The ups, downs, ins and outs of Rosemary Lane. Raised as the ward of Lord and Lady D'Arcy, after coming of age she discovers that her guardians' generosity is boundless—as they contribute to her carnal education! $4.95/3078-4

HELOISE Sarah Jackson
A panoply of sensual tales harkening back to the golden age of Victorian erotica. Desire is examined in all its intricacy, as fantasies are explored and urges explode. Innocence meets experience time and again in these passionate stories dedicated to the pleasures of the body. $4.95/3073-3

PAULINE
From rural America to the royal court of Austria, Pauline follows her growing sexual desires. "They knew not that I was a prima donna, sought after by royalty, indulged and petted by the elite of all Europe. I would never see them again. Why shouldn't I give myself to them that they might become more and more inspired to deeds of greater lust!" $4.95/129-2

THE ROMANCES OF BLANCHE LA MARE
When Blanche loses her husband, it becomes clear she'll need a job. She sets her sights on the stage—and soon encounters a cast of lecherous characters intent on making her path to sucksess as hot and hard as possible! $4.95/101-2

MAUDE RIVERS
Under the tutelage of Charles, Maude learns to abandon the restraints of her strict upbringing and embrace the rewards of unbridled sexual indulgence. The lustful Charles leads his lovely charge on an erotic journey of breathtaking variety, and introduces her to a cast of insatiable accomplices. $4.95/3087-3

KATE PERCIVAL
Kate, the "Belle of Delaware," divulges the secrets of her scandalous life, from her earliest sexual experiments to the deviations she learns to love. Nothing is secret, and no holes are barred in this titillating tell-all that reveals the hidden lives of turn-of-the-century lads and ladies. $4.95/3072-5

THE AMERICAN COLLECTION

LUST Palmiro Vicarion
A wealthy and powerful man of leisure recounts his rise up the corporate ladder and his corresponding descent into debauchery. Adventure and political intrigue provide a stimulating backdrop for this tale of a classic scoundrel with an uncurbed appetite for sexual power! $4.95/82-3

WAYWARD Peter Jason
A mysterious countess hires a tour bus for an unusual vacation. Traveling through Europe's most notorious cities, she picks up friends, lovers, and acquaintances from every walk of life in pursuit of unbridled sensual pleasure. Countless orgies, outrageous acts, and endless deviation! $4.95/3004-0

LOVE'S ILLUSION
Elizabeth Renard yearned for the body of Dan Harrington. Then she discovers Harrington's secret weakness: a need to be humiliated and punished. She makes him her slave, and together they commence a journey into depravity that leaves nothing to the imagination—*nothing!* $4.95/100-4

THE RELUCTANT CAPTIVE
Kidnapped by ruthless outlaws who kill her husband and burn their prosperous ranch, Sarah's journey takes her from the bordellos of the Wild West to the bedrooms of Boston, where she's bought by a stranger from her past. $4.95/3022-9

DANCE HALL GIRLS
The dance studio in Modesto was ruthless trap for men and women of all ages. They learned to dance under the tutelage of sex fiends. So grateful were they for attention, they opened their hearts—and legs! $4.95/44-0

RICHARD KASAK BOOKS

RUSS KICK
OUTPOSTS:
A Catalog of Rare and Disturbing Alternative Information

A huge, authoritative guide to some of the most offbeat and bizarre publications available today! Dedicated to the notion of a society based on true freedom of expression, *Outposts* shines light into the darkest nooks and most overlooked crannies of American thought. Rather than simply summarize the plethora of controversial opinions crowding the American scene, Kick has tracked down the real McCoy and compiled over five hundred reviews of work penned by political extremists, conspiracy theorists, hallucinogenic pathfinders, sexual explorers, religious iconoclasts and social malcontents. Better yet, each review is followed by ordering information for the many readers sure to want these remarkable publications for themselves. From radical left to super-conservative, no one with a "need to know" can afford to miss this ultra-alternative resource. $19.95/*0202-8*

WILLIAM CARNEY
THE REAL THING

Carney gives us a good look at the mores and lifestyle of the first generation of gay leathermen. A chilling mystery/romance novel as well. —Pat Califia

Out of print for years, *The Real Thing* has long served as a touchstone in any consideration of gay "edge fiction." First published in 1968, this uncompromising story of New York leathermen received instant acclaim—and in the years since, has become a highly-prized volume to those lucky enough to acquire a copy. Now, *The Real Thing* returns from exile, ready to thrill a new generation—and reacquaint itself with its original audience. $12.95/*280-9*

LOOKING FOR MR. PRESTON

Edited by Laura Antoniou, *Looking for Mr. Preston* includes work by **Lars Eighner, Pat Califia, Michael Bronski, Felice Picano, Joan Nestle, Larry Townsend, Sasha Alyson, Andrew Holleran, Michael Lowenthal,** and others who contributed interviews, essays and personal reminiscences of John Preston—a man whose career spanned the industry from the early pages of the *Advocate* to various national bestseller lists. Preston was the author of over twenty books, including *Franny, the Queen of Provincetown*, *Mr. Benson*, and *The Big Gay Book*. He also edited the noted *Flesh and the Word* erotic anthologies, *Personal Dispatches: Writers Confront AIDS*, *Hometowns*, and *A Member of the Family*. More importantly, Preston became a personal inspiration, friend and occasionally a mentor to many of today's gay and lesbian authors and editors. His life and writing will be remembered and celebrated in this unique collection. Ten percent of the proceeds from sale of the book will go to the AIDS Project of Southern Maine, for which Preston had served as President of the Board. $23.95/*288-4*

AMARANTHA KNIGHT, EDITOR
LOVE BITES

A volume of tales dedicated to legend's sexiest demon—the Vampire. Amarantha Knight, herself an author who has delved into vampire lore, has gathered the very best writers in the field to produce a collection of uncommon, and chilling, allure. Including such names as Ron Dee, Nancy A. Collins, Nancy Kilpatrick, Lois Tilton and David Aaron Clark, *Love Bites* is not only the finest collection of erotic horror available—but a virtual who's who of promising new talent. $12.95/*234-5*

RICHARD KASAK BOOKS

MICHAEL LOWENTHAL, EDITOR
THE BEST OF THE BADBOYS

...[W]hat I like best about Badboy is the fact that it does not neglect the classics.... Badboy Books has resurrected writings from the Golden Age of gayrotic fiction (1966-1972), before visual media replaced books in the hands and minds of the masses....
—Jesse Monteagudo, *The Community Voice*

A collection of the best of Masquerade Books' phenomenally popular Badboy line of gay erotic writing. Badboy's sizable roster includes many names that are legendary in gay circles. Their work has contributed significantly to Badboy's runaway success, establishing the imprint as a home for not only new but classic writing in the genre. The very best of the leading Badboys is collected here, in this testament to the artistry that has catapulted these "outlaw" authors to bestselling status. John Preston, Aaron Travis, Larry Townsend, John Rowberry, Clay Caldwell and Lars Eighner are here represented by their most provocative writing. Michael Lowenthal, one of gay literature's new generation, both edited this remarkable collection, and provides the Introduction. $12.95/**233-7**

GUILLERMO BOSCH
RAIN

An adult fairy tale, *Rain* takes place in a time when the mysteries of Eros are played out against a background of uncommon deprivation. The tale begins on the 1,537th day of drought—when one man comes to know the true depths of thirst. In a quest to sate his hunger for some knowledge of the wide world, he is taken through a series of extraordinary, unearthly encounters that promise to change not only his life, but the course of civilization around him. $12.95/**232-9**

MICHAEL LASSELL
THE HARD WAY

Michael Lassell's poems are worldly in the best way, defining the arc of a world of gay life in our own decade of mounting horror and oppression. With an effortless feel for dark laughter he roams the city, a startling combination of boulevardier and hooker.... Lassell is a master of the necessary word. In an age of tepid and whining verse, his bawdy and bittersweet songs are like a plunge in cold champagne.   —Paul Monette

The first collection of renowned gay writer Michael Lassell's poetry, fiction and essays. Widely anthologized and a staple of gay literary and entertainment publications nationwide, Lassell is regarded as one of the most distinctive talents of his generation. As much a chronicle of post-Stonewall gay life as a compendium of a remarkable writer's work. $12.95/**231-0**

SAMUEL R. DELANY
THE MOTION OF LIGHT IN WATER

"*A very moving, intensely fascinating literary biography from an extraordinary writer. Thoroughly admirable candor and luminous stylistic precision; the artist as a young man and a memorable picture of an age.*"   —William Gibson

The first unexpurgated American edition of award-winning author Samuel R. Delany's riveting autobiography covers the early years of one of science fiction's most important voices. Delany paints a vivid and compelling picture of New York's East Village in the early '60s—a time of unprecedented social transformation. Startling and revealing, *The Motion of Light in Water* traces the roots of one of America's most innovative writers. $12.95/**133-0**

RICHARD KASAK BOOKS

THE MAD MAN

For his thesis, graduate student John Marr researches the life and work of the brilliant Timothy Hasler: a philosopher whose career was cut tragically short over a decade earlier. Marr encounters numerous obstacles, as other researchers turn up evidence of Hasler's personal life that is deemed simply too unpleasant. Marr soon begins to believe that Hasler's death might hold some key to his own life as a gay man in the age of AIDS.

This new novel by Samuel R. Delany not only expands the parameters of what he has given us in the past, but fuses together two seemingly disparate genres of writing and comes up with something which is not comparable to any existing text of which I am aware.... What Delany has done here is take the ideas of Marquis de Sade one step further, by filtering extreme and obsessive sexual behavior through the sieve of post-modern experience.... —Lambda Book Report

Reads like a pornographic reflection of Peter Ackroyd's Chatterton *or A.S. Byatt's* Possession.... *Delany develops an insightful dichotomy between [his protagonist]'s two worlds: the one of cerebral philosophy and dry academia, the other of heedless, 'impersonal' obsessive sexual extremism. When these worlds finally collide ... the novel achieves a surprisingly satisfying resolution....* —Publishers Weekly

$23.95/193-4

KATHLEEN K.
SWEET TALKERS

Here, for the first time, is the story behind the provocative advertisements and 970 prefixes. Kathleen K. opens up her diary for a rare peek at the day-to-day life of a phone sex operator—and reveals a number of secrets and surprises. Because far from being a sleazy, underground scam, the service Kathleen provides often speaks to the lives of its customers with a directness and compassion they receive nowhere else. $12.95/192-6

LUCY TAYLOR
UNNATURAL ACTS

"A topnotch collection..." —Science Fiction Chronicle

A remarkable debut volume from a provocative writer. *Unnatural Acts* plunges deep into the dark side of the psyche, far past all pleasantries and prohibitions, and brings to life a disturbing vision of erotic horror. Unrelenting angels and hungry gods play with souls and bodies in Taylor's murky cosmos: where heaven and hell are merely differences of perspective; where redemption and damnation lie behind the same shocking acts. $12.95/181-0

ROBERT PATRICK
TEMPLE SLAVE

...you must read this book. It draws such a tragic, and, in a way, noble portrait of Mr. Buono: It leads the reader, almost against his will, into a deep sympathy with this strange man who tried to comfort, to encourage and to feed both the worthy and the worthless... It is impossible not to mourn for this man—impossible not to praise this book.
—Quentin Crisp

This is nothing less than the secret history of the most theatrical of theaters, the most bohemian of Americans and the most knowing of queens. Patrick writes with a lush and witty abandon, as if this departure from the crafting of plays has energized him. Temple Slave *is also one of the best ways to learn what it was like to be fabulous, gay, theatrical and loved in a time at once more and less dangerous to gay life than our own.* —Genre

Temple Slave tells the story of the Espresso Buono—the archetypal alternative performance space—and the talents who called it home. $12.95/191-8

RICHARD KASAK BOOKS

DAVID MELTZER
THE AGENCY TRILOGY

...'The Agency' is clearly Meltzer's paradigm of society; a mindless machine of which we are all 'agents' including those whom the machine supposedly serves.... —Norman Spinrad

With the Essex House edition of *The Agency* in 1968, the highly regarded poet David Meltzer took America on a trip into a hell of unbridled sexuality. The story of a supersecret, Orwellian sexual network, *The Agency* explored issues of erotic dominance and submission with an immediacy and frankness previously unheard of in American literature, as well as presented a vision of an America consumed and dehumanized by a lust for power. $12.95/216-7

SKIN TWO
THE BEST OF *SKIN TWO* Edited by Tim Woodward

For over a decade, *Skin Two* has served the international fetish community as a groundbreaking journal from the crossroads of sexuality, fashion, and art, *Skin Two* specializes in provocative, challenging essays by the finest writers working in the "radical sex" scene. Collected here are the articles and interviews that established the magazine's reputation. Including interviews with cult figures Tim Burton, Clive Barker and Jean Paul Gaultier. $12.95/130-6

CARO SOLES
MELTDOWN!
An Anthology of Erotic Science Fiction and Dark Fantasy for Gay Men

Editor Caro Soles has put together one of the most explosive, mind-bending collections of gay erotic writing ever published. *Meltdown!* contains the very best examples of this increasingly popular sub-genre: stories meant to shock and delight, to send a shiver down the spine and start a fire down below. An extraordinary volume, *Meltdown!* presents both new voices and provocative pieces by world-famous writers Edmund White and Samuel R. Delany.
$12.95/203-5

BIZARRE SEX
BIZARRE SEX AND OTHER CRIMES OF PASSION
Edited by Stan Tal

Stan Tal, editor of *Bizarre Sex*, Canada's boldest fiction publication, has culled the very best stories that have crossed his desk—and now unleashes them on the reading public in *Bizarre Sex and Other Crimes of Passion*. Over twenty small masterpieces of erotic shock make this one of the year's most unexpectedly alluring anthologies. Including such masters of erotic horror and fantasy as Edward Lee, Lucy Taylor and Nancy Kilpatrick, *Bizarre Sex and Other Crimes of Passion*, is a treasure-trove of arousing chills. $12.95/213-2

PAT CALIFIA
SENSUOUS MAGIC

A new classic, destined to grace the shelves of anyone interested in contemporary sexuality.

Sensuous Magic is clear, succinct and engaging even for the reader for whom S/M isn't the sexual behavior of choice.... Califia's prose is soothing, informative and non-judgmental—she both instructs her reader and explores the territory for them.... When she is writing about the dynamics of sex and the technical aspects of it, Califia is the Dr. Ruth of the alternative sexuality set.... —Lambda Book Report

Don't take a dangerous trip into the unknown—buy this book and know where you're going!—SKIN TWO $12.95/131-4

RICHARD KASAK BOOKS

GAUNTLET

THE BEST OF *GAUNTLET* Edited by Barry Hoffman

No material, no opinion is taboo enough to violate Gauntlet's *purpose of 'exploring the limits of free expression'—airing all views in the name of the First Amendment.*
—Associated Press

Gauntlet has, with its semi-annual issues, taken on such explosive topics as race, pornography, political correctness, and media manipulation—always publishing the widest possible range of opinions. Only in *Gauntlet* might one expect to encounter Phyllis Schlafley *and* Annie Sprinkle, Stephen King *and* Madonna—often within pages of one another. The most provocative articles have been gathered by editor-in-chief Barry Hoffman, to make *The Best of Gauntlet* a riveting exploration of American society's limits. $12.95/202-7

MICHAEL PERKINS

THE GOOD PARTS: An Uncensored Guide to Literary Sexuality

Michael Perkins, one of America's only critics to regularly scrutinize sexual literature, presents sex as seen in the pages of over 100 major volumes from the past twenty years. *The Good Parts* takes an uncensored look at the complex issues of sexuality investigated by so much modern literature. $12.95/186-1

JOHN PRESTON

HUSTLING:
A Gentleman's Guide to the Fine Art of Homosexual Prostitution

John Preston solicited the advice of "working boys" from across the country in his effort to produce the ultimate guide to the hustler's world.

...fun and highly literary. What more could you expect from such an accomplished activist, author and editor?` —Drummer $12.95/137-3

MY LIFE AS A PORNOGRAPHER
And Other Indecent Acts

...essential and enlightening...His sex-positive stand on safer-sex education as the only truly effective AIDS-prevention strategy will certainly not win him any conservative converts, but AIDS activists will be shouting their assent.... [My Life as a Pornographer] is a bridge from the sexually liberated 1970s to the more cautious 1990s, and Preston has walked much of that way as a standard-bearer to the cause for equal rights.... —Library Journal

My Life as a Pornographer...is not pornography, but rather reflections upon the writing and production of it. Preston ranges from really superb journalism of his interviews with denizens of the S/M demi-monde, particularly a superb portrait of a Colt model Preston calls "Joe" to a brilliant analysis of the "theater" of the New York sex club, The Mineshaft.... In a deeply sex-phobic world, Preston has never shied away from a vision of the redemptive potential of the erotic drive. Better than perhaps anyone in our community, Preston knows how physical joy can bridge differences and make us well. —Lambda Book Report
$12.95/135-7

LARS EIGHNER

ELEMENTS OF AROUSAL

Critically acclaimed gay writer Lars Eighner develops a guideline for success with one of publishing's best kept secrets: the novice-friendly field of gay erotic writing. In *Elements of Arousal*, Eighner details his craft, providing the reader with sure advice. Because *Elements of Arousal* is about the application and honing of the writer's craft, which brought Eighner fame with not only the steamy *Bayou Boy*, but the illuminating *Travels with Lizbeth*. $12.95/230-2

RICHARD KASAK BOOKS

MARCO VASSI

THE STONED APOCALYPSE
"...Marco Vassi is our champion sexual energist."—VLS

During his lifetime, Marco Vassi was hailed as America's premier erotic writer and most worthy successor to Henry Miller. His work was praised by writers as diverse as Gore Vidal and Norman Mailer, and his reputation was worldwide. *The Stoned Apocalypse* is Vassi's autobiography, financed by his other groundbreaking erotic writing. $12.95/**132-2**

A DRIVING PASSION
While the late Marco Vassi was primarily known and respected as a novelist, he was also an effective and compelling speaker. *A Driving Passion* collects the wit and insight Vassi brought to his infamously revealing lectures, and distills the philosophy—including the concept of Metasex—that made him an underground sensation. An essential volume. $12.95/**134-9**

THE EROTIC COMEDIES
A collection of stories from America's premier erotic philosopher. Marco Vassi was a dedicated iconoclast, and *The Erotic Comedies* marked a high point in his literary career. Scathing and humorous, these stories reflect Vassi's belief in the power and primacy of Eros in American life, as well as his commitment to the elimination of personal repression through carnal indulgence. $12.95/**136-5**

THE SALINE SOLUTION
During the Sexual Revolution, Marco Vassi established himself as an intrepid explorer of an uncharted sexual landscape. During this time he also distinguished himself as a novelist, producing *The Saline Solution* to great acclaim. With the story of one couple's brief affair and the events that lead them to desperately reassess their lives, Vassi examines the dangers of intimacy in an age of freedom. $12.95/**180-2**

CHEA VILLANUEVA

JESSIE'S SONG
"It conjures up the strobe-light confusion and excitement of urban dyke life, moving fast and all over the place, from NYC to Tucson to Miami to the Philippines; and from true love to wild orgies to swearing eternal celibacy and back. Told in letters, mainly about the wandering heart (and tongue) of writer and free spirit Pearly Does; written mainly by Mae-Mae Might, a sharp, down-to-earth but innocent-hearted Black Femme. Read about these dykes and you'll love them."
—Rebecca Ripley

A rich collection of lesbian writing from this uncompromising author. Based largely upon her own experience, Villanueva's work is remarkable for its frankness, and delightful in its iconoclasm. Widely published in the alternative press, Villanueva is a writer to watch. Toeing no line, *Jessie's Song* is certain to redefine all notions of "mainstream" lesbian writing, and provide a reading experience quite unlike any other this year. $9.95/**235-3**

SHAR REDNOUR, EDITOR

VIRGIN TERRITORY
An anthology of writing about the most important moments of life. Tales of first-time sensual experiences, from the pens of some of America's most uninhibited literary women. No taboo is unbroken as these women tell the whole truth and nothing but, about their lives as sexual women in modern times.

Included in this daring volume are such cult favorites as Susie Bright, Shannon Bell, Bayla Travis, Carol Queen, Lisa Palac and others. They leave no act undescribed, and prove once and for all that "beginner's luck" is the very best kind to have! $12.95/**238-8**

THE MASQUERADE EROTIC LIBRARY

Title	Code	Price
2069 TRILOGY	244-2	$4.95
AFFINITIES	3113-6	$4.95
AGENCY, THE	216-7	$12.95
AL	302-3	$4.95
ALIZARIN LAKE READER, AN	3106-3	$4.95
ALL THE WAY	3023-7	$4.95
ALL-STUD	3104-7	$4.95
AMERICAN PRELUDE	170-5	$4.95
ANDREA AT THE CENTER	206-X	$4.95
ANGELA	76-9	$4.95
ANIMAL HANDLERS	264-7	$4.95
ANTH. OF CLASSIC ANONYMOUS EROTIC WRITING, AN	3140-3	$6.95
APPLICANT, THE	306-6	$4.95
ARENA, THE	3083-0	$4.95
ASK ISADORA	61-0	$4.95
AUTOBIOGRAPHY OF A FLEA III	94-7	$4.95
B.M.O.C.	3077-6	$4.95
BAD HABITS	3068-7	$4.95
BADBOY EROTIC LIBRARY, V.1	190-X	$4.95
BADBOY EROTIC LIBRARY, V.2	211-6	$4.95
BADBOY FANTASIES	3049-0	$4.95
BAYOU BOY	3084-9	$4.95
BEAST OF BURDEN	3105-5	$6.95
BEST OF GAUNTLET, THE	202-7	$12.95
BEST OF MARY LOVE, THE	3099-5	$4.95
BEST OF SKIN TWO, THE	130-6	$12.95
BEST OF THE BADBOYS	233-7	$12.95
BIG SHOTS	3112-8	$4.95
BIZARRE DREAMS	187-X	$4.95
BIZARRE SEX & OTHER CRIMES OF PASSION	213-2	$12.95
BLACK TONGUE	258-2	$6.95
BLUE TANGO	037-7	$4.95
BONE	177-2	$4.95
BY HER SUBDUED	281-7	$5.95
CANDY LIPS	182-9	$4.95
CANNIBAL FLOWER	72-6	$4.95
CAPTIVE MAIDENS	3014-8	$4.95
CARNAL DAYS OF HELEN SEFERIS, THE	3086-5	$4.95
CAROLINE'S CONTRACT	3122-5	$4.95
CAROUSEL	3051-2	$4.95
CARRIE'S STORY	228-0	$4.95
CATALYST, THE	3015-6	$4.95
CHAINS	3158-6	$4.95
CHARLY'S GAME	221-3	$4.95
CHINESE JUSTICE & OTHER STORIES	3153-5	$4.95
CINDERELLA	305-8	$4.95
CIRCLE OF FRIENDS	250-7	$4.95
CITADEL, THE	198-5	$4.95
CLAIRE'S GIRLS	3108-X	$4.95
COMPLETE EROTIC READER, THE	3063-6	$4.95
COMPLETE PLAYGIRL FANTASIES, THE	3075-X	$4.95
CONFESSIONS OF A CONCUBINE	154-3	$4.95
CONSTRUCTION WORKER, THE	298-1	$5.95
CRUMBLING FAÇADE	3043-1	$4.95
DANGEROUS LESSONS	32-7	$4.95
DARKER PASSIONS: DRACULA	147-0	$4.95
DARKER PASSIONS: JECKYLL & HYDE	227-2	$4.95
DARKER PASSIONS: FRANKENSTEIN	248-5	$5.95
DARLING • INNOCENCE	3047-4	$4.95
DEADLY LIES	3076-8	$4.95
DEMON HEAT	79-3	$4.95
DEPRAVED ANGELS	92-0	$4.95
DISCIPLINE OF ODETTE, THE	3033-4	$4.95
DISTANT LOVE	3056-3	$4.95
DOCTOR IS IN, THE	195-0	$4.95
DOUBLE NOVEL	86-6	$4.95
DREAM CRUISE	3045-8	$4.95
DRIVING PASSION, A	134-9	$12.95
DUKE COSIMO	3052-0	$4.95
ECSTASY ON FIRE	3080-6	$4.95

THE MASQUERADE EROTIC LIBRARY

Title	Code	Price
EIGHTH WONDER	200-0	$4.95
ELEMENTS OF AROUSAL, THE	230-2	$12.95
ENTER WITH TRUMPETS	197-7	$6.95
EQUINOX	3157-8	$6.95
ERIC'S BODY	151-9	$4.95
EROTIC ADVENTURES OF HARRY TEMPLE, THE	3127-6	$4.95
EROTIC COMEDIES, THE	136-5	$12.95
EROTOMANIA	3128-4	$4.95
EVIL COMPANIONS	3067-9	$4.95
EXPOSED	3126-8	$4.95
FANTASY BOARD	212-4	$4.95
FAUSTUS CONTRACT, THE	167-5	$4.95
FEAST UNKNOWN	276-0	$6.95
FESTIVAL OF VENUS	37-8	$4.95
FIRE AND ICE	297-3	$5.95
FIRST PERSON	179-9	$4.95
FLESH FABLES	243-4	$4.95
FOR SALE BY OWNER	3064-4	$4.95
FRAGRANT ABUSES	88-2	$4.95
FULL SERVICE	150-0	$4.95
GARDEN OF DELIGHT	3058-X	$4.95
GAY ADVENTURES OF CAPTAIN GOOSE, THE	169-1	$4.95
GLORIA'S INDISCRETION	3094-6	$4.95
GOLDEN YEARS	3069-5	$4.95
GOOD PARTS, THE	186-1	$12.95
HARD WAY, THE	231-0	$12.95
HAREM SLAVE	226-4	$4.95
HAREM SONG	73-4	$4.95
HAVEN, THE	165-9	$4.95
HEAT WAVE	3159-4	$4.95
HEIR • THE KING, THE	3048-2	$4.95
HELEN AND DESIRE	3093-8	$4.95
HELOISE	3073-3	$4.95
HIGHWAYWOMAN, THE	174-8	$4.95
HITTING HOME AND OTHER STORIES	222-1	$4.95
HOT BAUDS	285-X	$5.95
HUCK & BILLY	245-0	$4.95
HUSTLING: A GENTLEMAN'S GUIDE...	137-3	$12.95
ICE MAIDEN, THE	3001-6	$4.95
IF THE SHOE FITS	223-X	$4.95
ILLUSIONS	3074-1	$4.95
IMAGE OF THE BEAST, THE	166-7	$6.95
IMRE	3019-9	$4.95
IN THE ALLEY	3144-6	$4.95
IN THE BLOOD	283-3	$5.95
INITIATION OF PB 500, THE	3141-1	$4.95
INITIATION RITES	3120-9	$4.95
INSTRUMENTS OF THE PASSION, THE	3010-5	$4.95
JADE EAST	60-2	$4.95
JAZZ AGE, THE	48-3	$4.95
JENNIFER	3107-1	$4.95
JENNIFER AGAIN	220-5	$4.95
JESSIE'S SONG	235-3	$12.95
JOY SPOT	301-5	$4.95
JUDITH BOSTON	273-6	$4.95
JULIETTE II: REVENGE ON THE LORD	240-X	$5.95
KATE PERCIVAL	3072-5	$4.95
KATY'S AWAKENING	308-2	$4.95
KIDNAP	90-4	$4.95
KIM'S PASSION	162-4	$4.95
KISS OF LEATHER	3161-6	$4.95
KUNG FU NUNS	3031-8	$4.95
LADY F.	3102-0	$4.95
LAVENDER ROSE	208-6	$4.95
LEATHERWOMEN	3095-4	$4.95
LEATHERWOMEN II	229-9	$4.95
LESSONS AND LOVERS	196-9	$4.95
LETHAL SILENCE	3125-X	$4.95
LEWD CONDUCT	3091-1	$4.95
LONG LEATHER CORD, THE	201-9	$4.95
LOOKING FOR MR. PRESTON	288-4	$23.95

THE MASQUERADE EROTIC LIBRARY

Title	Code	Price
LOVE AND SURRENDER	3082-2	$4.95
LOVE BITES	234-5	$12.95
LOVE IN WARTIME	3044-X	$4.95
LOVE'S ILLUSION	3100-4	$4.95
LOVING DOMINANT, THE	218-3	$6.95
LUST	82-3	$4.95
LUSTFUL TURK, THE	163-2	$4.95
MAD MAN, THE—HARDCOVER EDITION	193-4	$23.95
MAN SWORD	188-8	$4.95
MAN WITH A MAID	307-4	$4.95
MAN WITH A MAID II	3071-7	$4.95
MAN WITH A MAID: THE CONCLUSION	3013-X	$4.95
MANEATER	3103-9	$6.95
MANSEX	3160-8	$4.95
MANY PLEASURES OF IRONWOOD, THE	310-4	$5.95
MARKETPLACE, THE	3096-2	$4.95
MASQUERADE READER, A	84-X	$4.95
MASTERING MARY SUE	3005-9	$4.95
MAUDE RIVERS	3087-3	$4.95
MELTDOWN!	203-5	$12.95
MEMBER OF THE CLUB	3079-2	$4.95
MEN AT WORK	3027-X	$4.95
MEN WHO LOVED ME	274-4	$6.95
MIKE AND ME	3035-0	$4.95
MILES DIAMOND & DEMON OF DEATH	251-5	$4.95
MILES DIAMOND	3118-7	$4.95
MIND MASTER	209-4	$4.95
MISS HIGH HEELS	3066-0	$4.95
MISTRESS MINE	3109-8	$4.95
MOROCCO	148-9	$4.95
MOTION OF LIGHT IN WATER, THE	133-0	$12.95
MR. BENSON	3041-5	$4.95
MUSCLE BOUND	3028-8	$4.95
MY DARLING DOMINATRIX	3055-5	$4.95
MY LIFE AND LOVES (THE 'LOST' VOLUME)	52-1	$4.95
MY LIFE AS A PORNOGRAPHER	135-7	$12.95
NADIA	267-1	$4.95
NAUGHTIER AT NIGHT	3030-X	$4.95
NECESSARY EVIL	277-9	$5.95
NINA FOXTON	145-4	$4.95
OBSESSIONS	3012-1	$4.95
ODD WOMEN	3123-3	$4.95
ORF	3110-1	$6.95
OUTPOSTS	316-3	$19.95
OUTWARD SIDE	304-X	$6.95
PARLOR, THE	291-4	$5.95
PASSAGE & OTHER STORIES	3057-1	$4.95
PASSION IN RIO	54-8	$4.95
PAULA	3036-9	$4.95
PAULINE	3129-2	$4.95
PERSUASIONS	183-7	$4.95
PETER THORNWELL	149-7	$4.95
PINK CHAMPAGNE	282-5	$5.95
PRISONERS OF TORQUEMADA	252-3	$4.95
PRIVATE LESSONS	3116-0	$4.95
PRIVATE LIVES	309-0	$4.95
PROFESSIONAL CHARMER	3003-2	$4.95
PROTESTS, PLEASURES & RAPTURES	204-3	$4.95
RAIN	232-9	$12.95
RAWHIDE LUST	55-6	$4.95
REAL THING, THE	280-9	$12.95
RELUCTANT CAPTIVE, THE	3022-9	$4.95
REPENTANCE OF LORRAINE, THE	3124-1	$6.95
RETURN TO TIMBERLAND	257-4	$5.95
REUNION IN FLORENCE	3070-9	$4.95
RITUALS	168-3	$4.95
ROMANCES OF BLANCHE LE MARE, THE	3101-2	$4.95
ROPE ABOVE, THE BED BELOW, THE	269-8	$4.95
ROSEBUD SUTRA	242-6	$4.95
RUN, LITTLE LEATHER BOY	3143-8	$4.95
SABINE	3046-6	$4.95

THE MASQUERADE EROTIC LIBRARY

Title	Code	Price
SACRED PASSIONS	21-1	$4.95
SALINE SOLUTION, THE	180-2	$12.95
SCARLET PANSY, THE	189-6	$4.95
SCHOOL FOR SIN	89-0	$4.95
SCORPIUS EQUATION, THE	3119-5	$4.95
SCRAPBOOK	224-8	$4.95
SEASON OF THE WITCH	268-X	$4.95
SECRET DANGER	3111-X	$4.95
SECRET RECORD, THE	3039-3	$4.95
SENSATIONS	3081-4	$6.95
SENSUOUS MAGIC	131-4	$12.95
SEX SHOW	225-6	$4.95
SEX. ADV. OF SHERLOCK HOLMES, THE	3097-0	$4.95
SEXPERT, THE	3034-2	$4.95
SHADOWMAN	178-0	$4.95
SILK AND STEEL	3032-6	$4.95
SINS OF THE CITIES OF THE PLAIN	3016-4	$4.95
SISTER RADIANCE	215-9	$6.95
SKIN DEEP	265-5	$4.95
SKIRTS	3115-2	$4.95
SKYDIVING ON CHRISTOPHER STREET	287-6	$4.95
SLAVE ISLAND	3006-7	$4.95
SLAVE PRINCE, THE	199-3	$4.95
SLAVE, THE	173-X	$6.95
SLAVES OF CAMEROON	3026-1	$4.95
SLAVES OF SHOANNA	164-0	$4.95
SLAVES OF THE EMPIRE	3054-7	$4.95
SLOW BURN	3042-3	$4.95
SOME WOMEN	300-7	$6.95
SORRY I ASKED	3090-3	$4.95
SPANISH HOLIDAY	185-3	$4.95
STASI SLUT	3050-4	$4.95
STOLEN MOMENTS	3098-9	$4.95
STONED APOCALYPSE, THE	132-2	$12.95
STORY OF A VICTORIAN MAID	241-8	$4.95
SUBMISSION HOLDS	266-3	$4.95
SUBMISSIONS	207-8	$6.95
SWEET DREAMS	3062-8	$4.95
SWEET TALKERS	192-6	$12.95
SWEETEST FRUIT, THE	95-5	$4.95
SWITCH, THE	3061-X	$4.95
TABLEAUX VIVANTS	3121-7	$4.95
TAILPIPE TRUCKER	296-5	$5.95
TALES FROM THE DARK LORD II	176-4	$4.95
TEARS OF THE INQUISITION	146-2	$4.95
TELENY	3020-2	$4.95
TEMPLE SLAVE	191-8	$12.95
THONGS	217-5	$4.95
THREE WOMEN	3025-3	$4.95
TERROR	247-7	$5.95
TITIAN BERESFORD READER, A	3114-4	$4.95
TOURNIQUET	3060-1	$4.95
TRINKETS	246-9	$4.95
TUTORED IN LUST	78-5	$4.95
UNNATURAL ACTS	181-0	$12.95
VELVET TONGUE, THE	3029-6	$4.95
VENUS IN FURS	3089-X	$6.95
VICTORIAN ROMANCE, A	175-6	$4.95
VIRGIN TERRITORY	238-8	$12.95
WAYWARD	3004-0	$4.95
WET DREAMS	3142-X	$4.95
WET FOREVER, THE	3117-9	$6.95
WHIPS	254-X	$4.95
WHISPER OF FANS	259-0	$4.95
WHITE THIGHS	3009-1	$4.95
WILD HEART	3007-5	$4.95
WOMEN AT WORK	3088-1	$4.95
YELLOW ROOM, THE	96-3	$4.95

ORDERING IS EASY!

MC/VISA orders can be placed by calling our toll-free number
PHONE 800-458-9640 / FAX 212 986-7355
or mail the coupon below to:
**MASQUERADE BOOKS
DEPT. W54A, 801 2ND AVE., NY, NY 10017**

BUY ANY FOUR BOOKS AND CHOOSE ONE ADDITIONAL BOOK, OF EQUAL OR LESSER VALUE, AS YOUR FREE GIFT.

QTY.	TITLE	NO.	PRICE
			FREE
			FREE

W54A

SUBTOTAL
POSTAGE and HANDLING

We Never Sell, Give or Trade Any Customer's Name.

TOTAL

In the U.S., please add $1.50 for the first book and 75¢ for each additional book; in Canada, add $2.00 for the first book and $1.25 for each additional book. Foreign countries: add $4.00 for the first book and $2.00 for each additional book. No C.O.D. orders. Please make all checks payable to Masquerade Books. Payable in U.S. currency only. New York state residents add 8¼% sales tax. Please allow 4-6 weeks delivery.

NAME _____

ADDRESS _____

CITY _____ STATE _____ ZIP _____

TEL ( ) _____

PAYMENT: ☐ CHECK   ☐ MONEY ORDER   ☐ VISA   ☐ MC

CARD NO. _____ EXP. DATE _____

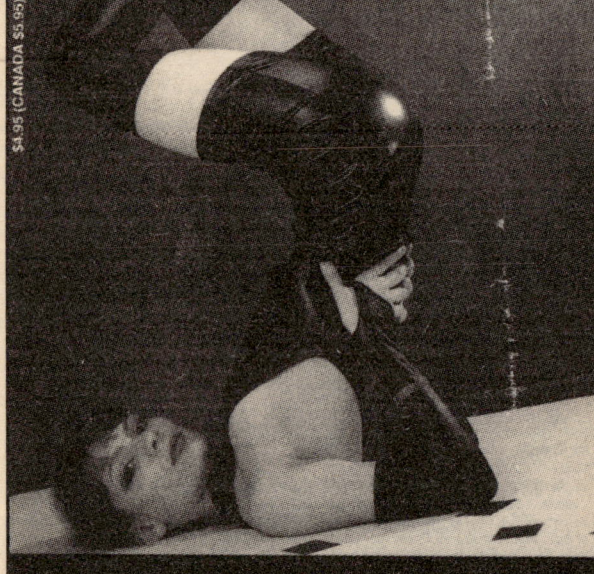